NO ILLUSION

Lynnette Kent

A KISMET® Romance

METEOR PUBLISHING CORPORATION
Bensalem, Pennsylvania

First Printing March 1993.

ISBN: 1-56597-053-5

Printed in the United States of America.

For my husband, who always knew I
could do it.

LYNNETTE KENT

Lynnette Kent began reading romances in the third
grade. Thirty years and hundreds of scribbled pages
later, her husband's encouragement launched her into
a serious writing career. Presently, she and her family reside in a suburb of Washington, D.C., where
she draws on her travels and experiences as a military
wife to provide settings for the stories she loves to
create.

ONE

"This is the wrong bus!"

The man sleeping in the seat across the aisle jerked his head at her exclamation but didn't wake up; the driver glanced at her through the mirror and turned the wheel.

Chloe dropped back against her seat with a stifled groan. Of all the stupid things to do, this had to be the worst. Already running late, she needed every spare second to be sure she got to work on time. But instead, of turning south on Wisconsin Avenue toward downtown Washington, D.C., this bus had turned north, heading even farther into the suburbs. Now she would have to get off, cross the street, wait for another bus going in the other direction, go back to the station, wait for the *right* bus . . .

Barely restraining a potent curse, Chloe pulled the rope that would keep her from moving any farther in the wrong direction. Then she stood up and made her way quickly to the front of the bus.

At least I don't have to carry much equipment today, she thought, trying to find a splinter of sunshine in the situation. *And no crowds this early on a*

Sunday morning. No wedging through the mob to get to the door.

"Do you know what time the next 34 bus will be in the station?" she asked the driver as she waited for the stop.

"Sure, lady," he replied sarcastically. "I carry all the bus schedules right up here in the old noggin."

So much for the sunshine. "I hope you have a good day, too," she told him as she stepped out into the street.

The bus pulled away with a roaring belch of smoke as Chloe hurried to the nearest corner, still chastising herself for her stupidity. She'd made this mistake before, but not usually with such a tight schedule to worry about. And she should have realized that on a Sunday morning she'd probably be alone at the bus stop; she should have been prepared to cope. It was always easier when somebody else was waiting with her. Then she could ask, casually, if this bus was the one she wanted. No such luck today, though, which was how she got in trouble to begin with.

It had *looked* like the right number. Of course, she did have trouble with threes—they tended to look a lot like eights and fives. And, today, like E's. But she'd really thought it said 34, not E4. It would help if she had read the destination, but she'd gone with the numbers, feeling sure she was right.

Wrong, Chloe thought with a sigh as she waited for the light to change. It just goes to show, you should never take anything for granted. Especially this gorgeous weather, she reflected as the wind caught her long skirt and blew it around her legs. It was a perfect spring day in a town where spring was always special. The traffic was light, so she wouldn't have to breathe car exhaust while she waited for the bus. And the sun was shining. Maybe she could walk down to Lafayette Park after work and see how the tulips looked this year. That would be fun.

Twenty minutes later, she was still on the corner and what was left of her optimism had evaporated. She would be late for work, no question about it. And although they probably wouldn't fire her, they would knock down her pay. *Damn!* she said to herself. *I've got a mortgage payment due next week. Where is that bus?*

She didn't even bother to look at the sign when the blue and white monster finally pulled up in front of her; she couldn't read it anyway. But, learning from recent experience, before she dropped her money in the box she first asked the driver, "You *do* stop at Friendship Heights, don't you?"

"Sure," he replied. Chloe dropped into the front seat with a relieved sigh, then recalculated her schedule. Ten minutes back to the station, maybe ten waiting for the right bus, then fifteen or twenty more to get downtown. It wasn't great, but it was the best she could do.

If you could drive, whispered a little voice in her mind as she sat down, *it would be about a thousand times better*. But she had to have a license to drive a car. To get a license she had to be able to read. End of that discussion.

And anyway, she comforted herself as the bus swayed into the station, *if I could drive, I'd have to pay for parking. Public transportation conserves energy. Reduces traffic. Cuts down on air pollution. All those good things*.

Not that such public-spiritedness offered much consolation when the manager of the restaurant informed her that being an hour late cut her pay by a third. Chloe took the bad news with composure, though, lifting her chin to rise to the challenge.

"That's quite all right, Mr. Chafee. I'll get to work right now."

Transferring equipment from her canvas satchel to her pockets, she didn't waste time on regrets. But when the mirror in the bathroom reflected her flushed cheeks and angry eyes, she knew she had to take the time to recover. She needed to be calm and relaxed in order to enjoy the next two hours, or else no one else would, either. And if they didn't enjoy it, there wasn't any point.

"Breathe deeply," she told herself. "Focus." She let her eyes close, her shoulders slump, her chin drop. After a few moments in the cool quiet, she had acquired the serenity she needed. Now her eyes smiled confidently, her shoulders were square and high, her back straight. Lifting her hands in front of her, she made an intricate flourish and produced a red rose from, apparently, thin air.

"Who needs to read," she asked herself, flashing a smile at her reflection, "when you can work magic like this?"

Once out in the large, light dining room she forgot the irritations of the day, the problems in her life, and concentrated on her performance. There were plenty of children in the restaurant; she enjoyed making them giggle and smile, loved the light that brightened their eyes at some impossible trick. Birthday parties had given her a start years ago when she lacked the confidence to perform magic for adults. Now it seemed that the better known she got, the fewer offers she received to work with kids. But she took every one that came her way. Children were so special, so important—and so much fun!

Like the little boy at the corner table whose eyes hadn't left her since she walked in the door. Chloe recognized the signs of a real magic lover and worked her way toward him. The man with him—it had to be his dad, they looked so much alike—seemed to share the passion, too, since every time she glanced their way she met his eyes.

She arrived beside them at last and placed a hand lightly on the boy's shoulder. "Excuse me," she said, in a voice pitched to carry clearly over the restaurant patter, "but did you know you have a golf ball behind your ear?"

The little boy looked up in amazement as her fingertips fluttered on his neck. When she pulled her hand away from his ear, his mouth dropped open. He stared up at her, speechless, and took the white ball she extended to him.

"I don't know what it is," she continued with a smile and an open-handed shrug, "but everyone seems to be wearing golf balls! Even grown-ups!" Carefully, she touched the smooth skin at the side of his dad's head and came away with another ball: fluorescent orange this time.

"Cool! Can you do it again?" The boy bounced on his chair with nine-year-old enthusiasm.

She cocked her head to the side and pretended to study him closely. He really was adorable, with lots of blond curls and the biggest brown eyes she'd ever seen. "What's your name?"

"Eric Carroll," he said earnestly.

"Well, Eric, you don't seem to be wearing anything else unusual right now. But I do have some bunnies you might like to meet." Reaching into the pocket of her dress, she brought out a pair of sponge rabbits. "Hold out your hand." She placed the smaller of the two on the chubby palm and closed his hand with hers. "This is the mother bunny. And I have the father. We need to be careful, though, to keep them apart, or we'll have a whole bunch of baby bunnies hopping around." She clenched her fist tightly. "So you keep your hand closed and I'll close mine." He followed her directions with dedicated attention. "Now look at her again."

Eric opened his hand and squealed with delight. The little rabbit had become a group. "Neat!" he exclaimed. "Seven of them—how'd you do that?"

"It's just the way rabbits are," she explained as she gathered them out of his hand. "Oops!" She looked at the table and his half-finished lunch. "Would you believe it? I left my handkerchief under your plate!'' As he laughed, she lifted the plate with her left hand and used the fingers of her right to pull a scrap of red silk out from underneath the dish. She pulled. And pulled. The red flowed into yellow, swirled green, billowed to blue. With a last tug she flourished the ten-foot-long rainbow above her head.

"Thanks," she said. "I wondered where this was!"

Father and son applauded as the scarf fluttered down around her shoulders. She smiled and made them a bow. "Thank you, kind sirs. But, before I go," she said, extending her hand one more time, "isn't it uncomfortable to carry this in your nose?''

Her thumb touched his upper lip and then her hand drew away. On her open palm rested a large piece of candy. She laid it by his glass and, with another bow and a smile, moved away.

Eric turned a beaming face to his father. "Did you see how she did that, Dad? Wasn't it neat? Wow, I love magicians!'' Two tables over, three little girls were giggling over the magical appearance of a frog in their dad's water glass. Entranced by the magician, Eric munched on his candy and followed her every movement with his eyes, gasping with delight each time she made the impossible happen.

Another, older gaze pursued her as well. Peter Carroll had been aware of the woman's striking presence for quite some time before she'd arrived at their table to enchant his son. Tall and slender, dressed in a sleeveless black dress which looked elegant and sophisticated compared with the fussy springtime pastels other women were wearing, she'd caught his attention as soon as she entered the room. The confident grace of her movements invoked images of an elegant black cat, secure in itself, mistress of all it surveys. It would take a lot of self-confidence, he thought, to perform in a situation where every move could be closely examined.

Now, waiting patiently for his son to finish his meal,

Peter let his eyes dwell on the magician again, noting with pleasure the width of her smile and the sparkle of eyes that, even across the room, shone amethyst between her black lashes. While Eric was mesmerized with feats of prestidigitation, Peter acknowledged an attraction of a more basic, less mysterious origin. Her talents as a conjurer might be remarkable, but one flash of those eyes would have most males ready to let her saw them in half if that was her wish. No matter what their age and range of experience.

His eyes came back to his own table, where Eric was bouncing on his chair seat again. "Can we go over there, Dad? Please? I want to see some more!" He stood up and peered over the room divider at the table now enjoying the magic show. "Look at that—she's juggling the salt and pepper shakers, Dad! Wow, I could do that!" Inspired, the boy turned to grab the shakers from their table, only to find them already confiscated.

Peter raised an eyebrow and shook his head. "*I* remember the last time you tried to juggle, my boy. I spent the afternoon cleaning eggs out of the living room carpet. And no," he went on in response to the coming question, "you can't go over and disturb someone else's meal. Are you finished with your lunch?"

Eric slumped into his chair with the typical I-can't-have-what-I-want sulk. "Yes, sir," he moaned in the drawn-out voice familiar to parents the world over.

His father shrugged with parental indifference. "That attitude, as you very well know, will get you nowhere." The folder with the bill and credit slip had been placed next to his elbow. Reaching into his shirt pocket for his pen, Peter discovered the edges of some sort of paper there as well. Not aware of having put anything into his pocket, he pulled it out. He found himself staring at a black business card. *Chloe* the first line proclaimed in white lettering, with *Mistress of*

Magic below it. A phone number occupied the lower right corner.

He closed his mouth with a snap. How had she done it? How had she slipped her card into the pocket of his shirt, underneath his jacket? Peter allowed himself to watch her again as he thought it out. The card must have been planted during the time she was at the table. But he would swear she had never touched him, had only been close to his shoulder at the very beginning, when she'd "discovered" the golf ball behind his ear. Yet somehow she had managed a gesture which seemed, well, almost intimate. The image of those long, slender fingers stroking down over his shoulder and underneath his jacket was surprisingly vivid, given the fact that it had never happened.

Peter shook his head abruptly, signed his name to the bill and picked up his credit card. The woman was good; he'd give her credit for that. And, after all, what did it really matter? Just some sleight-of-hand from a stranger. Without examining his motives, he slipped the black card into his wallet.

"Come on, Eric," he said, getting to his feet, "let's go. You're supposed to go over to Alex's house in an hour. Unless, of course," he suggested, looking at the pout on his son's mouth, "you'd rather spend the afternoon in your room. That, too, can be arranged."

Eric responded to the threat and leaped to his feet, challenging his father to a race from the dining room. Peter clamped a hand on his shoulder instead and forcibly extracted the correct behavior expected from a nine-year-old leaving an expensive hotel restaurant. Only ten years or so, he thought, and the lesson will finally sink in!

They made it all the way to the door before the wheels turning in Eric's mind clicked into place. Without warning he stopped, whirled, and made a beeline back into the restaurant. Peter waited for a few seconds, thinking his son had left something on the table. When

Eric showed no sign of reappearing, he started back across the lobby, half-worried, half-irritated. This boy and his impulses were going to be the death of someone, sometime—if not his father, then certainly himself!

From the doorway, he surveyed the restaurant. As he'd feared, Peter found his son at the magician's side, watching with wide-eyed wonder as she pulled the scarf out from under someone else's plate. As soon as she presented the children with a treat and began to move away, Eric caught hold of her arm, forcibly stopping her in the middle of the room. As he proceeded to assault her with words, Peter cast a rueful glance at the ceiling and started toward them, irritation gaining the upper hand in the struggle with worry.

"Eric . . ." he said, in a voice dense with warning.

A shining, excited face turned his way. "I just had the greatest idea, Dad! My birthday! She could come and do magic for the guys at my birthday party! Wouldn't that be cool? And I wanted to ask her, since it's not very far away, so I came back. Isn't it a fantastic idea, Dad?"

The magician lifted her eyes from Eric's face to his father's. Peter met her laughing gaze with a smile of his own, aware of the amused glances from the diners around them. "I apologize for my son. I know he's interrupting your performance." He could have said more, but he wanted to hear her voice again.

Her wide smile answered him first, then the husky voice he'd waited for. "There's no problem," she assured him. "I need a break anyway. Let's talk outside, where there's not so much noise." With a graceful gesture she ushered them out of the restaurant; for the second time Peter found himself standing in the lobby. Eric had never let go of her arm, and she focused her attention on him. "I would be delighted to perform at your party, Eric. Why don't you discuss it with your parents and then get in touch with me if they decide it's a good idea.''

Eric was practically jumping up and down, in the process cranking her arm like the handle for a well pump. "That's what I'm doing! This is my dad and he can decide right now, can't you, Dad?"

Peter grabbed his son's shoulder in an effort to anchor him to the earth before he took the woman's arm off. "No, I can't decide right now, Eric. Believe it or not, magicians have other commitments besides birthdays for rambunctious boys." Eric's face fell, but at least he stopped moving. A quick squeeze from his father's strong fingers even prompted him to loosen his hold on the magician's arm.

"Since I already have your card," Peter went on, "I'll call in a day or so to arrange a date for the party that will fit your calendar. What is the best time to reach you, Miss . . . ?"

"Just Chloe." She allowed her hand to rest briefly on Eric's tousled blond curls and then stepped back, as if to distance herself from them both. "I'm usually at home until about noon. If not, please leave a message on my answering machine—I always call back!" With a flash of that brilliant smile, she turned and made her way back to the dining room.

She looked as good from the back as from the front, Peter decided. Straight, silky black hair curved under at the line of her jaw, exposing a gracefully long neck and its vulnerable nape. The severe black dress dropped to a deep V between her shoulder blades, revealing a supple spine and directing his imagination toward slim hips and a gently rounded bottom. Although the folds of her skirt hid all but her ankles, the elegance of her stride hinted at long, sexy legs.

A fantasy-come-true, Peter decided appreciatively. He had no explanation for his uncharacteristic need to scrutinize every detail of this strange woman's appearance; he considered himself as far removed from a girlwatcher as any man could be. But—just this once!—he enjoyed the sensation while it lasted and kept his eyes on her until she disappeared inside the restaurant. With a wistful sigh he came back to consciousness to find that Eric had vanished again.

"Damn!" Turning on his heel, Peter let anger propel him across the spacious room, calling his son's name with every ounce of authority he possessed. "Eric! Eric, where are you? I want you here—right now!"

"Here I am, Dad!" He hadn't gone very far, really, just halfway *up* the *down* escalator. With a jogging step he was keeping himself in place there. "I always wanted to do this!"

Peter stood at the bottom. "Get down here, Eric. Now."

Whatever danger was implied in the quiet tone got through to the boy, because without protest he did as he was told. Hands in the pockets of his pants, Peter waited for the escalator to deposit his son in front of him before he continued in the same voice. "We are going to the car. You are going to walk with me and you are going to keep your mouth shut. I am angry and disappointed that I can't take my eyes off of you for more than a minute without having to find you and get you out of some new predicament. If this behavior does not stop, you will be left at home with a babysitter when I want or need to go out. Do you understand me?"

Nine-year-olds are experts in the art of hanging their heads; Eric was a master. "Yes, sir," he said quietly.

Without another comment Peter walked quickly to the revolving door, expecting his son to follow without further delay. Such confidence was, in fact, justified; except for the extra two circuits in the door, the strange gyrations along the sidewalk that looked like a cross between kick-boxing and sword-fighting, and the detour to check out the ceramic swans supporting the glass table in the store window, Eric was right behind him.

That Peter was well aware of these embellishments to the stated program could be seen in the resigned half-smile he wore and the sigh of relief that lifted his shoulders when finally the seatbelts were buckled and the car motor turned on. Safe at last, he thought.

Wrong. "Hey, Dad," Eric exclaimed with excitement as a new thought struck him. "Maybe the magician could put me in a box and saw me in half at my birthday party—like that trick we saw on TV! Wouldn't it be cool to have somebody cut you in half on your birthday? The guys would go wild—they'd love it. Will you ask her about it, Dad? Will you?"

With a helpless laugh, Peter gave in. "Sure, Eric, I'll ask her. Anything you say." *Or maybe*, he thought, *I'll get her to put you in a box and make you disappear for a week or so—just long enough for me to catch my breath. That's a trick every parent would like to know!*

But as he made the drive home, Peter found himself speculating on some of this particular magician's less arcane talents, the ones that would fulfill the promise of that wide, red mouth and the texture of her soft, clear skin. Chloe. Her very name conjured up visions of romance and sensuality. And hands that were accomplished enough to perform such dexterous manipulations could, no doubt, work a different kind of magic on a man's body. . . .

Peter leaned over, punched the air-conditioning up to high and opened the vent as wide as it would go. His mind had slipped off the leash today, no doubt about it. He hadn't panted over a woman this way since long before Eric was born. Well, it would pass. A good hour or two with a stack of exam papers would wear it out of him. And he had lecture notes to review for tomorrow's classes. Yes, life was quite full enough, thank you, without the complications violet eyes could bring to it.

For instance: "Tell, me, son, what do you want for your birthday?"

Eric didn't even hesitate. "A boogie board. And a boom box. My own stereo, a TV for my room . . ."

My fault for asking, thought his father.

"Now, watch closely. Can you see it?"

"Sorry, sweetie, the answer's still yes. But maybe I just know what to look for."

"No, even an expert should be confused. Let's try it again. I take it *so*, move around this way, shift, and . . ."

The phone rang just as Chloe had attempted a new illusion involving paper flowers which were *supposed* to vanish into her sleeve and appear, magically, of course, behind her ear, remaining uncrushed in the process. The abrupt jangle broke her concentration, however, and the blossoms rained all over the floor instead. With a glare at the laughing man on the couch, she blew a frustrated breath off her lower lip to lift her bangs out of her eyes and reached for the receiver. "Shut up, Dallas, and let me answer the phone. Go get yourself something to drink."

Grinning, her audience levered himself off of the low sofa and passed by, close enough to give her a sympathetic pat on the head. Dallas Page, Texas native, assisted Chloe on stage, drove her equipment around the city, and could be counted as her closest friend; his irreverent, devil-may-care attitude also drove her crazy sometimes. Another ring went by as Chloe calmed down and remembered her manners. You never knew which call meant a job. It paid to be polite.

And so she was. "Chloe speaking. May I help you?"

The voice on the line was instantly familiar. "This is Peter Carroll. You may remember captivating my son at lunch on Sunday."

She closed her eyes. Oh, yes. She remembered everything about the feisty little boy with wheat-colored curls and deep brown eyes. "Of course, Mr. Carroll. What can I do for you?" And she remembered even more about the sleek man who was Eric's father, whose hair was the same blond, strictly tamed, but whose eyes were a stormy gray. Whose voice, like thunder, had set up vibrations along her spine. Then.

Now.

"You have inspired in my son an unwavering desire to be sawed in half on his birthday," he said. When she gave a gasp of laughter he chided, "This is not funny, my dear. It's all I've heard for two days. If I can tell him tonight that I've made definite arrangements for you to attend his birthday party, I might actually find out what happened in school this week. He may even do his homework. Your cooperation would be an act of kindness, Miss, uh, Chloe."

Chloe moved to the desk and picked up her cassette recorder. "What date do you want, Mr. Carroll?

The sound of flipping pages filled a pause. "Eric's birthday is the sixteenth, but that's a Friday. Are you free on the afternoon of the seventeenth? About two o'clock?"

Chloe pressed the record button and spoke into the microphone. "That's 2:00 PM on the seventeenth, for Eric Carroll." Releasing the button, she spoke into the phone. "Also, Mr. Carroll—"

He interrupted, "If I'm to call you Chloe, I think you can use my name, too. I'm Peter."

"Oh." She swallowed. It was stupid to be so nervous. This was just business. "Well, Peter, I need to see the room in advance of the performance, to get my setup in mind and that sort of thing. Would it be possible to come over when Eric isn't there, a day or two ahead of time?"

"Of course. He'll be in school during the day. I have classes in the mornings on Mondays, Wednesdays, and Fridays. How about early Tuesday afternoon?"

Chloe remembered her rehearsal schedule. "No, I'm afraid not. Would Thursday morning be possible? If you are busy, perhaps Mrs. Carroll could be there."

His voice came over the phone with an inflection she didn't quite understand. "There is no Mrs. Carroll, Chloe. But I can be here Thursday morning, if that works out better for you."

Again she pressed the button on the recorder: "That's great, Mr., uh, Peter. I'll plan to be there about 10:00 AM on the fifteenth. And your address is?"

When she had repeated the address and directions after him, she put the recorder down. If Peter sensed the awkwardness of her method he didn't comment but said, warmly, "This will be a real load off of Eric's mind, Chloe. He knew he couldn't tell his friends until I set up the arrangements, and keeping quiet has practically killed him."

She laughed again. "I understand the temptation. But you might want to break it to him that I don't saw people in half. Mine is a nonviolent sort of magic."

"It'll be a blow," Peter warned, a hint of teasing in his voice. "Are you sure you can't manage it?"

"I'll give it all my most special effects. I think I can promise he won't be disappointed."

The silence at the other end of the line lasted long enough to worry her. His voice came back, at last, almost reluctantly. "I feel certain, Chloe, that you could never be a disappointment." Another pause. "To anyone." And before she could reply, he'd said goodbye and hung up.

Chloe placed the receiver in its cradle but left her fingers clasped around the handle, as if to keep hold of the voice of the man who was no longer there. For a long moment she stared at her thumb rubbing up and down across the plastic, while she chewed on her bottom lip and pondered the feeling of loss that wouldn't go away. *It's just a job*, she tried to tell herself. *Not the rest of your life!*

But he's not married.

A clatter from the kitchen behind her, followed by a loud, drawling "Damnation!" shattered the dreary mood. She shook her head and turned to her desk where another microcassette recorder, identical to the one she'd used on the phone, waited. From the rack of minitapes hanging above the desk she chose the fifteenth and popped it in.

"Performance at Charlie's Place, 9:00 PM" her own voice informed her when she pushed the "play" button. "Special requests: audience participation, adult format, quote, unquote, sexy costume. Be prepared for drunks." A click, a whir, and another message. "Call back from Charlie's Place, requesting disappearance of audience member for effect. Get a plant—maybe Marsha." Click, whir. "Marsha available for thirty dollars and drinks. Will rehearse Tuesday. The end."

She listened to the silence for a moment, then rewound the tape and played just to the end of "Tuesday." With her finger on "Record," Chloe continued. "Appointment 10:00 AM, Peter Carroll's house, 1098 Winston St., to preview setting for birthday performance on Saturday. Eric will be nine or ten; young boy format. Check out possibility of disappearance closing. Party at 2:00 PM on the seventeenth; see further notes. Directions to house on the seventeenth. The end."

Rewind. Eject. Find the tape for the seventeenth. Insert. Review: no messages on this tape. Good, the whole day would be free. Record: "Birthday party for Eric Carroll, 2:00 to 4:00 PM. Young boy format. Notes to follow. Directions. . . ." Here Chloe took the easy way out: she found the place on the working tape where she had repeated Peter's telephone instructions and simply played it into the other recorder. "The end."

"Whew!" She turned to look at Dallas as he leaned against the doorway to the kitchen, a soft-drink can in his hand. "That's some method you got there," he said. "I'm always amazed that you never get confused."

Chloe carefully replaced the last tape in its slot and the cassette recorder on the desk. She shook her head.

"I can't afford to get confused. The whole system depends on keeping the tapes in precise order, and business depends on the system. One mix-up could mean missing a job; missing a job would mean missing a mortgage payment. Or a week's worth of meals. Not to mention equipment, clothes, heat. . . ."

He levered himself away from the wall and came over to put his arm around her. "Still living on the edge, honey?"

With a shrug she nodded. "It's not so bad, really. In fact, it's exciting, most of the time." She looked up at him with an uncertain smile. "The pit is awfully deep, though, Dallas. I'd hate to fall in."

He hugged her in silence for a minute. His voice came at last, muffled by her hair. "You know," he began, and Chloe could hear his hesitation, "I've seen some advertisements for study courses. Adult classes, special programs. You could—"

"When do I have time for school, Dallas?"

She felt a kiss drop on the top of her head. "It's just a thought. Anyway, as long as you've got me, you'll be fine. And I'm always around somewhere, Chloe. Just call me if you need me." A squeeze that threatened to break bones pressed her against his chest, then he let her go. "By the way," he continued as he walked back to the sofa, "I brought you another tape. More poetry and that new biography you wanted."

Chloe watched Dallas fish through his jacket pockets. He'd had more than his share of propositions from the audience in the time they'd been together; tall, lean men with a devilish grin and bedroom eyes appealed to the vast majority of women. But she never asked if he took the offers he got. The boundaries of their relationship, as close as it was, were strictly defined and such a personal question would be completely out of line. They worked well together, Chloe thought, precisely because they kept their privacy, gave each other space and independence.

Not that she hadn't wondered, occasionally, if there was someone special in his life. Dallas was far too lovable—and sexy—to be alone. When they first met, she'd even considered the possibility that they might fall in love—an idea that had lasted as long as it took to remember the lessons she'd learned. She couldn't feel that way about Dallas. Not about anyone. All she needed was a good, close friend. If he needed more, she was sure he felt free to find it with someone else.

Dallas straightened up with the tape in his hand. "What're you thinkin' now, magician," he asked suspiciously.

Chloe straightened her shoulders and shook off the somber mood. "Oh, just wondering if we shouldn't work up one of those sword tricks—you know, I could close you up in a basket and stick nice, sharp sabers into it. Those little boys would love it, especially if we had some blood running out the bottom."

Moving with lazy grace, Dallas caught up his jacket and crossed the room again. When he stood in front of her, he tapped her on the nose with the cassette. "Yeah, right," he drawled. "*My* blood, you mean? Didn't I hear you say somethin' about your magic bein' nonviolent? Thanks, lady, but I think I'll pass. I learned *my* lesson the first—and last!—time I rode a bull at the rodeo. My job description doesn't include workin' with anything that has a sharp point."

He picked up her hand and dropped the tape on her palm. "Got to go. See you later, sweetie." A gentle kiss on her forehead and he was gone.

Chloe stood where he'd left her, tapping the tape against the side of her leg, laughing quietly. Dallas helped her out in a lot of different ways, but the most important was the way he always made her smile. Plus the fact that, of all the men she'd met over the years, only Dallas could settle for what she had to offer. Not love, not sex, not commitment. Just friendship. Just a sharing of time and thoughts, without the word "forever" to ruin it. She'd tried forever once and found out how short it really was. And once, as they say, is enough.

Taking a deep breath, she dropped her chin to her chest and rolled her head gently from one shoulder to the other, trying to release her tight neck muscles. Where had all this tension come from? Except for the ever-present problem of money, her life proceeded very much according to plan. A small, comfortable house, a profession that gave her freedom and creative satisfaction, and a few good friends to fill her time—what more could she ask?

Something, whispered a voice in her mind *is missing*.

Well, what is it? she whispered back.

You'll know when you find it.

"Oh, right!" Chloe exclaimed out loud. "Now I'm getting mystical. Give me a break!" Bending down, she swept the scattered paper flowers up into her hand and then went to stand in front of the full length mirror that took up a wall of her living room. An hour or two of concentrated practice would improve the effect she wanted to create.

More important, it would help her forget the disturbing shiver of anticipation that passed over her when she thought about seeing Peter Carroll again. She had enough trouble without *that*!

Jack Evans apologized again as they rode the escalator to the hotel's mezzanine level. "I'm sorry about this, Peter. I've been trying to catch up with this guy all day. I just have to see him for a few minutes at the reception and then we can go on to dinner."

His college roommate had always been the anxious type. Shaking his head, Peter reassured his friend—again. "Don't worry about it, Jack. I'm glad to get the chance to see you while you're in town. I'll have a drink while you talk. No problem."

The crowd waiting to get into the ballroom for the

reception was unexpectedly large. Catching up on fifteen years of Jack's life while they waited in line, Peter had to wonder what could be drawing such interest at a relatively sober chiropractors' convention. It must be, he decided, a fantastic buffet.

They crossed the doorway at last. Jack spotted the man he needed to see in the corner by the bar and headed briskly that way with a promise to be quick. Peter wandered over more slowly and got his own drink, then turned to survey the room. From what he could see, the medical supply company sponsoring the reception had, in fact, provided a lavish spread. But the tables stood untouched, almost unnoticed.

The crowd which should have been attacking the buffet had collected at the other end of the room around some kind of performance. Curious, he made his way toward the crush, but all he could see from the back row were the heads in front of him. The laughter of the audience was tantalizing, the voice he could hear explaining and entertaining even more so.

And it was, he thought, a voice he knew. With a finesse developed during years spent attending Eric's ball games and school plays, where every parent wanted to be in front to see *their* kid, Peter flattened himself against the wall and edged carefully up the side of the crowd until he stood just behind the front row, out of sight but able to see everything. Able to see *her*.

A woman in evening dress—white tie and tails—was making an elaborate task of tying another woman into a chair. Judging by the amount of rope involved and the number of knots tied, Peter felt sure the prisoner would never leave the chair again.

"Now I'll flip the end over and tuck it under," Chloe was saying. "Yes, that's it," she asserted, pulling hard. "I don't think there's any way you can escape now, without my magic to help you. No matter how hard you . . ." Her voice died away as the woman, with no visible effort, stood up, stepped over the puddle of rope at her feet and walked away. ". . . try."

The crowd laughed heartily at the dismayed look on the magician's face as her intended victim escaped unscathed. "I guess that knot isn't the right one. Let me practice a moment . . ." she requested, pretending embarrassment, while her hands twisted and tangled a long rope into a bundled mess around her fingers.

After a few seconds she attempted to pull her hands free of the snarl. A brief struggle brought her eyes back to the audience. "Um, I think I have a problem," she apologized. "I seem to have gotten caught up in my work.

"Perhaps, sir," she suggested, walking up to a man in the middle of the front row, "you could just pull that end, there," with a tilt of her hands that showed him the frayed rope, "and get me out?"

"Sure," he said good-naturedly, and proceeded to yank the rope hard enough to jerk Chloe off her feet.

With a lithe twist she kept her balance. "Have you considered calf-roping as a hobby?" she asked, turning a mean prank into a joke. The group took her cue and chuckled, especially when she held up her hands. "But I'm still caught. Would someone else like to try?"

Several healthy tugs later, no one had released the rope. "Oh, well," sighed Chloe. "I guess I'm stuck. A magician without her hands isn't very entertaining. I wonder if they'll pay me for part of the night?" Lifting her shoulders in a big shrug, she sharply jerked her wrists apart. The audience gasped in collective surprise as the tangled rope slipped in a single smooth motion to the floor.

She bowed to their applause and retrieved the rope. "Thank you very much. Enjoy your evening."

Released, the crowd broke apart, laughing and shaking their heads, interested at last in the food and the bar. Chloe carefully coiled the rope and walked back to hang it on the post of the chair, then moved to the table behind the chair to rearrange her equipment.

Undecided about whether to approach her or not, Peter stayed where he was, propped up by the wall, as the crowd dispersed. He had a few seconds, he figured, to remain unnoticed and calculate the risks attached to talking with a woman who so completely upset his equilibrium.

A week ago he hadn't known she existed; now he couldn't seem to get her out of his mind. Of course, it didn't help that Eric's conversation, from the time he awoke in the morning until he fell sleep at night, centered around the magician who would perform at his birthday party. But Eric wasn't responsible for the seductive fantasies that made getting to sleep more difficult for his father, or the restless dreams that rendered what sleep he did get unrefreshing. And whether it would be wiser to get to know her and dispel the mystery or simply ignore the attraction and walk away, he could not say.

Peter was about to choose the coward's path and leave when the man who had nearly pulled the magician down during the rope trick stepped up behind her. She turned when he tapped her shoulder; her delicate eyebrows arched in surprise as he used two fingers to tuck something between the studs of her dress shirt.

"That's some act, sweetheart," Peter heard him mutter in a slurred voice. "How about a private performance?"

Without a second's pause Chloe pulled the cash out of her shirt. "I'm afraid not," she replied with a cool smile, rolling the bill between her palms until it had become a narrow tube. Picking it up between her thumb and first finger, she tapped the end of the tube against her palm. Once, twice. "But thanks for the tip!"

On the third tap she snapped both of her hands closed. When she opened them again, the tube of cash had disappeared.

"Hey! Where's my money?" The drunk gripped her arm and twisted. "That was a hundred bucks! What'd you do with it, you little b—"

Peter took a stride forward, intending to intervene. Before he could take another, there was a flash of white shirt cuff as Chloe lifted her hand. He couldn't see exactly what had happened, but all at once she stepped free.

"There is a security guard at the door who will be happy to take you to the police if you can't behave," she told the bully, who was rubbing his wrist with a pained expression on his face. "Perhaps you should find another party." As he started to brush past her, she put her hand for an instant on his arm. "Have a good evening!" she suggested graciously.

His reply was obscene. Undisturbed, the magician watched with a slight smile as her tormentor lumbered out of the room. Her eyes were still focused on the doorway when Peter reached her side.

"Very impressive," he said quietly. "But where *is* his money?"

TWO

Chloe snapped her head around. "Mr. Carroll!" she exclaimed in a voice she couldn't control. "What are you—I mean, how nice to see you again!"

"Thanks. The name is Peter. And where is his cash?"

She had to grin. The man had been such an easy mark. "Oh, in his coat pocket. He'll find it when he sends the suit to be cleaned."

Peter Carroll smiled in return, a genuine expression that lightened the somber gray of his eyes. "It's a good trick. So was the rope. Do you do this kind of thing," he asked with a wave of his arm that took in the crush of people around them, "frequently?"

Chloe nodded. "Conventions are bread and butter work. The pay is pretty good, the overhead is low, and you get free food." She glanced at the buffet across the room. "And since I'm on my break now I better take advantage of it," she explained, feeling a rumble in her stomach and a dryness in her mouth that made food a priority. "Would you like to join me?"

He made a gesture that instructed her to lead the way. She moved across the ballroom, smiling and nodding at the compliments thrown at her by the people who had been her audience, but hardly hearing anything they said. They reached the buffet; distracted, Chloe went through the line filling her plate with whatever came to hand, more aware of the man behind her than the food on the table.

What, she wondered, could he be doing here? She might, if she'd been asked, identify Peter Carroll as a lawyer, or a stockbroker, maybe even a government official. But a chiropractor? He didn't seem to fit, somehow. Not that it mattered, she thought, studying the cheese tray with an intensity that had nothing to do with a choice between Cheddar and Swiss. Except that if she'd known he would be here she wouldn't have taken the job. The last thing she needed was to have her concentration broken, to be thinking about how good he looked instead of what was happening with the audience. *If he stays to watch*, she told herself in despair, *I might as well have my hands tied!*

Almost before she realized it, she'd reached the end of the buffet. Looking down at her plate, Chloe saw with dismay the mound of food she'd picked up: steamed shrimp, artichoke dip, cheese cubes and crackers, fettucini in cream sauce and roast beef with bearnaise sauce on a roll. A cherry tomato and a pineapple cube topped the huge stack. Wondering how she would balance the heavy dish, let alone eat all of the food on it, she examined the room for a place to sit, but since the one amenity lacking was a free chair, they had to settle for an empty spot next to the wall. *Too bad I can't actually levitate*, Chloe thought. *I may drop this food before I get to eat any of it!*

It didn't help to notice that Peter had taken one slice of smoked salmon and a single cube of melon. *Now I look like a glutton*, Chloe groaned silently. Then she stiffened her shoulders. *Who cares what he thinks, anyway? I don't need his approval!*

But, after a munching silence, he confirmed her worst fears. "Do I take it," he asked with a pointed look at her still-full plate, "that the only time you eat is when you're working?"

"What an atrocious thing to say!" she protested. "Of course not." Then, despising herself for the need to explain, she admitted, "But I haven't eaten today. I had rehearsals all morning and afternoon. And anything that's in my refrigerator is eligible for medical experimentation." She looked at her plate and sighed. "I may have overdone it, though. I don't think I can finish."

Peter took her plate from unresisting fingers and left it with his on a tray, returning with a drink for them both. "It's water," he explained when she hesitated before taking hers.

"Thanks. That's just what I wanted. How did you know?"

"Lucky guess." Something in his expression held her gaze and brought a flush she could feel to her cheeks and throat. What was he thinking? When his eyes dropped to her mouth and stayed there, she thought she knew. Suddenly, trying to breathe normally took immense concentration.

With an effort she could almost feel, he dragged his gaze away and looked over the crowd. "Does this kind of work advance you professionally?" he said then, sounding as if he, too, had trouble controlling his breath. "It doesn't seem likely to make you famous."

It took her a second to realize he was referring to their previous conversation. "Emily Dickinson says that fame is like spoiled food—it might kill you if you eat it." Thinking of the meal she'd just finished, Chloe had to grin. "I don't know that I want to be famous."

His brows lifted in astonishment. "A magician who reads poetry?" He thought for a minute, then offered a quote of his own and commented, "It is a precarious perch, I suppose, being well-known."

Indignation that he would be surprised gave way to a need to identify the source of his quotation. She considered carefully. "Not, I think, Walt Whitman. It sounds too early for Eliot. Oh, wait," she cried, delighted with her success, "I know! It's Robert Frost! 'Provide, Provide' is the name of the poem."

Grinning, he nodded. Their shared pleasure in poetry seemed to draw them closer somehow, to forge a bond that Chloe knew she wasn't ready for.

I don't want to like him this much, she thought. *I can't.*

She looked around the room for a diversion. "I've never visited a chiropractor," Chloe confessed with a nod toward the boisterous conventioneers. "What do they do?"

The lift of his right eyebrow and the ironic light in his cool gray eyes told her he'd understood her change of subject. "I have no idea. I'm here with a friend," he explained casually. "He came into town for the convention. We're supposed to have dinner, but he got roped into this party so I tagged along. And found . . ." he said in a low voice, which dragged her eyes away from the crowd and back to his face, ". . . you."

What she saw there brought an instant denial to her lips. "Peter, I—"

"Frost can be quite a useful poet," he interrupted seriously. "In one of his poems he wonders whether the world will end in fire or in ice, and decides that, if desire is any indication, fire is the way to go. I," Peter said, lifting his hand to draw two fingers lightly along her jawline, "have to agree." For an endless moment his eyes held hers. The possibilities of a relationship shimmered in the air between them, the promise of excitement, fulfillment, perhaps even contentment.

But then, with a shake of her head, Chloe pushed the opportunity away. "I won't be here much longer if I don't get back to work," she said brightly, attempting a nonchalance he could no doubt see right through. "It was a pleasure to meet you again, Peter," she assured him, backing away with her hands behind her back, to be sure she didn't reach out to him. "I'll look forward to Eric's birthday."

Moving back to her table on the other side of the ballroom, she sat down, pulled out some coins and a glass and placed them on the cloth-covered top. Soon another group had gathered around her and the shouts of laughter drew glances from around the room. Fighting to keep her attention on her work, Chloe nevertheless noticed exactly how long Peter stood where she'd left him, watching the performance, a curious smile twisting his mouth.

And she knew exactly the instant when he left. Not because she saw him go, but because the room felt suddenly empty, and when she looked up, he was gone.

All well and good, she told herself, going through the motions of the ages-old shell game and managing to hide her distraction from the people at the table. It would never have worked out, anyway. She had too much to do, and he would just get in the way.

So why should she feel so profoundly disappointed?

And so irrationally pleased that she would see him again on Thursday?

The address Peter Carroll had given her was in Georgetown, that venerable old section of Washington, D.C., characterized by elegant town houses, beautiful gardens—and no subway stops. One of the reasons she'd picked Washington as a place to settle was the excellent public transportation system, but for some unknown reason, the D.C. Metro had avoided Georgetown. Since Chloe didn't drive, her choice for the appointment on Thursday the fifteenth was either the bus or a cab. Although she couldn't really afford the expense, she took a cab.

She rode across town in air-conditioned comfort, trying not to watch the meter and trying, with even less success, to calm the butterflies that were doing acrobatics in her stomach. Far too easily for her peace of mind,

Chloe recalled the cool, controlled impression Peter Carroll conveyed each time she'd seen him: not a blond hair out of place, not a speck on the navy blue blazer and perfectly creased gray slacks. His expensive loafers were blindingly polished, and the crispness of his starched buttoned-down shirt as she'd slipped her card into his pocket still tingled under her fingers.

There was no way she was going to arrive on his doorstep on a humid, sticky morning in May, feeling equally sticky and humid after a twenty-minute walk from the bus stop. She refused to examine her motives for this piece of extravagance, but felt justified when the taxi stopped in front of a very elegant brick house on a circular street near the river. You just couldn't show up here looking anything less than your best!

In keeping with most of its neighbors, this house had no front lawn. A graceful sweep of brick steps brought her to the front door, which was stained a beautiful golden brown with a brass kickplate across the bottom and a huge brass door knocker in the shape of a lion's head at waist height. She let the lion crash two times and then stepped back on the porch to examine the front of the house while she waited. Each window possessed a pair of working shutters, painted a steely blue, and a wrought iron window box, in the same blue, planted with bright red geraniums. The window glass sparkled in the sunlight, testifying to the loving care with which the house was maintained. Just another indication of how precisely Peter Carroll conducted his life. So very different from her own. . . .

"May I help you?" The door had opened. Chloe jerked her head around to see a very small, very lovely Asian woman looking out at her.

Feeling tall and awkward, she stuttered, "Uh, yes. I . . . I . . . my name is Chloe. I'm here about Eric Carroll's birthday."

With a slight smile, the woman bowed. "Ah, yes. Please come in." She stepped back and pulled the door open wide as Chloe did as she was told. After the door closed with soft, well-oiled eased, she turned. "I am Maia, Mr. Carroll's housekeeper. He said you would be here today. He expected to be here to meet you but there must be some delay. You are to make yourself free of the house, do whatever is necessary for your performance. Would you like some tea?"

Feeling a little like Alice in Wonderland, Chloe pulled herself together enough to accept the offer. "In about half an hour? Would that be convenient?"

Maia bowed again. "Certainly, Miss Chloe. I will bring it to the drawing room, here," she indicated, opening a set of double doors on the right side of the entry hall. "Please make yourself comfortable." With exquisitely small steps she made her way past the curved staircase and disappeared through a door underneath.

Chloe could scarcely breathe, so overwhelming was the beauty of the house. The staircase rose, unsupported, in an elegant arc to the second floor and then coiled even further to the top of the house. Through the center of the spiral hung an immense crystal teardrop chandelier. Marble squares in deep green and grayed white tiled the floor, the walls were papered in a dark green and burgundy stripe, and there could be no doubt about the antiquity of the upholstered bench against the wall, or the grandfather clock in the corner.

The "drawing room" maintained the image with more antique furniture, a Turkish carpet, and graceful, obviously expensive window swags. Not, Chloe thought, a room in which to entertain small boys with magic, even if those charming curtains closed to darken the room, which they didn't. She wasn't sure she even wanted to drink a cup of tea there; how horrible it would be to dribble on that rug!

Three other doors opened out of the entry hall. Chloe peeked into the one nearest her, directly across from the drawing room, to find a rather large coat closet. In all this splendor, at least the small size of the boots and sneakers inside assured her that the mischievous, adorable Eric really did live in this stately house! On the same wall was a set of double doors which opened into a gracious dining room, with a silver tea service on the glossy table and a corner cupboard full of china and crystal. It was a magical room, yes, but not a room for magic.

One more to go. Crossing the foyer, she grasped the knob and turned. Probably a powder room, Chloe told herself. I can't perform in a powder room, either. But the door swung wide to reveal a room as large as the drawing room, but of entirely different character. Dark, cozy, cluttered, it beckoned with a musky, musty scent that spoke of work. And books.

There were hundreds of them. Every available wall space had been lined with darkly stained bookcases. Every available inch of shelf space was filled with books. One window peered through the shroud of shelves, but since it was covered with wooden blinds, three-quarters closed, very little light made its way into the dimness. A huge, flat-topped desk occupied the center of the room, the lamp on its top providing the only other source of illumination. Stacks of paper were arranged neatly around the edges, leaving the space in front of the leather chair cleared for work. A cup filled with pens sat to one side, next to a rigidly aligned ruler.

Chloe absorbed it all, standing frozen at the door. This had to be Peter Carroll's study. It seemed like trespassing to even think about going in. And yet it would be perfect for her performance: dark and eerie, with a compelling aura of mystery that would enhance every illusion. She loved it. As her mind drifted among the possibilities, Chloe took one step inside, and then another, until without inhibitions she was exploring the corners, the fireplace, and the kneehole of the desk, nothing but magic on her mind. Tape recorder resting against her cheek, she spoke softly but clearly, in a one-woman brainstorming session, about the dimensions, characteristics, and potential of the room. The big desk, with its deep recesses and many drawers, fascinated her, and she had just knelt down for a closer look when someone spoke.

"Hello, there!"

"Oww!" she yelped in reply. On her knees underneath the desk, Chloe jerked up at the sound of Peter Carroll's voice; to say the edge of the desk was sharp and hard as her skull cracked into it would be a vast understatement. She sat back down and cradled her head in her arms, blinking back tears and, literally, seeing stars.

"Chloe? Where the devil are you?" His voice was coming closer; in another second he would find her crouched under his desk. "What are you—?" The leather chair scraped backward across the bare floor, and he dropped on his knees in front of her. "Are you all right?"

Taking a deep breath, she raised her head slowly and looked at him. His eyes were almost level with hers. "Except for feeling stupid," she said breathlessly, "I'm fine."

"Can you get up?"

She nodded and winced. He stood up and stepped back, then braced one hand on his knee and extended the other to Chloe. She slid out from underneath the desk, took his hand, and came easily, if shakily, to her feet. "Thanks," was all she could manage.

His hand came startlingly, gently to her cheek. "You're awfully pale. Are you dizzy? Sick to your stomach?"

Again Chloe could hardly breathe—but for reasons that had nothing to do with the bump on her head. The palm against her cheek and the strong fingers around her waist sent a vibrant singing along her nerves. They were almost the same height, and gray eyes met violet directly over the short space between them. Through the confusion, she realized he had asked a question. She shook her head, then wished she hadn't.

"Really," she whispered, with another wince. "I'm okay."

Peter appeared unconvinced. "Turn around," he said, letting her go. With her back to him, Chloe felt his fingers probe gently through her hair. She gasped as he moved lightly across the knot rising on her crown. "Oh, yes, you've got a great big goose egg up there," he murmured. "I'll bet it does hurt."

His hands dropped away. Chloe knew it was only her imagination that made the withdrawal seem reluctant, especially when his voice came back strong and assured. "You need some ice on that lump, my dear. Right now," he declared firmly over her protest.

A strong hand in the center of her back steered her out of the study and behind the staircase, through the same door the housekeeper had used earlier. Blinking in the bright light, Chloe stepped into a spotlessly white kitchen, filled with the aroma of baking and the songs of birds. The songs, she realized, came through the huge open windows that looked out into a classically perfect Georgetown garden. Enchanted, she stepped over to a set of French doors for a better glimpse of the brick-walled courtyard, completely forgetting her host until, suddenly, he stood close behind her, pressing an ice-cold cloth against her head. His other hand held her shoulder as a brace against the pressure. Trapped between the window and Peter's warmth behind her, Chloe felt her breathing quicken, felt a flush take her face and throat. Her knees had developed a treacherous weakness that tempted her to sag against him and force him to catch her in his arms, draw her closer still.

Fortunately, he spoke, and the mists of fantasy evaporated. "How's that? Better?"

Chloe put up a hand to replace his on the ice pack. With a step to the side she was free. "Much better, thanks." She turned to face him and took a quick, startled breath. And then she started to laugh.

Peter stood before her, hands on his hips, a puzzled look taking over his face. "What's funny?" Still laughing, Chloe made a motion of her hand that took in his appearance from head to toe. Not understanding, he looked down at his shoes, pulled at his clothes, and ran his fingers through his hair in a general inventory that assured him he was appropriately covered.

Then he looked back at her in bewilderment. "What is it?" he demanded. "I've got all my clothes on. I'm not wearing anything bizarre—no paint, no dog droppings, no rotten eggs. Chloe?" He stepped closer, suddenly concerned. "Are you hallucinating? What do you see?"

Wiping her eyes, Chloe took a deep breath and then another, trying to calm down. "I'm sorry," she said when she could finally speak. "I'm not laughing at you. I'm laughing at myself. It's just, well, I got intimidated on the way over. It *is* Georgetown, after all, where ambassadors and congressmen live, historically important and socially correct. And then, seeing your elegant house and the way it's furnished, I thought that nobody would ever come here unless they wore their best clothes and their best behavior."

"You're kidding!"

She nodded. "I know, it's pretty silly. But when I finally get to look at you . . ." She made the same motion again, pointing out his damp hair and flushed face, the sweatsoaked t-shirt and nylon shorts he wore, the well-worn running shoes and the splashes of mud on his socks and legs. "This is a real place, just like any other."

The amusement in his eyes echoed her own. "You'd better believe it! With Eric running around, it could hardly be more 'real.' " With a hand on her arm Peter led her beyond the kitchen into a pleasant sitting area with more windows, more books, and a television.

"You see," he said, with a nod in that direction, "we even have the most vicious vice of the century. Eric loves that cartoon about the weird family—the Simpsons, is it?

"But look," he continued, shoving her gently onto a comfortable sofa, "you need to rest for a few minutes. And I, as you mentioned, need to change." As she sat up, trying to protest, he held up a hand. "No, I am a wreck—you're right. I was supposed to finish my run and be back before you got here, but I got held up, if you'll believe it, by traffic, had to take a detour, and ended up lost for about thirty minutes. *I* will go take a shower, while *you* put your feet up and sip the tea Maia brings. Then we can talk about the party. Okay?" She nodded and he extended a finger to brush the tip of her nose. "Thanks," he said with a grin, and was gone.

Stepping under the steaming spray a few minutes later, Peter had to congratulate himself. He'd managed to keep control of his impulses, in spite of almost irresistible temptation. First, in the study, she'd trembled under his hands, wide-eyed and uncertain; he could easily have offered her a very real and physical comfort. She would have been so light in his arms . . . God, the feel of her hair, flowing like water over his fingers! He wasn't sure what had stopped him, except that she was hurt and in pain. Maybe some remnant of decency still harnessed this crazy, consuming passion.

But then, in the kitchen, it had taken every ounce of his strength to keep from pulling her back against him, molding her softness into his body. Only the gentle clatter of a dish, reminding him that Maia stood nearby, had saved Chloe that time. Now, standing directly under the flowing water, Peter rubbed his face into his soapy palms and groaned. He'd barely slept at all last night, anticipating the morning. The hour-long run had been an attempt to get rid of some energy, calm himself down enough to be rational about this woman he barely knew.

Yet one glimpse had set his heart pounding and his hormones racing. Most women wearing a black shirt and black slacks would look simply severe. Chloe seemed exotic, as if the starkness of the outfit was somehow colored by her personality. Those eyes, that mouth . . .

He reached over and flipped the hot water off. Damn, it was cold. And it didn't help, much.

Wrenching the water off completely, Peter stepped out onto the mat and reached for a towel. Never in his thirty-seven years, not even in high school, had he lusted after a woman this way. The only solution to his problem would be to bring the lovely Chloe upstairs, leaving Maia horrified and disapproving in the kitchen, of course, lay her out on this big bed he had all to himself every night, and start fulfilling every fantasy he'd conceived during the last ten days.

Walking through the bedroom to the closet, toweling his hair dry, Peter had to laugh. Of all the probable outcomes for that scenario, Maia's resignation would be the most devastating; the house wouldn't run without her. *So*, he told himself, buttoning a conservative blue shirt, *I guess that's another impulse restrained. There's probably some union rule about magicians fraternizing with clients anyway.*

He ran a comb through his hair, avoiding his eyes in the mirror and trying to ignore the voice in his head reminding him that he wouldn't be her client after Saturday. "Life is full enough, Peter, my boy," he said out loud, "without trying to complicate it. And women universally mean complications." Leaving the bedroom and bath looking as if he'd never been there, he closed the door and hurried eagerly down the stairs.

Peter's absence gave Chloe a chance to recover. Not so much from bumping her head—Maia's sweet, hot tea quickly chased away the slight headache which was all she'd suffered. Chloe was more concerned with regaining her sanity. Over a lifetime of struggle, she had acquired self-confidence and poise. She valued her ability to perform, competently and even powerfully, difficult illusions in front of large groups of frequently uncooperative spectators.

But since meeting Peter Carroll, she found herself behaving less like the rational adult she knew she could be and more like a blushing adolescent. She'd noticed him, that first day, even before she'd stopped by his table. The night of the convention had only deepened the fascination; he'd been in her thoughts—far more often than she wanted to admit—ever since. And now, here in his house, she found the attraction almost overwhelming. If she closed her eyes—and she stared straight ahead so she wouldn't—she could see him again: dirty, sweaty, and very male. He had incredible legs, long and well-shaped, lightly tanned, covered with fine golden hairs. The light shorts and damp t-shirt had left very little else to the imagination; he didn't carry an ounce of spare flesh, that she could see, just well-toned muscle. Smooth skin that she wanted to touch. White, even teeth behind a mobile, generous mouth that would feel so warm against hers . . .

Chloe shifted against the couch, aware of desire swirling in her blood, awakening needs she'd long ago renounced. And all for a man as far removed from herself and her life as the moon. *No, she thought, I could create an illusion and bring the down the moon. Peter Carroll will never be more than just a distant, unreachable—*

"Earth to Chloe! Are you here?"

With a start she found him, not unreachably distant at all, but, instead, tantalizingly close, sitting on the coffee table in front of her, their knees almost touching. His nearness took her breath, left her all too aware of what she'd been thinking about, and how incredibly simple it would be to touch him. Now.

Instead she spilled the tea. "Oh, no!" she cried in dismay as the still-warm brew soaked into the cushion beside her. "I'm so sorry! Do you have a towel?"

Peter got up calmly and pulled a dishcloth from the counter. He came around to the sofa and knelt down to mop up the small damp spot. "No problem, Chloe, really. I shouldn't have startled you, but it seems to be a habit today. Believe me," he said firmly, with one warm hand closing over her agitated fingers as she continued to sputter, "Eric wreaks far worse damage than some weak tea. You see that dark area in the corner over there?"

Her eyes followed his pointing finger to notice a brown blotch. If she hadn't been looking for it, she would have thought it just part of the floral print of the fabric. "That was the Saturday he made himself a chocolate sundae, spilled it doing flips over the arm of the couch, and put a pillow over it so no one would see it until Maia came in on Monday."

Her mouth widened in horror as he continued. "Oh yes! And behind one of these cushions is a unique cluster of marks made by olives."

"Olives?" she squeaked helplessly.

Peter nodded. "I quote: 'They sort of just rolled under there, Dad, and I forgot about them.' "

Chloe dissolved into laughter. "I guess a little tea is almost a blessing, when you think about it."

His grin widened as he watched her, and he let his eyes roam her face, drinking in the pink flush across her cheeks, the sparkling amethyst of her eyes, and the soft, generous curve of her lips. She had relaxed against the cushions again, and her fingers rested quietly under his palm. With a simple movement he could be beside her, could pull her close and test that generosity for himself. And something in his face must have given his thoughts away, because her laughter faded, those incredible eyes widened, and her lips parted on a small, quick breath. *This time*, he thought, *I don't think I can stop it. I'm not strong enough, I want too much, I—*

"Mr. Peter?" said Maia from the doorway, "I am leaving for the market. Is there something special I should get you?"

Saved—foiled—again! Standing up, Peter left temptation on the couch and walked into the kitchen, aware that the magician followed closely behind. "Uh, Maia, could you wait until after lunch? I probably need to make a list of supplies for the party. Chloe might have some ideas," he suggested, "but we haven't discussed it yet."

The housekeeper was obviously displeased to have her schedule rearranged. "Will you be able to be here when Eric gets home, Mr. Peter? If I wait until after lunch, I will not be able to get back in time."

"I have a class at four o'clock, but I can be here until then. Will that work?" Maia bowed and went back through the doorway, her back rigid with disapproval. Peter gave a shrug and a rueful laugh. "Now she's in a huff. I'll have to coax her into forgiving me in a few minutes. Or else we'll get liver for dinner."

Chloe stood beside him and worried. "I'm sorry to get in the way and disrupt her schedule. I hope she isn't too angry."

Peter turned and found her eyes level with his. His comment was unrelated and unexpected. "You're very tall, aren't you? I'm about five eleven, myself."

"I have heels on, but I'm five nine in bare feet."

He nodded. "I thought so." Of all the things he could think of to say, only one would guarantee that they wouldn't end up upstairs. So he chose that one. "Do you have an idea about the performance for the party?"

Chloe allowed herself to be diverted from the ridiculous, sensual direction of her thoughts. It was for the best. "I think your study would be perfect, if you don't mind. And I've got some great illusions that will work beautifully with the fireplace, the bookshelves, and the desk.''

Without being directed she had started walking back toward the front of the house, explaining to Peter as they went into the study. ''The boys can sit on the floor. I'll have everything ready before they arrive. The program should last about forty-five minutes, don't you think? With, maybe,'' she said slowly, as the idea occurred to her, ''a little something extra at the end?''

Peter caught the spark of mischief in her eyes. ''Are you planning something devilish, my dear?'' he asked as they stepped back into the study. ''Something wicked for ten-year-olds?''

She would only smile. ''A magician's secrets must remain a mystery.'' Glancing around, she felt the now familiar twist of need in her chest as she caught sight of this strange, yet strangely familiar man. With his hips propped against the edge of the desk, his legs stretched out long, and his arms across his chest, he looked very much the lord of all he surveyed.

Including, Chloe thought with despair, *myself*. The dark intimacy of the room made her fantasies come to life. Seeking a diversion, she turned away. ''This really is a lovely room,'' she said. ''But I can't imagine owning so many books.''

''Occupational hazard, I'm afraid,'' he replied, his eyes never leaving her face. ''English professors have to read.''

She looked back at him in surprise. ''Why didn't I realize? Of course, you *have* to be a professor!''

His face twisted wryly. ''It's that obvious, hmm?''

With a smile, she confirmed it. ''And an author, I bet. Mysteries?''

He shook his head. ''Poetry.''

Chloe lifted her eyebrows, impressed. ''Really? Published?''

He left the desk and moved to a place on the bookshelves. Under his hand were several slim, colorful books. "Volume four is coming out in the fall. Who are your favorites?"

"I love John Donne, and Whitman and Eliot. And, of course, Emily Dickinson."

He smiled. "Not Frost?"

She answered with a smile, refusing to rise to the bait, refusing to acknowledge his reference to that incredibly provocative quote he'd used. But the silence was not uncomfortable as his long, slim fingers hovered, then pulled on a red binding with gold-tooled letters.

He held it out to her. "If you'd like, you can read some Carroll, too. I'm not Donne, but I'm honest."

Chloe stared at the book, hoping her face hid her panic. A second before the silence would have looked rude, she accepted his offering. "Thank you, I'm sure I will enjoy this." With a deep breath she met his eyes, expecting a look of puzzlement. She found instead a hint of uncertainty, even anxiety, as if her opinion mattered a great deal. Before she could be certain, it was gone.

In its place was simple warmth and amusement. "So Eric and I will label this the 'Magic Den,' or something equally mysterious, and usher all the boys in here on Saturday. When do you need to set up?"

Thank goodness for the darkness; perhaps he hadn't seen her blush. Chloe stepped back and responded lightly. "I'll come over about eleven o'clock with my equipment. Does the door lock? If anyone comes in exploring, the effect might be spoiled."

After some discussion about the lock, and the logistics, Peter escorted her to the front door. "I'm looking forward to this almost as much as Eric is, you know," he said as he pulled the door open. "I've always enjoyed a good magician."

He hadn't intended the words to have a double meaning, but his tone changed the simple sentence into something very, very complicated. Chloe looked away, briefly, and then back, determined to ignore the implications. "I can assure you it will be good, Peter," she said, and then bit her lip at her own slip of the tongue. Stepping out on the porch, she settled for a simple unambiguous, "Good-bye. I'll see you on Saturday."

Not trusting himself with another word, Peter lifted his hand in farewell and watched her walk down the steps. *You should not*, he pointed out to the lecher in his mind, *be noticing the way her slacks pull across her bottom as she walks or the sway of her hips. And wishing her hand held you as tightly as she holds your book is a piece of adolescent foolishness.*

Nevertheless, his eyes followed her down the street until she turned the corner. His mind pursued her farther still, until a blaring horn made him realize he stood like an idiot with the front door still ajar. With a slam that set the crystal teardrops tinkling he remedied that situation. If only his other problem could be solved with a good, loud thud!

Chloe arrived home again every bit as rumpled and sticky as she'd expected after a ride on the bus, but her little bungalow made no pretense to grandeur and accepted her just as she was. When she unlocked the door, she stepped directly into the living room where a comfortable, well-used couch, a big, broken-in armchair with an ottoman, and several oversized throw pillows all invited her to relax. It might not be Georgetown elegance, but it was good to be home!

Kicking off her shoes by the door, Chloe padded barefoot over the worn blue carpet to her desk, where she placed Peter Carroll's book carefully on the top. Her hand remained resting on the cover, as if she could absorb the words inside through her skin. Maybe Dallas would read some of it to her so she could tell Peter what she thought of his work. He didn't need to know she couldn't read it for herself; it was a secret she shared only with her most trusted friends—which meant Dallas and nobody else. Certainly not a college professor from Georgetown, with money to burn and published poetry of his own on his shelves.

She stood there for a long time, head down, thinking about the past, the present, and the possibilities in the future. Robert and Mikey were the past: the man who had fought her and won and the little boy he'd taken away. Peter Carroll was the present: a client, a father, an attractive man who stirred her as no one ever had. Then there was Eric: a handful of active, happy boyhood who reminded her, in too many ways, of all that she'd lost. And Dallas, of course: loyal friend, undemanding confidant, unfailing supporter. The one who stayed when everyone else turned away.

What did the future hold? Not Mikey, she knew. Dallas would be here—she could count on that. But what about Peter? She'd read the signs in his face today; she knew he was attracted to her, wanted her, had thought about her after they met. So what, then? Could she handle a brief affair—a few nights spent together, a few steamy, sensual afternoons of love, and then end it? Where would that leave her? Could she possibly give everything to him and then just walk away? Could she walk away from Eric?

No. And the possibility of a lasting relationship was just as unthinkable. Peter lived in a world she knew nothing about, an elegant, fastidious world with housekeepers and books and college classes. How long would it take him to realize her handicap, to pry out her secrets, to despise her for her past? The pain of that rejection, she knew, might be more than she could bear. It made any commitment between them impossible.

Chloe drew her fingers slowly across Peter's book and, finally, away. It would end on Saturday, she decided. She would do the performance, take a check, and walk away from them both. She and Dallas would get a pizza and some wine, spend the evening listening to tapes and feeling good. That's all she needed.

It's all she could have.

With a loud sigh Chloe plowed her fingers through her hair, turned, and headed into the kitchen. All at once she felt hungry and thirsty, felt the need to do something besides think. Tonight's show needed to be set up, and Eric's party needed planning; she had a million things to do. But thinking about making love to Peter Carroll would not get any of them done.

A single candle flickered in the darkness. Its waver-
ing light glazed ten small faces, reflecting equal parts
of excitement and apprehension as they gazed around
the room, searching in vain for a familiar outline, a
shadow or a surface, to give them a reference point.
Blackness crept out of the corners and shrouded the
walls, pushing the boys closer together for the reassur-
ance of bodily contact. Their usual ten-year-old noise
faded abruptly into an enjoyable panic as the door behind them slammed shut.

The flame faltered and died. Music came to their
ears, quiet, intense, nearly as dark as the room itself.

A trumpet blared and a face came out of the blackness above their heads: a woman's face, very white,
but not frightening, really, with a gentle, if mysterious,
smile. Her eyes sparkled and flashed as she looked them
over. "Welcome," she said in a soft, compelling voice.
"I am Chloe. Let us explore the realm of magic
together."

Two white hands appeared beside the face. With an
intricate flourish they produced a glittering gold handkerchief, waved it in the air, then folded it carefully in
half, in half again, and again, until it was small enough

to be hidden in one palm. The right hand flattened, circled once, twice, over the left fist, then moved below, palm up, to receive the shower of gold coins that flowed clinking over her fingers. Amid cries of delight, the closed hand revealed itself to be, in fact, empty. The gold cloth had vanished.

Against the crashing music, Chloe threw the coins up in the air and caught them again in a silver cup which, when it was turned to pour, proved that the coins, too, were gone. And then, with another wave of her hand, the magician reached two slender fingers inside and pulled the gold cloth out of the empty cup. The boys cheered wildly.

With a sharp clap of her hands, Chloe summoned a series of bright metal rings, which seemed to materialize by themselves out of the darkness to be caught in first one hand and then the other. In a few moments she had them twisting and sailing through the air, soaring higher and higher above her head. When they rested, tinkling, in her palms again, she spoke. "Eric, could you help, please?" When he came to stand where she pointed, Chloe involved him in an intricate and ultimately hilarious routine involving juggling, linking and unlinking rings, and, miraculously, the reappearance of the gold coins in Eric's pocket. The boy returned to his seat in a state of total enchantment.

The rasp of a striking match preceded the flare of flame on the candle they'd seen before, and then another. In the comparatively brilliant light Chloe was revealed in more detail, standing behind a table draped in black. The pace of the performance increased, as balls appeared, disappeared under a small golden bowl, and then reappeared out of thin air between her fingers, or, several times, behind young boys' ears and elbows and knees. Where there had been one bowl, there were suddenly three, and the balls leaped from one to the other accompanied by laughter and applause. And then the bowls and balls became juggling props, flashing and glittering in the candlelight until they sailed, too quickly for the eye to follow, back into the dark.

The applause died slowly. Chloe held up her hands, asking for silence. "I would like to perform for you now a feat of incredible concentration and intensity. I ask that you remain quiet, and help me to visualize as I bring something out of nothing." With a quick breath she extinguished the candles, explaining, "For such a difficult task we require the blessings of darkness." Placing her hands carefully together, palm against palm, she closed her eyes slowly and whispered, softly but clearly, "Now—think!"

The tension in the room vibrated around them all, heightened by the pulsing rhythm of the music. Some of the boys sat, eyes closed, adding their strength to the will of the magician. Others stared intently into the blackness, waiting for they knew not what. The most observant of the boys noticed a shimmer on the table in front of them, which soon became a glitter, and then a sheen. As they gasped in amazement, the music swelled and the image gained strength and substance until at last before their eyes appeared a pair of shining brass scimitars, curved edges wickedly gleaming, with bright red silk tassels curled around the hilts. Last of all, Chloe opened her eyes and, with a brilliant smile, lifted one mighty weapon in each hand and crossed them above her head.

There was a flash, a crash, and a plume of brilliant purple smoke rose before their eyes. While they exclaimed, confused and concerned, the door behind them opened, allowing light once again into the room. Excited beyond words, the boys turned to look, and then turned back, as their eyes adjusted, to Chloe.

She had, of course, disappeared. Only the swords remained, crossed on the velvet-covered desk, attesting to her presence. Bewitched, the boys called and searched, looked behind the curtains and under the desk, to no avail. More than a little bemused himself,

Peter Carroll eventually herded the boys out of the study and back toward the garden, where a table with cake and the trimmings awaited their assault. He gave the room one last look before he closed the door, but there was, indeed, nothing to be seen.

"Whew!" Chloe heard the Texan's exclamation echo around her in the chimney. "What a job! You outdid yourself this time, honey," Dallas said, his voice coming closer as she reached, toes pointed, for the floor of the fireplace. "You had those kids in the palm of your hand, no doubt about that."

Chloe dropped down on her haunches to clear the top of the firebox; then she straightened up. "It *was* good, wasn't it? You handled it all perfectly, Dallas." She used one of the white gloves she'd been wearing to wipe her face, then noticed with a grimace the amount of soot she'd managed to pick up. "Too bad they haven't had the chimney cleaned recently. I thought the disappearance went well, didn't you? Although I was sure one of them was going to start looking up the chimney—he was standing there for quite a while. Fortunately Peter got them out."

"I was holdin' my breath, that's for sure. If those boys had seen me behind the door, lookin' like some horror show murderer in a black mask, they would have freaked out." He held out his hand for her soiled gloves and wrapped them up with his mask. "Slip that apron off, sweetheart, before you drop dead," he suggested, referring to the long black tunic she wore. Its pockets held the props she produced for her illusions; when filled with balls and bowls and cups and coins, it could get very heavy.

Obediently Chloe turned so that he could undo the zipper and sighed with pleasure as Dallas took the weight off her shoulders. "The only thing harder than climbing a chimney," she reflected, stretching her arms wide and twisting her shoulders to get the kinks out, "is climbing a chimney carrying ten pounds of metal that mustn't make noise. I didn't realize until I did it how tough that would be."

"You know," Dallas said, laying the apron carefully across the desk, "you could always get a job as a chimney sweep, when you get tired of magic."

"Thanks, but no thanks."

"Or mountain climbin'—I hear there's good money in sponsorship for mountain climbin'." Dallas was wearing an apron of his own, where he stored the linking rings and the other props she had thrown to him during the performance. With the ease of long practice, he transferred items between the two garments until each held its original property.

"I'm not very good with heights, Dallas. I think I'll leave the mountains to somebody else—David Copperfield, maybe. Are you ready to get the drape?"

They moved to either side of the black velvet curtain that had been erected across the entire back wall of the room to serve as a backdrop for the performance. Supported by telescoping legs and what amounted to a long curtain rod, the cloth made many of her illusions possible, since black against black is completely invisible. The boys had looked carefully behind it in their search for the vanished magician, finding nothing, of course; only the bookshelves and the window rewarded their efforts. Which was just what Chloe had intended: misdirection is the key to most magic.

In five minutes the velvet was stowed in its specially made sack, the aprons tucked in, and the room returned to its more practical self. Dallas was just reaching up to the highest bookshelf in the corner behind the door to get the rest of his tools when a decisive knock startled them both.

Chloe put a finger to her lips, hoping that silence would be taken for emptiness if one of the boys wanted to come in.

It was not, however, one of the boys. Peter Carroll looked around the door and, seeing only Chloe, slipped in carefully to avoid exposing her to prying young eyes. A wide grin lighted his face as he came across the room. "That was a remarkable performance, my dear. I had no idea—and the boys can't stop talking about it! Even the birthday presents are taking second place to a moment by moment retelling of the mystery!" He bent slightly, offering his hand to help her up from her knees. When she stood before him, he forgot to let go. "I have this crazy wish to know how you did it all, but I doubt you'd tell me."

Mesmerized as she was by his smile, Chloe could only shake her head. "I—I think you'd be disappointed. It's more fun if you don't know the secret," she said breathlessly. Something about this man made nonsense of all her good intentions, transformed her usual independence to a weak-kneed submission. A lift of that arrogant eyebrow, a smiling glint from those stormy gray eyes and she would, as the saying went, follow him anywhere. His thumb stroked lightly over the backs of her fingers, and she shivered with a sudden chill.

Her gaze held his as he continued the light caress, and then she watched as his eyes dropped to her lips. His grip tightened, suddenly; his arm tensed, and it was only a matter of seconds before he would draw her close enough to kiss. . . .

A loud thump broke the silence, followed by a painful clang. The two in the center of the room jumped, and Peter whirled around. "What the hell?"

Chloe put her hand on his arm and threw Dallas an angry, knowing look. "I'm sorry, Peter. Let me introduce you to Dallas Page, my assistant. Dallas, this is Peter Carroll, Eric's father." *The owner of the house, you idiot. The man who writes our check!*

Dallas bent to pick up the heavy tool belt he had dropped on the hardwood floor, then sauntered over and extended a long, lean hand. "Pleased to meet you, Mr. Carroll."

Peter's narrowed eyes looked over the whip-thin frame and tousled brown hair even as he shook hands. It annoyed him to have to look up into the tanned face, annoyed him that he'd been caught on the edge of, well, whatever he'd been about to do. And most of all it annoyed him that Chloe should work so closely with a man—any man.

"How do you do, Mr. Page." He did at least remember his manners.

After the briefest of contacts, they both stepped back. Dallas managed to look casually busy, putting away the spotlight, gathering up the last of their belongings, but Chloe didn't miss the far-from-casual glances he threw at the other man in the room, and his usual smile had been replaced by a thin, taut line. Peter returned the favor, standing cool and calm with his hands in the pockets of his gray slacks, pale yellow oxford cloth shirt rolled up at the sleeves, his speculative gaze following the man in the black jumpsuit as if to make sure he didn't steal something. Meanwhile, the uncomfortable silence stretched on and on. Getting the rest of her gear together, Chloe watched, bewildered, as the two men circled each other like rutting stags. *What in the world*, she wondered, *had gotten into Dallas?* She'd never seen him so . . . so jealous.

Finally she decided that somebody needed to say something. "Dallas is, um, part of the magic," she explained, trying not to sound apologetic. "Some of those illusions can't be produced without two people, at least not in a room like this."

Peter's eyes swung back to her. "I see." What he saw was not clear, exactly, except that it seemed to mean more than just the performance. And it didn't make him smile. "Well, I came in to congratulate you on an excellent performance and to invite you, uh, both, into the kitchen for coffee and cake."

He extended his invitation as he walked back to the door. Feeling abandoned, Chloe followed, saying, "I had planned to make an appearance at the end of the party, with a treat for the boys to take away with them. Dallas can't be seen at all, or they'll guess some of the secrets.'' She tried to restore his good mood with a grin of her own. ''I think boys should keep their illusions as long as possible, don't you?''

Failure. His eyes were a frosty gray as they met hers. ''I think everybody should keep their illusions. But it's not always possible.'' With a deep breath, he finished, ''Thanks for the great show. I'll see you after the party and write you a check.'' He shut the door, literally, in her face.

Chloe stood for a minute with her forehead pressed against the closed door, fighting the urge to beg for something she knew she shouldn't have. She could feel the Texan's eyes on her back like the heat of the sun on a summer afternoon and knew that if she turned around the turmoil of her emotions would show on her face. Even with Dallas, she couldn't face that kind of exposure.

But when at last she got up the courage to confront him, he wasn't looking her way. ''Hey, there, Ms. Magician,'' he threw over his shoulder as he rifled through one of their trunks of tricks. ''You gonna stand there all day or are we gonna get this last trick ready?'' His voice held only its usual irreverence.

With relief, Chloe straightened her back and let him change her mood. ''Keep your shirt on, Dallas. I'm coming,'' she returned with a good imitation of her own insouciance. ''Let's leave them with something to remember us by!''

Their last impression was the most sensational. Under Peter's indulgent eye, ten little boys were tearing around the entry hall, sliding and slipping over the marble, barely missing the furniture and leaving more than one scuff for Maia to deal with. And then the music returned, louder and more demanding than before. With a flash like lightning and a crack of thunder, the magician reappeared in front of their eyes in an envelope of smoke. They gasped in astonishment as she floated forward in a cloud of iridescent designs and mystical symbols that seemed to vibrate on her flowing, shimmering robe of black silk. Without a word she passed among them and her hands produced, from the air it seemed, a small scimitar for each of them—no bigger than a small ball, not large enough to get hurt with, but sufficient to keep her memory alive. Awed, the boys left silently with the parents who collected them, only to explode in feverish explanation once the magic spell dissolved.

Eric, of course, remained caught in the enchantment; he stood still and, for a short time, speechless with wonder. At last he found his voice.

"That was so cool!" he whispered. He looked at Peter. "Did you see that, Dad? Look at this—just like the ones she used!" he exclaimed, showing his father the small sword. Whipping himself around the foyer, pretending to fight a host of enemies with his tiny weapon, Eric brought himself up short in front of the magician herself. "I can't believe you did all that stuff! Will you show me how?"

She looked down at the little boy whose big brown eyes met hers so beseechingly. With one more tug at her heart he could have anything she had to give. "If I told you the secrets, it wouldn't be as much fun," she said, just as she had to his father. "I think you'd rather not know, at least for now."

Surrender, as Peter could have told her, was not in Eric's vocabulary. "Please?" he begged. "Just one trick?"

Those eyes! Chloe sighed. "Okay. Watch carefully." From her right pocket she took the silver cup he'd seen before and from the left she drew a handful of coins. Lifting her arms, she dropped the coins, clinking merrily, into the cup. With a kiss on the brim, she raised the cup, tilted it: no coins fell out.

"Cool! Where'd they go?"

Chloe smiled at the boy, at the same time suppressing the shiver of awareness that told her his father stood behind her shoulder, watching carefully. "They're still there," she explained. "Watch." With another twist of the cup, the coins poured back into her palm. "It's all in how you position the cup, Eric," she continued, lowering the cup. "Put your finger inside and move it around."

He did so, concentrating so intently that his eyes almost crossed. Then, suddenly, he gave a triumphant crow. "There's a secret compartment inside the cup! The coins fall into that side if you hold it right—and it's lined with felt so they won't make noise! How neat! Can I try it?"

She relinquished the coins and the cup to Eric, who sat down on the bottom step of the staircase and proceeded to practice his first magic trick. A warm hand on her shoulder turned her to face Peter Carroll, who gave her a wry look. "I had hoped he would grow up to be an architect, or maybe president. It looks like I'll be talking about my son, Houdini, instead!"

Chloe lifted an eyebrow, trying to decide if he'd meant the comment as an insult or a joke. "Magic is an honorable profession, if it's done well, Peter. It can even be a profitable one, for the right person. Houdini himself was quite a wealthy man."

He stepped back, hands raised in surrender. "I didn't mean to offend you—I'm very impressed by what you do. Speaking of which," he paused, reaching into the pocket of his shirt, "let me make it a little more profitable for you." Handing her a check, he couldn't help adding, "And, of course, Mr. Page."

She closed the check in her palm without looking at it. "Thank you, Peter."

There should have been something else to say, but the frost in his gray eyes stopped the words. With a shake of her head that set her hair swinging, she turned

toward Eric. "Have you got it yet?" she asked the boy.
Teeth clenched, he gave a small shrug and continued
his practice.

"Well, I'll leave the cup and coins with you, then,"
Chloe said, ignoring his father's startled refusal in favor
of Eric's delighted crow. "Sort of a birthday present.
Maybe one day I'll see you perform." Unfastening the
clip at her throat, she allowed the silk robe to fall off
her shoulders and slip down her arms, where she caught
it with her fingers and gathered the slippery folds together over one arm. Unable to resist the impulse, she
rested her hand for a second on Eric's soft curls.

"Happy Birthday, Eric. Good luck."

When she reached the front door, Chloe turned to
look once more at the slender man who remained in
his chosen place, leaning with elegant composure
against the wall. "Good luck to you, too, Peter." Their
gazes clashed. In his she could read, all too easily,
rejection and denial, firmly supported by anger and
pride. Whatever he had read into her relationship with
Dallas must have driven him away. Maybe she should
explain. . . .

No. With a lift of her chin, Chloe retrieved her own
pride. *She'd* decided to end it here. Let *him* be the one
left hurting and wondering why. "It's been a pleasure
working for you, Mr. Carroll," she said in her most
professional voice, with her most professional smile.
"If you ever need a magic act again, don't hesitate to
call. Dallas and I will be happy to help you out." She
waited a second, but his only response was a lift of
that arrogant eyebrow. "Good-bye," Chloe said, with
a firmness she was proud of, and slipped out the door.

And that, thought Peter, congratulating himself, was
that. Beautiful women meant trouble, especially when
they came equipped with jealous male "assistants."
Throughout the remainder of the evening, preparing
Eric's requested birthday dinner of grilled hamburgers,
in the middle of a shower of rain, and enduring a dem-

onstration of every birthday present received, Peter comforted himself with a prediction of the problems he had escaped by letting Chloe walk away.

Eric is all the trouble I need in my life, his father silently reflected later in the evening, as he applauded the tenth performance of the disappearing coin trick. *I have no time for an affair, or a flaming romance. And anyway, it's just a physical reaction. She's gorgeous. I've been alone for awhile. It will pass. It has to.*

As the coins vanished for the twelfth time, Peter stirred himself to action. "Okay, Eric the Magnificent, it's time for all magicians to hit the sack. Upstairs, into your pajamas, brush your teeth. I'll come up in ten minutes to say goodnight."

"Aw, Dad, do I have to?" came the traditional protest, but less forcefully than usual after the excitement of the day. In less than fifteen minutes, with Eric soundly asleep, Peter had the house to himself. He sat in his study with a blank sheet of paper in front of him and his favorite pen curled in his fingers, trying to ignore the exotic, unfamiliar scent the magician had left behind. The combination of smoke and velvet and sweet, womanly perfume tantalized him and stirred the longings he had attempted to put aside.

But, he had to admit some time in the early hours of the morning, it also inspired the first decent poem he'd written in months. Stretching his arms high above his head, Peter ignored the wreck of his desk to focus on his achievement: a single sheet of paper with a symmetrical arrangement of words flowing down the center of the page:

Smoke
pouring, choking,
blinding me.
Perfume
of the ancients,
musk, incense,

in alabaster and silk.
Mystery
of the ages,
cold, fiery,
enchantment.
Illusion promises perfection.
Reality
shreds
the image.
I stand
removed, remote.
Safe.
Alone.
Empty.
Hurt.
Dead.
Embalm me with your precious oils.
Rest me on my raft and push me swiftly out to sea
that I might drown this pain,
unsought,
and set my spirit free.
The vastness of the universe might serve
as space enough
between myself and thee.

As a statement of his confusion over Chloe, it was,
he thought, a success; as a confession of the depth of
his feelings, he found it much less comfortable. The
words had come easily, once he accepted the need to
write about her, but what they revealed disturbed him.

"Removed"? "Remote"? Was he really so distant?
How could he be, with a spitfire like Eric dragging him
through life? And yet, there it was again: did he need
to be "dragged"? Why wasn't he moving under his
own steam, so to speak?

How did Chloe come into all of this? He'd thought
it was simply sex: desire for a woman whose looks

promised, as he'd said, enchantment. Was there more? Had he let her get away with something he needed?

With a curse, Peter pushed away from his desk with such force that the chair fell over backwards as he stood up. The lateness of the hour, coupled with fatigue, was the problem. Everything would be clear in the morning. He had needed to work, and so he had. He might never publish this particular poem, but he had long ago learned that trying not to write, when the words pounded at his brain, guaranteed disaster in every other aspect of his life. Setting his reactions and emotions on paper provided a release that would at least let him go to bed with a reasonable hope of getting to sleep.

And if it wasn't what his body craved, well, too bad. As long as his mind remained clear, cold showers and abstinence would no doubt take care of the rest.

"More pizza?"

"Nope, I'm stuffed."

"More wine?"

"Nope. Not unless you want me to fall asleep on your floor."

Chloe chuckled. "It wouldn't be the first time."

"True. Hand me a pillow."

The last notes of a Beethoven piano sonata still vibrated in the dimly lit living room where she and Dallas sprawled comfortably on the floor, leaning back against the old couch, with their pizza feast on the coffee table at chin-level. Adrift in the comfortable glow of a little too much wine and a job well-done, Chloe decided that she could afford to explore the unknown. Reaching up a lazy hand, she pulled Peter Carroll's book off her desk. Then she tugged on Dallas's blue shirt sleeve to get his attention.

"Before you drift off, I want you to read something."

He lifted one lazy eyelid. "It's midnight, Chloe. I don't read that late."

"Oh, come on. You're a night owl, just like me."

Groaning, he pushed himself upright. "And *you* are a problem, you know that? What is this that can't wait 'til mornin'? A foreclosure notice? A demand for back taxes?"

She handed him the slender volume. He took it in his long, strong fingers and carefully turned back the cover. "Nice binding," he commented in the reverent voice of a connoisseur. "Great print. Who . . ."

Stretching out her arm for her wine glass, Chloe was struck by the quality of his sudden silence. When she turned to look, she found his head bent, his gaze focused on the title page. He didn't say anything for what seemed like a long, long time.

"What's wrong?" she said at last, seeing the tension in his body, knowing it forecast trouble.

Dallas closed the book firmly, without looking her way. "I, uh, think I'd better go."

She held him in place with a hand on top of his clenched fist. "I thought you were going to read to me."

"No!" he said too loudly, then seemed to regret the violence of his outburst. "I can't, Chloe. Leave it." He got up then, with a series of jerky, uncoordinated motions totally unlike his usual smooth control. The book slid unnoticed to the floor.

Chloe watched him walk away from her, felt the weight of fear settle in her chest. When he got to the door, the fear became panic and propelled her to her feet.

"Dallas?" she implored desperately. "You can't walk out of here without an explanation. We mean too much to each other for you to act like that!"

Keeping his back to her, he shoved his hands into the pockets of his jeans. "You don't want to do this, Chloe. I said leave it."

She crossed the floor in three strides and grabbed his

arm in a fierce grip. "Talk to me, Dallas Page. I want to know!"

Whether it was her words, or her touch, something inside him seemed to break. He whirled around; his hands clamped painfully over her shoulders. "How in hell," he demanded through gritted teeth, "can such an intelligent woman be so damned blind?"

"Blind? What are you talking about?"

All at once his face softened, his hold gentled. "Oh, Chloe," he said softly, a bittersweet smile twisting his mouth. "In all my dreams I never imagined havin' to say it like this." As his gaze held hers, his eyes filled with a laughing sorrow. "You want me to read you love poems, honey. Love poems written by another man—the one you want for your own. And in all these years you never even saw that I'm in love with you myself."

It couldn't be. Surely, she would have known. But as Chloe stared into his face, saw it stripped bare of all the defenses she'd never recognized were there, she knew the truth. "You never said . . ." she started tremulously.

Dallas shrugged. "Your feelin's have always been clear, Chloe. I respected how you felt. I just never realized that, when you changed your mind, I might not be the one you turned to."

She brought her hands up to clasp his. "Dallas, it isn't like that," she promised, trying to make him believe. "I'm not involved with him—never will be."

Gently, he disentangled his fingers. "You're lyin', darlin'. If not to me, then to yourself. Let's end this with honesty, if not love."

Chloe stood still as he stepped back, her mind unwilling to accept the meaning of his words. "End it? What do you mean?"

He didn't answer for several seconds. At last he took a deep breath, as if drawing in strength, and once again plunged his hands into his pockets. "I'm leavin', Chloe."

"You can't!" The agony in her voice shocked them both. She took a step toward him, trying for control with an effort that showed in the trembling hand she stretched out to him. "What are you going to do, Dallas?" she managed more moderately. "Where are you going?"

Leaning a shoulder against the door frame, he met her look one last time. "I'm thinkin' that it's time I went back to Texas, sort of surveyed the situation down there. God knows I'm tired of this town, without an inch of space to call my own or a foot of sky that's not filled with junk. I only stayed this long because of you, and I don't think I did you any favors. Or myself." His rueful grin was obviously forced. "I guess you could say this is my notice to quit. Sorry about the two weeks."

"What will I do without you?"

With the door open, he stopped. He had heard her question, even though it was barely a whisper. His fist clenched against the wall, and he spoke without turning around. "What will you do without me? Well, I guess you're gonna have to start thinkin' for yourself, Chloe. Start figurin' out how to feel again. Maybe open up a little to people instead of keepin' them behind that smoke screen you call magic.

"I thought I was the man to help you do that. And then I thought nobody could, but at least I'd be your friend. But now, well, I think you've come up against somethin'—somebody—who brings you outside of that prison you carry around. And forgive me, but it hurts too much for me to stand here and watch. I love you, sweetie. Goodbye."

Chloe slumped to the floor, her back to the door. With her head buried on her knees, her mind's eye followed Dallas. She saw him open the door to her van and toss the keys onto the driver's seat, heard the slam as he closed it again. She saw him walking through the dark, narrow streets of her neighborhood and then out to the main avenue leading down to the city. Would he catch a cab? A bus? He lived down near the National Zoo, about seven miles away. Knowing Dallas, he might walk.

And then what? He would stuff his clothes into that old duffle bag he carried wherever he went, and he'd be gone. He'd hitch a ride south, headed for Texas. Would he ever call? Would he answer the phone if she tried to call him now?

From where she sat by the door, Chloe could lift her head and see herself in the mirror, could see the fear and panic in her face. Dallas had been the mainstay of her life for so long, she really didn't know what to do without him. And it wasn't just that she needed him to drive her around, write checks for her, make poetry tapes and read the paper. She needed him to talk to, to laugh with. How would she survive without *anybody* to share with?

"Damn you, Peter Carroll!" She shouted into the empty house, struggling to her feet, rubbing away tears. "I wish I'd never seen you—this is all your fault!" With furious energy she threw out the pizza and poured the wine down the sink, spent an hour scrubbing her kitchen and another cleaning the bathroom. And then, exhausted, she threw herself on her bed. And still, in the dark, there were two images in her mind: Peter Carroll, angry and aloof, and Dallas Page, a solitary figure walking with long, clean strides down the interstate to Texas.

"Heave-ho!"
"That's it, babe. Pump it up!"
"Nice view!"
It was the last straw. Pulling her fingers out from underneath the third wooden chest she'd unloaded from the van so far, Chloe straightened up and turned to face

her audience. "I've had it with you guys," she said, flashing a warning look at the bartender and the janitor who stood in the doorway, offering suggestive remarks and no help. "If you don't keep your comments to yourselves, you might just find one of these boxes on your foot as we go by."

"Aw, don't be mean, sweetheart. Give us a smile."

Pushing her wet bangs off her forehead, Chloe bent over to pick up the box again, giving the woman on the other end a nod to lift her end. They were only halfway into the process of moving her equipment into the Street Scene nightclub where she would be performing for the next four weeks, but one hundred percent humidity and a temperature of ninety-six degrees guaranteed that Chloe's temper was shredded and her attitude hostile. Setting up had never been this hard before—but then, she'd never done it before without Dallas. Her new assistant, Kirsten, was athletic and coordinated, but no match for the Texan in the strength department. *Oh well*, she told herself, groaning a little at the weight of the box on her wrists, *women have more stamina, to make up for the brute strength. We'll make it.*

Breathing hard, they made it across the sidewalk and up to the door, where the two men leaned against the wall, grinning widely and looking as if they had rooted to the spot. They didn't give an inch as Chloe started to back through the doorway. She took a deep breath and looked over at Kirsten with a question in her eyes. Kirsten stared back and, without moving a muscle, let Chloe know she understood.

They dropped the box.

"Hey!"

"What the hell are you doing?" The two men moved fast when they wanted to, and got their feet out of the way just in time.

Chloe gave them an innocent look. "Oh, I'm sorry. Do you think it's too heavy?"

The two men stared at her, half-angry, half-ashamed, and she stared expectantly back. Finally, the bartender spoke up. "Look, you need some help? Maybe we could . . ."

The janitor seemed less convinced. "If I give you twenty-five apiece," Chloe offered at last, although she winced inside at the cost, "will that make it easier?"

In a miraculously short time, all the equipment was in place backstage. Then began the painstaking process of arranging the stage for maximum effect. Dallas, Chloe couldn't help but remember, would have known exactly what she needed and done it before she thought of it herself. Kirsten couldn't be blamed for her lack of experience, but explaining every detail pushed them to the very limit as far as the schedule went. The first show started at eight-thirty; they left the club at seven fifteen needing showers, costumes and makeup. But Kirsten drove nearly as recklessly as Dallas, and they made it back to the club with four minutes to spare. At exactly the right moment Chloe took her place in the center of the darkened stage.

The magic worked.

Afterward, they both collapsed in the pint-sized dressing room. The airless, windowless space, crammed with boxes of junk, hardly cushioned them in luxury, but at least the manager had remembered her request for sandwiches and tea and had left a bountiful tray perched on one of the sturdier cartons. "He must have liked the show," Chloe remarked as she and Kirsten attacked the food.

For a long time, only the sound of discreet munching broke the silence, until with a last soothing sip of ice-cold liquid Chloe felt the relaxation of hunger well-fed. Leaning back in the ragged arm chair, she drew in a deep breath and let it out very slowly. "You did a great job out there," she told Kirsten with a smile. "Everything was there when I needed it. And you look good under the lights. How did you feel?"

Kirsten stretched back in her turn. "It was . . . okay," she replied in the soft, slightly accented voice which hinted at her childhood in Germany. Ice-blond hair and eyes as clear as a blue Alpine lake complemented the image and, coupled with a tall, statuesque body, created a remarkable stage presence. "I was very, very nervous, at first," she continued, "but the audience was concentrating on *you* and somehow it seemed most important that nothing break that focus, if you know what I mean, so I was able to stop worrying about myself and to think only about what you would need next."

Chloe grinned at her with delight. "That, dear Kirsten, is *exactly* what should happen! You are an assistant beyond compare! Now all we need to do is get through two more shows tonight, and then we can call it a day."

She leaned her head against the back of the chair and closed her eyes against the scorching light from the bare light bulb overhead. Kirsten left the room—to find the restroom, Chloe presumed, but then knew different when the door opened again almost immediately. The heat from above cooled abruptly as the searing glare was replaced with a soft glow from the battered lamp Kirsten had found. As Chloe stared in speechless gratitude, her assistant smiled and shrugged.

"There is no need for you to suffer when you have to perform again in an hour," she said. "I thought you might rest more comfortable this way."

Overwhelmed, Chloe allowed her lashes to drop against her cheeks, holding in quick, startled tears. For the first time in the six weeks since Dallas had left, she began to believe that things might actually work out. Getting along without him had proved harder than she could have imagined. Just getting an advertisement into the trade papers for a new assistant had been a nightmare. The interviews were worse, as half the weirdos in Washington showed up at her door wanting to be a magician. And her trips around town, looking for jobs like this one, had meant endless bus rides carrying an oversized satchel of equipment for demonstrations to prospective club owners. She had come across Kirsten on one of those trips. The lounge owner wasn't interested, but Kirsten, tired of working as a waitress, was fascinated, and over a series of cold drinks the two women discovered a comfortable rapport. By late that evening, after some practice at home, they had agreed to work together.

Which solved the professional problems, at least. In the personal sphere, nothing had improved. Kirsten, although a concerned and caring friend, had a life of her own with a tall, blond husband and a pair of twin boys to occupy her free time. Without Dallas to pal around with, Chloe spent most of her time alone, practicing her magic which kept her mind away from the regrets and the aching emptiness that filled her when she stopped. Days like this one, in fact, were good, because she would be so exhausted by the time they got home that nothing, not the ache of missing Dallas, not even the image of Peter Carroll that haunted her dreams, would keep her awake. She hoped.

The 1:00 AM show was crowded, which was to be expected on a Saturday night, and rowdy and difficult. Chloe managed to keep her timing up, with Kirsten helping all she could, but the distractions of the drunks in the audience spoiled some of the effects. The final illusion, in which Kirsten disappeared from underneath the table, brought more skeptical hoots than amazed sighs. One man lurched toward the stage, intent on looking for the tall blonde himself, but the bouncer stepped in and caught him back before he caused any damage. Chloe took her final bow to sporadic applause and waited impatiently for the curtain to close before dropping her head as far back as it would go. She hated late shows, hated the people who came and the way they behaved. But this one had ended, and in, oh, about an hour she could be tucked up in bed and, with any luck, asleep.

Judging by the noise, the crowd had decided to see the night out in the Street Scene. As they stored the last of the equipment, Chloe and Kirsten could hear the rough laughter and the breaking glass that seemed to symbolize a good time. Without a word they double-checked each lock on her strong storage chests, making sure they couldn't be opened, before retreating to the dressing room to change into street clothes and pick up their makeup cases. A word from the manager assured Chloe that she would be welcome back on Tuesday, since Sunday and Monday were dark at the club, and then they were free to leave. Finally.

The van was parked behind the building, in an alley, under a street lamp. It had seemed like a good precaution in the early evening, with the sun still shining, but at almost three in the morning, when they realized that the street lamp didn't work, the situation looked worse. And when the shadow stepped out from behind the garbage dumpster, the whole night went to hell.

It was the same drunk who had tried to get on the stage. "Hi there, sweet face," he slurred, cutting off their escape to the street. "I liked your show. What else do you do?"

His left hand caught Kirsten by the arm. Before Chloe could move away or scream, his right hand held a ten-inch knife. "I wouldn't do anything, if I were you, Miss Magic," he sneered. "I might be tempted to do some carving." He flourished the knife in Chloe's face. When he smiled, the smell of liquor hit them in the face. "Back up!" he ordered, laying the knife along her cheek. "Both of you—against the wall."

FOUR

If anyone had asked him what he was doing in the middle of the Georgetown madness at midnight on a Saturday, Peter really couldn't have given a rational answer. The tourist/college crowd shoved and danced and lurched around him, caught up in their weekend fling, as he paced slowly along the sidewalk, trying to think and, at the same time, trying *not* to think. The noise deafened him, the heat of the day still radiated out of the asphalt, and the heavy smell of food from the open doorways of student hangouts set his teeth on edge. This was, he told himself, a rotten idea.

He turned a corner, thinking about going home. But the house was empty, with Eric sleeping over at a friend's, and Peter was nothing if not tired of entertaining himself with his own thoughts. Lifting his face to catch the slight breeze that came from the darkness, he saw a sign above his head.

OPENING TONITE! it read. THE STREET SCENE PROUDLY PRESENTS: CHLOE, MISTRESS OF MAGIC! YOU MUST SEE HER TO BELIEVE!

Oh God, he thought, *here we are*. He'd come out tonight intending to see this show, had changed his mind about a hundred times since leaving home, and now . . . He stepped under the awning. The billboard in front of the club held an incredible close-up photograph of Chloe and a series of performance pictures with a beautiful blonde whose name, according to the note, was Kirsten. Interesting. But his eyes strayed back to the face he'd spent over a month trying to forget. In every way known to man, he had occupied his mind, punished his body, and stifled his emotions. Still she was there when he closed his eyes at night. And she was there when he woke an hour later, or two. Or four—that seemed to be about as much sleep as she allowed him these days.

The decision had already been made, of course; he would be going in. The last show started at one. Perhaps if he spent the next forty-five minutes drinking hard, he could be numb by the time she appeared. And if he continued to drink through the show, he would be incapacitated by the time it ended, so that he wouldn't be hanging around the back door when she walked out. Begging to take her home. Pleading to see her again, needing to touch and hold . . .

Dragging his wallet out of his back pocket, Peter pulled out some money, paid his cover charge, and then let himself into the club.

"That's it—all the way to the wall. Now just relax and we'll have some fun."

Chloe did as she was told, stepping back until she felt the hot bricks of the building pressing into her shoulders. The man followed, pulling Kirsten with him, until he had both women against the wall and could control them with a whip of his knife. Paralyzed by fear and fatigue, Chloe could only stare at that blade, wondering where it would bite first. She could feel Kirsten trembling beside her. What could they do? How could this be happening—why wasn't there someone to see? Surely two strong women could overpower one drunk—but there was the knife.

With his left hand on the wall beside Kirsten's head, the drunk looked them both over, and then, slowly, inserted the tip of his knife into the neck of Chloe's dress. She gasped and braced her shoulders as the sound of tearing cloth filled the night. She knew, Kirsten knew, if either of them moved, the knife would be tearing flesh. Chloe drew in her stomach muscles as the knife pressed past her ribs, felt the caress of the air as the halves of the dress began to separate over her breasts. The drunk noticed that, too, and brought the knife back up to aid the process, pushing one flap of fabric away with the blade, exposing a delicate, puckered nipple to his glassy gaze . . .

Her concentration was so focused on the silver threat at her breast that she didn't realize, at first, how the situation had changed. But then Chloe saw the cold steel waver as the vicious fingers around its hilt loosened. She heard Kirsten gasp at the same time the knife hit the pavement with a painful, liberating clang.

She jerked her gaze up. Peter Carroll stood behind the drunk, holding him prisoner with a rusty metal pipe pressed into his windpipe. For a horrified moment she stared at the man's purple face, protruding eyes, and gaping mouth. His hands snatched helplessly at the immovable bar across his throat.

Peter's tight voice penetrated her paralysis. "Get the police, Chloe. Go!"

She didn't need to be told again. Clutching at Kirsten's arm, Chloe fled the alley. Her breathless call brought the police to the scene in an unbelievably short time. Peter frog-marched his captive to the front of the club and turned him over to the authorities with an expression of disgusted pity, then walked over to where Chloe wilted against the side of the building and opened his arms. She stumbled into his embrace; Kirsten somehow managed to hold onto both of them as they answered the necessary questions from the police.

An hour later Peter walked Kirsten to the door of her

house in Alexandria, and delivered her into the anxious arms of her husband. Chloe waited in the van, to all appearances asleep, except that he knew she wasn't. Her white-knuckled hands, clenched around each other, gave her away.

He got back in and turned on the engine. "I need directions, Chloe. Where do you live?"

She told him, in an empty voice, what he needed to know, and within twenty minutes he had pulled up in front of a little brick house with a light burning in the window. For a minute he just sat, letting his muscles loosen and his mind relax. In the silence he could hear Chloe breathing softly and evenly, really asleep this time, and he turned his head to watch. The seat of the van reclined and she lay curled on her side, facing him, with her hands pillowed under her cheek like a little girl. A curtain of black hair shadowed the other side of her face and fell into her eyes; with a trembling finger he drew it away and felt, for the first time, the softness of her skin. She still wore his beige linen jacket, although he couldn't really remember when he'd given it to her, couldn't remember several of the minutes that followed his first glimpse of that knife blade next to her throat. Didn't want to remember, for that matter. Heroics were not part of his style. Especially not during barroom brawls.

Shaking his head at the whole situation, Peter took the key out of the ignition and got out of the van. He stepped up onto the front porch and stood under the porch light while he looked for the right key. The big ring held probably twenty different keys, but trial and error worked its usual magic and the door opened. He came back to the van, opened the passenger door and reached across to unfasten the seatbelt. With one arm under her knees and the other around her shoulders, he drew the sleeping woman against his chest. Her head snuggled onto his shoulder as he walked up the short sidewalk, crossed the porch, and pushed his way into Chloe's house.

To the left he saw the living room. The hall stretched back into darkness. He moved carefully, looking for the room that was hers. In the blackness he found a bed covered in white, with a crumpled shirt and slacks on the floor that told him where she'd dressed. But when he lowered the light weight of her to the mattress, her arms clutched his neck with frenzied strength.

"Please, no, don't go! Please!" she begged, like a child chased by nightmares. Even in the dark he could see the diamond tears on her cheeks.

"I won't," he whispered soothingly, as he had to Eric so often, so many years ago. "I'm right here. It's okay." He set a knee to the bed on her other side and lifted himself up, over, and down, until they lay stretched out, closer than together, while his arms guarded her from the night. And then, with his lips in her hair, Peter fell asleep, too.

Chloe awoke, as she had so often dreamed, in his arms. And this time, she knew immediately, it was real. She had never felt so comfortable, so warm in her life. Even in sleep he held her tightly against him, and one leg had shifted to rest on top of her bare thigh where her dress had fallen away. Under her palm his heart beat steadily, and the hint of starch from his shirt mingled with something more personal to create a scent she found intriguing and exciting. By lifting her chin, she could bring her lips only an inch away from the slightly stubbled skin of his throat, but when she did so, she felt his heart rate jump. He wasn't asleep after all.

Reluctantly she pulled far enough away to rest her head on a separate pillow. Gray, smiling eyes were waiting for hers when she met his gaze. "Good morning," he whispered in a sleep-graveled voice. "How do you feel?"

She couldn't help smiling back. "Wonderful," she confessed in the same quiet tone. "How are you?"

He nodded slightly. "About the same." He lifted his hand to brush a strand of hair behind her ear; then it closed warmly around the top of her arm, keeping her close. "I haven't slept so well in weeks."

Her turn to nod. "Like a baby," Chloe admitted. Then she remembered. "You saved our lives last night," she reminded him.

Peter shrugged. "I'm glad I was there."

"But how did you come to be in that alley?"

For the first time his eyes cut away, as if to avoid the issue, but then came back with an honest, if rueful, look. "I saw the one o'clock show. And I heard that guy mumbling to himself, after the bouncer grabbed him. I would have gotten there sooner except I'd given my credit card to the waitress—and I guess I couldn't really believe he would hurt anybody. I'm sorry about that."

Chloe shook her head. "You were there when we needed you—that's all that matters. Thanks." The violet eyes dropped to her hands, still resting comfortably against his chest, and then came back to his face as another question occurred to her. "Peter, I don't understand. Why did you come to see me? And why the late show, of all things? It's always the worst."

Peter released her shoulder and rolled onto his back, using his free hand to rub his eyes. "Eric slept over with a friend last night. I . . . I got tired of the house and so I went for a walk through Georgetown, just drifting, really. And suddenly there I was, with your picture staring up at me."

Chloe lifted herself onto an elbow, releasing his other arm, if he chose to draw it away. But his hand clung firmly to the curve of her waist, moved to stroke her ribs and stayed there. "So it was an accident that you came to see me."

"No! That is . . ." he stumbled, and then stopped.

Chloe took pity on him. "It's okay, Peter. It was lucky for us, however you got there."

For a long moment she looked down at his profile, at the glint of early sun in the light stubble along his jaw, the proud slope of his nose, and the high bridge of bone above the flat planes of his cheeks. The shining gray of those eyes mesmerized her. They had never been so close before, and now she could see the fine lines at the corners of his mouth that told his age, along with a shimmer of silver in the hair falling over his brow.

It seemed possible, with all their barriers down, to ask, "How old are you, Peter?"

He turned to look at her and grinned. "Thirty-seven. Can you return the favor?"

She rewarded him with a generous smile. "Do I have to be honest?"

His right eyebrow lifted as if to underline the obvious. "Oh, well," Chloe sighed, "I guess I can tell you. I'm thirty. Almost thirty-one."

"A mere infant. Wait until you're looking at forty."

"Thanks, I'll put that off as long as I possibly can."

He had used the cover of the conversation for his own study, taking in the perfect oval in which violet eyes and rose-pink lips made an equally perfect triangle. She looked closer to twenty than thirty, with flawless skin and those black bangs almost hiding her eyes. Peter realized he'd always wondered how she looked without them and raised a hand to sweep the fringe back over her head.

Then he forgot what he'd meant to do. The touch of his palm against her skin ignited the banked fire in them both. He heard Chloe gasp, saw her eyes widen, and he drew in a ragged breath that hurt his throat. Her fingers tightened in his shirt as his slid through her hair, until his palm cupped the curve of her jaw and his fingers splayed over the sweet curl of her ear. The muscles in his arm tightened, bringing her hips into a sear-

ing, unsatisfying contact with his. Peter closed his eyes
against the waves of need washing over him. When he
opened them again, the same flood had engulfed Chloe,
and the purple eyes were almost black.

"I've never kissed you," he managed unsteadily.

Her response was breathless. "I know."

Watching her mouth, he could barely keep his head.
"I'm afraid I won't be able to stop."

"I know."

He dragged his eyes up to hers. "It's the same for
you?"

"Oh, yes," she whispered.

He closed his eyes again and blew out a long breath.
With an effort as great as any he had ever made, he
drew back, brought his leg away from hers and, at last,
sat up. Keeping his feet firmly on the floor, he turned
to face her as she lay on the bed, not angry or even
hurt by his withdrawal, only waiting for what he would
say.

"I've wanted you from the first moment I saw you,"
he explained. "But I didn't want an affair, didn't want
to get involved with something I couldn't handle."

He cleared his throat, looked away for an instant,
then went on. "Being there last night wasn't an accident. I've spent almost two months trying to stay away.
It doesn't work, and I left the house last night intending
to go to your show, and see you afterward. I changed
my mind about a thousand times between the house and
the club, but I ended up there anyway.

"I need to see you, to be with you. Whatever this is,
it's more than sex, more than just a physical attraction.
But, God knows, it's sex, too. I want you. . . ." He
stopped, unable to find the words he needed. When he
looked up from where their fingers were twined together, he found her eyes waiting. "What do you
think?"

Chloe smiled gently. He had never looked so much
like Eric, like a ten-year-old who had gotten himself in

trouble. At the same time, he was very much a man, with a man's desires and a man's effect on her.

"I feel the same," she said softly. "I've tried every way I know to stop thinking about you. Dallas warned me, but I wouldn't believe him. I—"

Peter tightened his grip. "What do you mean? What about him?"

Chloe lowered her eyes. This was one memory that still hurt. "He told me he loved me," she whispered. "All these years, and he never said a word, never let me know."

All at once she was alone on the bed. Peter stood by the window, two angry strides away, fighting for control. "You didn't see it?" he demanded in a rough, unsteady voice. "My God, Chloe, I took one look at the man and knew how he felt!"

"I guess I was stupid," she flashed back at him. "Or maybe I just saw what I wanted to see. But that night he told me the truth. And he said he couldn't stay and watch while I . . ."

Her voice died away. Silence stretched between them. The air seemed to shimmer with tension. Staring blindly out the window, Peter waited as long as he possibly could.

"While you?" he prompted at last.

"While I got involved with you."

Eagerly, he turned around. Chloe had not moved; the sight of her reclining gracefully against the pillows made breathing irrelevant. But the anguish on her face, as she mourned the friend who loved her, dimmed her beauty like a shadow across the moon. A shaft of sunlight caught the sparkle of tears in her lowered lashes and Peter realized, for the first time, the high price she had paid for this moment.

"I guess, then," he suggested awkwardly, as nervous as a teenager on his first date, "we need to give whatever this is a chance. Do you want to start out in bed?"

Her gaze flew up to his. He saw the dawn of laughter bring a glint to those violet eyes and answered it with some of his own. "I know, it's a pretty bald question. More like a truck driver than a poet. I haven't found my equilibrium in this situation yet. But—" He hesitated, then went the whole way. "I've never felt this strongly about anyone."

The intensity of his admission kept her motionless for a moment. Then Chloe stood up on the other side of the bed. "*I* think," she said seriously, "we should start out with breakfast."

His startled look prompted more laughter. And then, because she needed to know that they could be together without going up in smoke, she came across the room and put her hand on his arm. "Let's try friendship first, Peter," she proposed. Her grin turned cheeky and she gave him a playful slap. "If it doesn't work out, we can always fall back on sex!"

He chuckled as she eluded his seeking hands. "Wanton!" he called as she vanished out the door.

Over breakfast they discovered a mutual passion for croissants and raspberry jam and a source of disagreement in the appropriate degree of runniness for scrambled eggs. Strong coffee for Chloe and hot, sweet tea for Peter presented no problems, but the possible dangers from the preservatives in bacon kept them arguing the entire time she cooked. Only as Chloe put the plates down on the table Peter had set did he finally grant her the right to poison herself as she wished, as long as she didn't poison him.

"Thank you, sir! Eat your runny eggs."

He shook his head in mock disgust. "Yours are practically powder—all the nutrients cooked out of them. On top," he continued with a disdainful gesture of his fork, "of that toxic stuff you call meat."

Chloe bit off a piece of bacon with a defiant crunch. A change of topic seemed wise, before the conversation turned into a food fight. "You said Eric spent the night with a friend; what time will he be home?"

"Sometime this afternoon. Andrew has a big yard with a treehouse and all the trimmings; it's hard to pry Eric away. He doesn't have so much space at home."

"How's his magic trick?"

Peter rolled his eyes up. "I've wanted to thank you for that, magician! I must have marvelled at the disappearing coins *at least* five thousand times since you were so kind as to leave it with us. In self defense I found another magic shop and got him a book and some locking rings, just so I'd have something else to applaud! I'm looking forward to sending him to Greece this summer, to let his mother do the clapping for awhile."

Slowly, gently, Chloe set her fork on her plate. Took a sip of coffee. And another. Finally she looked across at Peter. "Did you do that on purpose?"

He nodded. The gray eyes smiled faintly, ruefully, into hers. "I thought we needed to talk about it, and hoped it would come easier this way."

"You're divorced?" She'd just assumed, all this time, that Eric's mother had died.

"Yes. Let me explain." He took a deep breath, propped his elbows on the table, and rested his chin on his clasped hands. "Elaine and I were undergraduates together, and married right after graduation. I got accepted into the graduate lit program at Princeton, she was accepted in archaeology at Brown. Okay, we thought, we're young, we can drive all night on weekends to be together. And, of course, it didn't work out very well."

After a sip of tea, he continued. "She had fallen in love with one of her professors, a specialist in Hellenic cultures, who begged her to come live with him in Greece. And after four years, about all we really had going was sex, anyway. Then she got pregnant."

Chloe made some sort of sound, and he looked up

from the egg design he'd been creating on his plate.
"Oh, I'm positive that Eric is mine—she didn't sleep
with the other guy until after the divorce. Elaine is very
fair and very moral. And, anyway, she insisted on a
paternity test, just to prove it to me. Because, you
see," and for the first time the anger showed in his
eyes, and in the flush across his cheeks, "she had no
intention of keeping the baby. She wouldn't, thank
God, have an abortion, but three weeks after Eric was
born, she left the country. A brilliant career in archaeology versus the call of motherhood? No contest."

In the silence, they could hear the refrigerator hum-
ming and the whine of the air conditioner. In a moment
it would be time for Chloe to volunteer some of her
own history, to tell him about *her* past. She stirred her
coffee as she faced the thought, and then pushed them
both away. Revealing her secrets would send him out
the door at a run—and she wasn't ready for that.

She looked over at Peter again and found the right
question to ask. "You brought him up all by yourself?"

"Pretty much. I made a visitation clause part of the
divorce agreement, because I didn't want to lie to him
about his mother. We've been over every summer since
he turned two, and he spends two weeks with her while
I hole up in a nice little cottage on the coast and write.
They aren't really close, but they do have a relationship. Polite, respectful, friendly. It's enough, I guess."
He stood up, picked up his plate, and walked over to
the sink. "I found Maia about six years ago to take
care of the house and to be there when Eric came home
from school. She's much more of a mother than Elaine
will ever be."

Chloe came to stand beside him as he rinsed his plate
into the garbage disposal. "You've done a good job
with him. You should be very proud."

Peter shrugged and then gave her his usual confident
smile. "You're right. He's a good boy, with a lot of

friends, and we get along very well. I don't think he's really missed much.''

They worked in silence for a few minutes, until another uncomfortable question occurred to Chloe. She turned from loading the last pot in the dishwasher to find Peter just behind her, hips propped easily against the kitchen table. Leaning back herself, to put some distance between them, she asked, in a hesitant voice, ''Have you been . . . alone? All this time?''

He knew what she meant. And, after the jealous anger he'd felt over Dallas Page, he liked it that she'd asked. ''Ten years of celibacy? Believe me,'' he said with a wicked glint in his eyes, ''if I'd been that noble, we wouldn't have made it out of the bedroom yet.''

''I—I'm sorry,'' she whispered. As he watched, a blush stained her cheeks. She dropped her chin, but he caught it in his fingers and lifted her face to his eyes. One step, and they were close enough to feel the current running between them, hot and strong.

''No, don't be. You have a right to know. I've had two fairly long relationships since Elaine. The last one ended a couple of years ago, and I haven't been with anyone since.''

Placing his hands on her shoulders, he drew her up against him. In bare feet the difference in their heights became apparent; the gentlest tilt of his head would be needed to join his lips with hers. Chloe brought her own hands together at the small of his back. The pressure of her softness drew a small groan from the back of Peter's throat. ''We're pushing it here, I think,'' he said, and then as she tried to pull back, ''No, don't move.''

His hands rubbed over her back, exploring the angles of her shoulder blades, the suppleness of her neck, the curve of her spine. Chloe could feel herself melting, and sensed the corresponding tightening in Peter. In another instant she would start an exploration of her own, across the contours hidden by his wrinkled shirt.

Or, maybe, underneath it. This was getting out of hand, very fast.

"You know," he suggested in an attempt at his normal voice, "I think now might be a good time for me to leave."

With her forehead buried against his shoulder, Chloe shook her head. He laughed. "Yes, I believe I'm right." When he stepped back, her hold broke easily enough, but the violet eyes were misted with regret. Enough provocation there to make a man forget every promise he'd ever made, every oath he'd ever sworn. Peter hadn't known he could be so strong.

Released from the spell of his closeness, Chloe shook her head violently, setting the fringe of her hair swirling and clearing the cobwebs out of her brain. Or what had once been her brain, but now seemed no more than mush.

"Of course it's time, Peter," she said strongly. "We both need a chance to clean up, if nothing else. Call a cab while I finish up with the kitchen." Wiping down the counter, she kept her back straight and her head high. She couldn't believe how close she'd come to begging.

Chloe waited in the living room while Peter retrieved his shoes and jacket from her room. He came in slowly, unwilling to leave, trying to think of something to say. Then he caught sight of his book on her desk. "Have you read it?" he asked. "What do you think?"

The emotional swings of this morning were getting beyond her control. For a second she fought down pure panic, unable to think of a single word to say. As she struggled, his face changed, and a look that was half-hurt, half-ashamed came over his features like a cloud over the sun.

"It's okay, Chloe, if you don't want to read it," he offered in a stiff voice. "Just let me take it back with me." He stepped over and put his hand over the book, but before he could lift it her fingers covered his own.

"No, please, Peter, leave it with me." Their faces were very close. "I . . . I just have been so tied up, I haven't read anything!" That was the absolute truth, if ever there was one. "I do want to keep it. Please?"

He turned his palm up and grabbed her hand. As he brought it to his lips, a horn sounded from the street. "That's my cab," he said into her fingers. His mouth moved against her skin, and then, slowly, he released her. She followed him to the door, where he turned to get one last look. "Have dinner with us tonight," he suggested. "Eric would love it. So would I." When she nodded, he gave a single quick smile and strode quickly out to the street.

Chloe watched until the cab had left her street, then closed the door again and leaned against it. She could still feel him in her house, setting her nerves on edge. No doubt if she went back to her room, his scent would linger on her bed. And it was all so precarious, so—so dangerous! With his arms around her, this morning, she'd felt sure, confident. Alone, now, she saw only the problems that getting involved with Peter—with any man—would create.

How had she let herself lose control like this? How in the world would she be able to hide the fact that she couldn't read from a man as intelligent, as observant as Peter Carroll? And how would he feel if he knew about Mikey—the son *she'd* left behind?

Well, it was too late for regrets. They had agreed to be together, and, given the passion they felt for each other, they would end up in bed. She decided to lay a bet with herself: if she hadn't made love with Peter in two weeks, she'd give up chocolate for a month. Or, better still, bacon.

Either way, it would be good for her. A flaming affair, physical and satisfying and short-lived, would burn this craziness out of them both. And then they could get on with their lives—separately. No confidences, no secrets revealed, just two ships, as they say, passing in the night. Otherwise, somebody would end up getting hurt.

With a stiff smile on her face, Chloe pushed herself away from the door and headed for the shower. Two weeks, or a month of no bacon—she had no idea which would be the healthier outcome.

FIVE

"Wow, Dad, look! She got it up!"

Peter *was* looking. Flying a kite on the Mall in July was a foolhardy enterprise; wind was a scarce commodity during summer in Washington, unless you counted afternoon thunderstorms. But Eric had insisted. And Chloe had stood patiently for half an hour as Peter struggled to send the orange box kite into the air. Only when his masculine pride was trampled in the dirt did she ask for a try.

At the first touch of her fingers on the string a breeze lifted her bangs out of her eyes. By the time she got the kite ready, the wind had freshened and the flags circling the Washington Monument were fluttering joyfully. Now Peter stood with his hands on his hips watching as the unwieldy contraption sailed cleanly above their heads, with no sign of ever coming down. All across the long stretch of grass running between the Monument and the Capitol heads lifted to look at that crazy, solitary kite.

"Here, Eric, come hold this thing!" she called over her shoulder. The line transferred easily to younger hands, and Chloe backed up to stand beside Peter. "What a wonderful kite!"

Peter threw her a sidelong glance. "Especially when it's in the air," he pointed out dryly. "How did you do that? Magic?"

"I'll never tell," she responded with a grin. "Wow, he's really got it up there, hasn't he?"

Walking slowly, they wove their way through the Saturday afternoon exodus from the Smithsonian Museums as Eric, his eyes on the heavens, navigated his kite through the sky, with the Capitol Building as a backdrop. The wind continued to blow, and Peter felt comforted by the black clouds rolling in from the west, foretelling a summer storm. It was a coincidence. Had to be. Even Chloe couldn't control the weather. Could she?

He started to ask, but was stopped by the panicked look on her face. "Peter," she said urgently, "he's not looking where he's going—we'd better . . . Eric!"

Peter whipped his head around. Eric was about a hundred feet away, running backwards, looking up at the kite. He hadn't heard the call over the noise. "Eric!" Peter shouted, adding his voice to Chloe's. They both started running, dodging the slow-moving throng, trying to get the boy's attention before it was too late.

With Eric, though, it was always too late. Chloe and Peter arrived just in time to pick him up out of the potato salad and baked beans of a family picnic. Fortunately, the family was laughing, the result of having three boys of their own, the mother said. *And* three girls. They always brought along a roll of paper towels, the father explained. Never knew when you would need them.

Wiping beans off Eric's legs, feeling his face turn red with embarrassment, Peter could only be thankful for the family's good humor. "Let me give you some money to replace the food," he offered, as Chloe took over the cleanup job. "It's the least I can do."

They wouldn't hear of it; they had been close to

finishing, anyway. Eric made his usual wide-eyed, cherubic apology, and the three of them backed away, with the string of the kite held firmly in Peter's palm. The wind died; the kite landed at his feet about twenty seconds later.

Chloe repressed her grin, and helped them untangle the string and carry the kite without a word. Peter hadn't criticized Eric, thank goodness, beyond a warning to watch where he stepped next time. And the resigned look on his face was lightened by a quirk at the corner of his mouth that told her he would be laughing about the whole episode in a few minutes.

Her memories of this week they'd spent together seemed to be framed with laughter. Eric's antics, his energy and boundless enthusiasm kept Peter alert and herself constantly entertained. By the end of their first day together she knew she'd fallen in love with the little boy who looked like an angel and whose diabolical impulses had shortened his father's life by several years. Or so Peter said.

And Peter, as the days went by, had said a great deal. She was constantly amazed to find that a man who seemed so controlled and reserved could talk so much. About so many different things! This must be what college did for you, Chloe thought wistfully, this wide acquaintance with the world and its wonders. On Tuesday, at the zoo, with Eric hanging off the fence and in immediate danger of falling in with the elephants, they discussed the destruction of the rain forests and the problems of game preserves in Africa. Thursday saw them in the Air and Space Museum, where Peter explained the history of flight to Eric and the principles of jet propulsion to Chloe. Their weekend kite expedition had been an illustration for what causes weather. Chloe could only shake her head; she'd never known someone who *knew* so much. How different her own childhood might have been with a father who shared himself so freely.

Then came the day she discovered another side of him. While Peter held a summer school seminar for graduate students on Monday and Wednesday afternoons, Eric was usually at loose ends, unless a play date could be arranged with one of his friends. On this particular Monday, the second one they spent together, no friend was available, and Chloe offered to take Eric out of the house for the afternoon. It started out well enough: she planned a picnic in a park near the house in Georgetown, some time on the playground, and then a walk to Peter's office to meet him after class. Simple, classic childhood occupations, she thought. What could go wrong?

Just after lunch the thunderclouds rolled overhead. Halfway through their walk to the university, the rain started, and within five minutes it poured down as if dumped from buckets, and lightning split the sky. They ran for the nearest overhead protection, a shop awning on a side street in the Georgetown shopping area. Even there, they got soaked. Eric suggested, and Chloe agreed, that the best idea was to go into the shop and get away from the weather.

It must have been Fate. Or the spirits. Or, more likely, her own subconscious that recognized and chose the magic shop of her good friend Vernon Cryer as a place to escape. Before she could catch her breath he had seen them. "Chloe, my dear!" he cried, enfolding her in his gigantic embrace. "It's been such a long time! How are you?"

Eric stood open-mouthed, astounded, at the sight of a fat, bald man dressed in what appeared to be a lime green genie's costume, standing with his arms around Chloe. "Vernon," she responded, trying to untangle herself from the scented scarves around his neck. "I'm fine. And it hasn't been that long—I seem to remember a wickedly expensive table you tried to sell me just last week."

"Ah yes," said the large man, with an even larger

smile, "but if you're here to reconsider, prepare yourself: I sold it yesterday. And for considerably more, I might say, than I offered to you."

"There's one born every minute, according to Barnum," Chloe responded dryly. She looked around for Eric, stepped back, and with a hand on his shoulder drew him forward. "Let me introduce a friend of mine, Eric Carroll. Eric, this is Vernon. He owns this magic shop—I get a lot of my supplies here." She flashed a smile and gave him a conspiratorial wink. "In spite of the ridiculous prices!"

Eric extended his hand. Vernon shook it and withdrew, leaving the boy with a very small, very real, garter snake curling in his palm. "Wow! Far out!" Eric ran the snake through his fingers as he stared up at Vernon. "How'd you do it? Where do you keep them?"

Ignoring Chloe's expression of distaste, Vernon laughed. "I just happened to find that one in my garden this morning, and brought him to work for fun. If you don't mind, I'll take him back when I go home tonight." Recapturing the slippery green reptile, he drew Eric over to one of the shelves. "I do have a very good supply of fake snakes, though," he pointed out. "You can have one, as a substitute, if you like."

"Cool!" Eric readily gave up the small, real snake for the chance to play with a ten-foot-long fake boa and an incredibly realistic cobra that came complete with basket, expanding hood, and Indian flute. Chloe watched as, with Vernon's instructions, the boy summoned the evil creature from its bed and caused it to dance and sway menacingly.

"What a neat trick," Eric exclaimed. "Don't you want to use it in your act, Chloe? It would be so cool and so scary! Nobody would know it wasn't real!"

She had to laugh. "No thanks, Eric. I don't like snakes much, even fake ones." Another illusion caught her eye. "Come look at this—it's a good trick for beginners: the disappearance box. See, you put something in this side, turn it and then, *voilà!* It's gone!''

Under Vernon's indulgent eye, Chloe and Eric explored every nook and cranny in the shop, trying out the tricks, trying on the costumes, exploring the mysteries of magic while the thunderstorm continued to roar outside, adding exactly the right background to their fun. And at last Eric obtained the wish of his heart: in a sublime example of the showmanship for which he'd been famous on the vaudeville circuit, Vernon, with Chloe's amused assistance, sawed the youngster in half. Or, actually, showed him how the classic trick was done. His eyes round with excitement, his face white with tension and, to be honest, a little fear, Eric allowed himself to be shut in the big box with only his head exposed. He very quickly discovered the secret, and laughed in triumph as Vernon drew the big sword all the way through the box and then separated the halves, bringing the ''feet'' all the way around next to Eric's ears.

''Look, Chloe!'' he called. ''Now I can really stand on my head!''

After such a supreme experience, any other illusion would seem anticlimatic. Eric discovered the bookshelf, with an excellent supply of how-to texts, and settled down to read. Vernon took the opportunity to offer Chloe a cup of herbal tea.

''What a charming boy,'' he said, spooning half a cup of honey into his own cup and a spoonful into hers. ''Where did you find him?''

''I performed at his birthday party a month or so ago,'' she replied, avoiding the shrewd green eyes of her friend. ''He really loves magic.''

''Yes, I can see that. But isn't he a little young for you, dear Chloe?''

''Just a little, dear Vernon,'' she responded sarcastically. ''Don't think you're going to find out anything juicy by being sneaky. I like Eric, and since his father has classes—'' Chloe stopped on a gasp, with one hand covering her mouth. ''What time is it?'' she asked urgently.

''Almost six. Why?''

She jumped off of the high stool at the counter, spilling tea in the process. ''Because his father finished his class about two hours ago and we were supposed to meet him at his office and walk home for dinner. I am in serious trouble! Where's your phone?''

Peter's line gave out a depressing beep: busy. She tried again in five minutes: busy. Peering out Vernon's dusty windows, Chloe decided that the storm had lightened enough to let them walk to the bus and get home. ''Come on Eric,'' she called, ''get the snake you want and let's go. We're very, very late.''

With the excellent manners that he displayed to everyone but his father, Eric chose a small (only four feet) snake—not the cobra—said thank you very much to Vernon, and followed Chloe quickly out into the mist. In fifteen minutes they were on the bus, and in twenty-five were hurrying up the brick steps to the house.

Eric burst in, screaming at the top of his lungs, ''Dad! Dad, come look what I got! We had the best afternoon—we went to a magic store and tried out everything! Dad, where are you?''

Chloe followed him inside, more slowly and much more quietly. At Eric's call, Maia had hurried in from the kitchen, her face undergoing the transition from worry to relief even as she pushed open the door.

''Look, Maia,'' Eric demonstrated, ''have you ever seen such a far-out snake? It looks real, doesn't it?''

Peter had been upstairs. She heard a door slam, and then he dropped down the spiral staircase in a rush, feet pounding against the polished wood. Her first look at his tense face and tight mouth warned Chloe of the trouble to come. He stopped on the next to last step, hands on his hips, eyes a steely, unwelcoming gray.

"Where," he ground out, "have you been?"

Eric rushed over to explain. "We got caught in the thunderstorm, Dad, and went into this really neat magic shop, and he had this cobra that looks real—boy, I'd love to have one of those, Dad, could I? The guys would be so jealous, really! And we looked at all the tricks, and—Dad! Maia!—he sawed me in half! Really! He put my feet up against my head and it was so cool, I couldn't believe it! You oughta see it, Dad!"

Peter's hand rested on his son's shoulder, firmly yet gently, as if to prove the boy's presence, back where he belonged, after a couple of very anxious hours. With a squeeze he stopped the flow of words. "That sounds great, son. Your dinner is waiting in the kitchen. Go in with Maia and get something to eat. I'll be in to hear the rest in a minute."

"Chloe, too, Dad? She showed me all the neatest tricks—she can tell you about some of them. . . ."

More strongly, Peter directed him toward the door. "Sure, Eric, in a minute. Go get started." He waited until both Maia and Eric had left the room and the door had closed solidly behind them before turning to look at Chloe.

The softness his face held for Eric had vanished. "What the hell did you think you were doing?" This voice was not the smooth, even tone she identified with Peter Carroll, but something much rougher and less controlled. "I have been calling all over town trying to find the two of you. Maia and I were worried out of our minds! Surely you know you don't just go off with a kid and not let anybody know where you are. What if something had happened? The very least you could have done was call and let us know you'd be late! I cannot imagine what you were thinking of—haven't you ever taken responsibility for a kid before? Don't you think D.C. is a little too big to wander around without telling somebody where you're going? Do you have any common sense?"

Chloe stood unflinching under the torrent of words. Her eyes narrowed, her lips tightened, and she felt the color drain from her face as she listened, but she let him finish without an interruption. As he asked the last question, she lifted her chin. "I have," she replied in a voice as frosty as the silver crystal of his eyes, "more than my share of common sense, or else I would not have made it this far by myself. I knew Eric was fine, I knew we were both safe, and I assumed—erroneously, it turns out—that I would be treated as a competent adult who could take care of herself and a child in unexpected situations. We did get carried away, and I apologize for not having called before dinner to let you know we'd be late. When I did try to call," she pointed out, "the line was busy and I couldn't get through."

She turned her back on Peter, walked to the front door, and then looked at him again, although she couldn't really see his face through the blur of unshed tears. "I am sorry you were worried—I know what it's like to be concerned about a child. I don't feel that the situation merits such hysteria, but then, I thought you understood that Eric's safety is as important to me as it is to you. I would never do anything to hurt him. If you don't trust me to be with him, it's just as well we found out now, isn't it? Give Eric my best, Peter. Good-bye."

Chloe allowed herself to slam the door; it felt great. She walked rapidly through the rain, which continued to fall gently but persistently in the deepening darkness, trying not to think of the scene just past, trying not to hear the echoes of Robert's voice coming down the years: "You what? Don't you know better than that? What did you think you were doing?" Shaking her head, she flung the tears from her eyes. Damn it, she should have known! You get involved and you always, always, *always* get hurt.

She'd gotten halfway down the block when she heard the door slam again and then Peter's voice calling her name. She picked up the pace and then broke into a run as she heard his steps pounding behind her. If she could make it to the bus stop, she'd get on on the first one, no matter where it went. *Three blocks away*, Chloe thought, her breath tearing in her throat. *I've got to make it three blocks*.

He caught her at the first corner, his fingers like steel bands around her upper arm.

"Let go!" she panted, attempting to pull away.

"Not on your life. Stop it!" he ordered, when she continued to struggle.

A couple stepped by them, looking curiously at the conflict. When the man turned back, as if to offer help, Chloe stopped trying to escape and stood still, fighting for breath, until her would-be rescuer moved on. What they didn't need, in this situation, was interference. Peter took advantage of the lull to pull her under the drooping branches of a large oak tree. He pushed her up against the trunk, trapping her there with a hand on either side of her head and his legs braced against her knees. Unlike herself, his breathing had hardly changed at all, and he waited patiently and in silence until her sobbing breath eased.

"You owe me a chance to apologize, Chloe," he said. "And you owe me a chance to explain how you misunderstood."

Explanations. Apologies. Did she want them? No. Escape was the only answer here, the only path to safety. Chloe moved, just slightly, and the pressure of his body against hers increased. Trapped, she thought. Even Houdini couldn't get out of this one.

But then she lifted her eyes to Peter's face. She always thought of him as cool and confident, but that control had slipped tonight; the line of his mouth was tight and his gray gaze pleaded with an intensity that melted her resolve. Shaken by his need, Chloe looked at him without a word, but something in her face gave him the permission he sought.

"I'm sorry I jumped on you. I really was worried, and I took it out on you," he said jerkily. "I should have had more control—I usually do. God knows Eric has pulled enough stunts in his short life that I'm used to dealing with surprises.

"But—and this is the part you misunderstood—it wasn't just Eric I was concerned about." He saw the skepticism in her eyes. "Don't look at me like that— it's true. I haven't forgotten that drunk at the club, and what he might have done. I'm not sure exactly what I was thinking, but I was afraid that something had happened to you, too."

Peter looked away for a second, then back into her eyes. "I worry about you every night," he confessed. "I have to fight the urge to go down to the Street Scene and make sure you get home safely. It's crazy, I know," he responded to her look of disbelief, "because you got along just fine before we met. But now, well, I'm afraid something will happen to you," he said, his voice low and rough. "And I just found you."

All at once Chloe was aware of his closeness, felt the light pressure of his arms against her shoulders and the heat of his legs on her thighs. Peter had been soaked to the skin, as she was, during their race; his hair clung darkly to his scalp, and the usual crispness of his white shirt molded his shoulders and chest with wet detail. Dropping her chin, she found the same state of exposure in her own cotton t-shirt; the soft mounds of her breasts and the peaks of her nipples showed clearly through the cloth. Peter's eyes followed her gaze. She felt him stiffen, heard his sharp breath, and looked up to see him attempting a ragged smile.

"We're a pair, aren't we?" he whispered. "I could take you right now," he said, watching her eyes widen at the suggestion. "I'm trying to be patient and it's killing me." He drew his hand away from the tree and used his thumb to wipe the raindrops off her full lower lip.

When he stroked across her mouth again, and again, she could feel herself weakening, knew that in a matter of moments she would let him take anything he wanted, anywhere. "Peter . . ." she moaned against his finger.

His hand cupped her jaw, slid down until his palm rested on the pulse at the base of her throat. She could feel his breath on her lips, almost, but not quite, a kiss. "Oh, Chloe," he muttered, "I want you so much." This time it *was* a kiss, soft and short and tantalizing. "Let me take you home and love you. Now. Tonight."

The press of his mouth against hers deepened, her lips parted. "Please?" Peter said, in a voice she could barely hear.

But then he joined his lips to hers again, with all the warmth and passion she'd ever wanted, ever needed, and Chloe couldn't remember the question, let alone the answer. She lifted her hands to the back of his neck, letting her fingers plunge into his damp hair and tangle in its fineness. The wind rushed around them, but whether the storm was outside or in her head, Chloe couldn't have said. Peter's heat against her and the press of his hips into hers were the only reality. She opened her mouth and, when his tongue sought hers, moaned deep in her throat. The taste, the feel of his invasion stole her breath; his shaking hand slid recklessly over her breast, twisting the already erect nipple until Chloe felt she might scream with need.

She gasped, instead. The sound, loud in the rain-filled silence, brought Peter to his senses. He stilled his hand and pulled his mouth away with something like a groan to hide his eyes against her shoulder. Chloe didn't try to bring his face back to hers. She stood absolutely still in the circle of his arms, listening to the rasp of their panting breaths in the darkness and being thankful that he'd had the strength to stop.

Only when she had control of her lungs again did she even try to talk. "We can't just run away, Peter. Eric needs you, has things he wants to tell you. I think," she said quietly, "we'd better get out of the rain."

He kept his face against her shoulder for a moment longer, then stepped away to set her free. Bending over to avoid the low branches, they came out from underneath the big tree and Peter took a few steps back the way he had come. When Chloe didn't follow, he turned. "You will let me take you home, won't you?"

She hesitated. Being in a dark car with Peter would test the very limits of her self control. "I—I could get a bus. . . ."

He came back and took her arm, realized she was trembling, and put an arm around her shoulders. "You will not take a bus. I will be a gentleman, I promise. You need to be in a warm, comfortable car, not the drafty bus. No arguments!"

She let herself be persuaded—*after* Peter had talked with his son. Soon enough, though, they were parked in front of her house. Peter had changed clothes before they left his house, and had loaned Chloe a sweatshirt. They were warm and dry and tired, after the stress of the day, and still not ready to separate for the night. So he turned, leaning his back into the car door, to watch her profile against the rain-spattered window and asked, "Why don't you drive?"

Chloe tipped her head back against the seat and sighed. She'd known he would ask this, so at least she was prepared. "I didn't learn, as a teenager. And now, well, I guess I'm just lazy. I can't really afford to maintain a car, anyway."

"But you have the van—"

Too bad he'd remembered the van. "I had to have a way to carry my equipment. Dallas helped me buy it several years ago, with some money I came into, but if it ever needs more than an oil change, I'll be out of luck. Since I use it just for business, it's tax-deductible." *Let that be the end*, she prayed. *This yarn is getting really thin!*

Peter stayed silent for such a long time she thought perhaps he'd fallen asleep, but when she turned to look she found his eyes open and waiting, with a kind of speculation in them that made her very nervous. She tried to hold his gaze, hoping to stare him down, but at last he spoke and she knew she was in trouble.

"It seems to me," he said with deceptive nonchalance, "that I've done all the talking this last week. You know my son and my house, you know about my divorce, and my sexual history. And yet I don't even know your last name. Is it just me, or is there an imbalance here?"

Chloe cleared her throat once. Again. "What do you want to know? I—I'm just what you see, no more, no less."

He shook his head. "Not true. Mona Lisa has nothing on you when it comes to mystery." A rueful smile crossed his mouth. "If I'd known I would have this opportunity," he said regretfully, "I would have written out a list of questions I'd like to ask. As it is, I'll have to make them up as I go along. First, the one I've already mentioned: what *is* your last name?"

"Would you believe Smith?"

He gave a shout of laughter. "If you tell me, seriously, that you are Chloe Smith, I guess I have to believe it."

She smiled back, relieved. "Well, as we've already established, I can't show you my driver's license, but that's my name. Not very impressive for a magician, is it?"

"No, I guess not." He thought for a moment, as if selecting his next question with care. "Are you a Washington native?"

Shaking her head, she replied, "No, I'm from what they call Southside Virginia, the bottom of the state near the North Carolina line. Very rural, not very rich, most of us." So far, so good.

"You have family there?"

Not so good. The length of her hesitation probably told him more than she intended. "I—yes, I guess so. We . . . we aren't very close. I don't keep in touch." When Chloe realized she was avoiding his eyes, trying to avoid his questions, she lifted her gaze to his face.

A lawyer or a judge could not have had a more penetrating stare. "Is that where your son lives?"

"No!" She sat up straight, panic pounding in her chest. "What in the world—why would you say that?"

"You're lying."

Unable to tear her eyes from his, Chloe searched for the door handle with her fingers, fighting to hold onto her composure and get out of the car before she fell apart. Her chances of success dwindled to nothing as she felt Peter's hand close around her wrist.

"Come on, Chloe, don't run away. It's a simple question."

"What—" she squeaked, and then tried again. "What makes you think I have children?"

"Child. One. A boy about Eric's age, I'd guess. Black hair, like yours, with your eyes. His dad's smile."

The picture by her bed. Understanding dawned as she stared at him. He'd seen Mikey's picture by her bed the morning after they'd slept together. Just a photograph, nothing more. No inscription *To Mom* or his name. Maybe she could get out of this after all. She took a deep, lying breath.

"No, Peter, I'm sorry. You've got it wrong."

"Really?" He let go of her wrist, folded his arms over his chest, and sat back to listen. "Tell me how."

"That's my nephew, Mikey. My sister's son. He's the only grandchild in the family so far. They sent that photo for Christmas last year." Sounded almost real, didn't it?

"You just said you don't keep in touch."

Damn. "Well, not with the people in Virginia. My sister and her husband live in Missouri," she explained, hoping he didn't ask for a town. She only knew St. Louis. "We send cards at Christmas, that's about it."

That right eyebrow, the one that signalled skepticism or outright disbelief, lifted high enough to hide under the hair falling across his forehead. "I see," he said, obviously unconvinced. But to her relief, he decided to let it go. "Okay, the interrogation is over for the evening." Getting out of the car, Peter came around to open her door and with a gentle, impersonal hand under her elbow, walked her up to the house. He waited until she'd stepped inside before speaking again. "How about lunch tomorrow?"

For more than one reason, Chloe was glad to have an excuse. "I'd love to, Peter, but I need to rehearse with Kirsten tomorrow. After about a week you have to change the act, or the management gets restless."

"Hmm. An early dinner?"

She shook her head. "I eat between shows, about nine-thirty." His face mirrored the regret she was experiencing. And in his eyes she could see darker, stronger feelings, the needs and desires gripping them both as they stood, close but not touching, in the shadowed doorway of her house.

He looked so good, leaning against the door frame, with his hair relaxed from its usual brushed back state into a looser, younger drift across his eyes, and his conservative button-down shirt replaced by a soft knit polo. Chloe wished she could ask him in, but she knew where that would lead. Even now she had trouble keeping her hands to herself; if they closed the door, there would be no chance for control. And tonight, with Eric waiting at home for his dad to return, just wasn't the right time. But, she thought, does that matter? It would be so good. . . .

Peter's self-discipline held better than her own. "Well," he was saying, "on Wednesday Eric goes to play with Andy all afternoon and I have class. Thursday and Friday I'm supposed to be in Baltimore for a conference. Eric is staying home if you'd like to—or wait, better yet," he paused, with a smile that did funny things to her stomach, "you could come with me!"

She looked at him warily. "Peter, I don't think—"

He took her hand. "Good—don't think. Just come. We could have two days by ourselves, with a pool at our disposal, all the best restaurants in Baltimore to choose from. Annapolis is a few minutes away. . . ."

Chloe pulled away. "Peter, *you're* not thinking. I have a show to do every night. You have seminars every day—we'd end up passing in the hallway. I don't think it's a good idea."

His face fell. "I guess you're right. It's just hard to accept that I can't see you until Sunday."

It was impossible not to ask. "Saturday?"

"No. A father/son event for Scouts. All day."

Chloe studied the floor and Peter stared at the top of her head as the prospect of nearly a week without time together suddenly overwhelmed them both. And then Peter straightened up. "Well, I guess that's that. But, Ms. Smith, I do have an invitation for you. On Sunday evening, the Kennedy Center is offering dinner and dancing on the terrace. Will you come with me?"

His grin was enough to make her agree. The sparkle in his eyes, the touch of his fingers under her chin, sealed the bargain. "I would be delighted, Professor Carroll. What time?"

"I'll bring the carriage around about six-thirty. Leave a light burning—I like to dance!" With a pinch of her chin he took off down the walk, literally bounced into the car, and roared away.

Well, Chloe thought, *bacon is really expensive. I should buy oranges with the money. Or spinach. Something healthy and full of vitamins. If this waiting continues, I'm going to need all my strength!*

This was not, Peter thought to himself as he finally got into the shower Sunday afternoon, an auspicious start to the evening. He liked to dance, sure, but usually he liked a full night's sleep in advance. Instead, he'd spent most of Saturday night sitting by the side of the bathtub, entertaining a boy who was covered from the tip of his nose to the tops of his feet with poison ivy. Or, rather, the rash from an allergic reaction to the stuff, encountered when Eric lost his grip on the rope swing and dropped into a leafy nightmare—in his swimsuit, of course, so that only his hip area escaped exposure.

At least there were no broken bones! But because he'd already been exposed once this spring, on a school picnic, it didn't take long for the itching to start. And after a sleepless night, with Eric in an acute state of misery, Peter called the pediatrician, who prescribed more oatmeal baths and an antihistamine, which at least kept the boy too sleepy to scratch. Maia added some Chinese herbal tea of her own, and that, combined with the latest samurai reptile videos and a chocolate cake, had made Eric fairly comfortable.

But now, instead of looking forward with energy and enthusiasm to the first real date he'd ever had with Chloe Smith—he still found it hard to believe that last name!—Peter wondered how he would even stay awake. A cool shower helped for about fifteen minutes, and a strong cup of coffee maintained his focus on the late Sunday afternoon traffic jam at the National Zoo. Still, by the time he pulled up in front of her house, he was dragging again. Should he cancel after all? Reschedule for next weekend? He debated with himself all the way up the walk, short as it was, and across the narrow porch.

Then he knocked on Chloe's door. It opened right away, and Peter realized that drowsiness would no longer be a problem. Every cell in his body stood on full alert.

After days without seeing her, he found himself bewitched all over again by the burnished ebony of her hair, swinging against her jawline like a fringe of silk. Drinking in every detail, he let his eyes caress her face—the clear violet eyes, rose petal lips, and porcelain skin, with just a trace of blush across her cheeks. Her scent reached out to him: flowers, incense, and something musky, dangerous, inviting. It took him a minute to remember how to breathe.

And then he forgot again, when his eyes dropped to her dress. Black, sheer fabric. Layers of it. There was a high, flat band around her neck and folds of soft black chiffon belted at the waist, leaving bare her shoulders and long, slender arms. More layers of the stuff, pleated, fell from the belt to just above her knees. And, as he'd always assumed, those gorgeous legs stretched forever, in sheer black stockings, to her high-arched feet. Which were, except for the stockings, also bare.

His eyes, filled with laughter, came back to her face. "I think," he said, "that shoes might be a good idea. As I remember, the terrace is a little rough."

Chloe stepped back to let him in. "Of course," she replied with mock disdain. "I'm waiting for my glass slippers!"

Peter snapped his fingers. "I knew I'd forgotten something! But then, you're the magician—I'm just the lucky prince who gets to take you to the ball."

He *could* be royalty, Chloe thought as she laughed at him, or the leading man in a film from the forties, when everyone dressed in evening clothes for dinner and danced their way through life. Peter wore his dinner jacket as comfortably as if it were an old sweatshirt, with no fidgeting or jerking at his bow tie, no pulling at the French cuffs of his pleated shirt, to hint that he didn't always dress this way. *Cary Grant, watch out*, she thought with a smile.

"Would you like something to drink?" she asked. "It should be a martini, the way you look, but I'm afraid all I have is a nice white wine. Or water."

But Peter shook his head. "Thanks, but no. After

being up all night with Eric, I'd probably fall asleep right away."

"Eric? Is he sick? What's wrong?"

"No, no, nothing too serious," Peter assured her, surprised at the concern in her voice. "He fell into the poison ivy yesterday at the Scout hike and now, well, he's *not* a happy camper."

Chloe studied his face worriedly, chewing on her lower lip, trying to decide whether Eric's health would be sacrificed for her pleasure. There was only one way to find out. "Listen, Peter, if Eric needs you at home, we can do this another time. You should have called and told me what happened. I understand that a sick child takes priority. Goodness knows, when I—"

She managed to stop just before she gave it all away. Stupid, Chloe, she told herself. That was a serious mistake.

And Peter's eyebrow told her he'd noticed it. But he didn't comment. "We appreciate your concern, Chloe, but I think Eric is fine. Maia is there, and she has the number if she needs me—which she won't. I'm not being callous; I wouldn't have left him if I thought something would go wrong. He's done this once every summer—sometimes twice!—since he was four; it lasts about a week, and then you'd never know."

And then for the first time that evening, he stepped close enough to touch her. He grazed her cheek with the back of his fingers, strayed one finger over her lower lip, and then closed his fist, tilting her chin up with his knuckle. "Tonight is just for us, Chloe," he murmured softly, roughly. "Let's take it." She closed her eyes, to savor the balm of his touch, and drove him over the edge.

With a sense of homecoming, Peter fitted his mouth to hers and kissed, gently. She tasted like water after a drought, cool, refreshing, life-giving. Intoxicating. With a murmur deep in his throat he sought more, cupping his hand behind her neck to deepen their joining.

Those lips *looked* soft—they *felt* like heaven. Her hands slid over his shoulders, down his back; the pressure of her palms urged him closer still.

At that instant, water turned magically to fire. He felt the flames in the tips of his fingers against her skin and in the pit of his stomach, burning, consuming him with need. Her mouth opening under his fanned the blaze, and her sigh rushed through him like a hot wind, threatening to ignite them both. The urge to crush her against him, to taste with his tongue and his hands every inch of her skin, overwhelmed him.

"This is crazy," he managed to breathe against her mouth in the middle of the inferno. "I knew it would be like this—I should never have . . ."

"Shh." Chloe stepped back, allowing air and space and coolness between them. "I'll get my shoes," she whispered and left him.

In her room, Chloe ignored the evening shoes waiting just inside the door and sat down, trembling, on the bed. Energy rushed through her. Tension stretched every muscle, every nerve. She stared at her hands, twisting and massaging each other in her lap, and then lifted her eyes to confront herself in the mirror.

This is it, she told herself apprehensively. *After tonight, no backing out. But you can still get out of it, if you want to. Do you want to?*

The answer was obvious, the decision already made. But still, for a few more minutes, Chloe put off the inevitable. She paced across to her window, stared out into the slowly darkening summer evening, and then went back to the mirror, where she brushed her hair and touched up her makeup. She put on the earrings she'd forgotten when he knocked on the door and, finally, slipped on the black satin slippers.

Peter called her name from the front of the house. "I'm coming!" Chloe responded and flipped off the light. Just before leaving, she glanced around her bedroom, out of habit more than anything else, and saw, as if in a spotlight, the picture of Mikey by her bed.

She picked it up, bringing her lips to the cool glass over his dear little face. And then, because she knew what the evening would bring, she opened the bottom drawer of the nightstand and placed the frame underneath the scarves and sashes it contained.

Just for a while, she promised the little boy. *It will be over soon. Then you can come back.*

Prince Charming had recovered his poise in her absence and stood by the front door waiting for Cinderella to appear. He took in the shoes right away, and grinned. "Black glass?" he queried.

"Obsidian," replied Chloe.

With a tilt of his head he acknowledged a score. "This is almost the twenty-first century, after all," Peter said thoughtfully. "In a few years, princesses will probably be wearing leather and chains. If they aren't already!"

Only after she'd locked the door and they had made their way down the flower-bordered walk, with his hand lightly, warmly, on her elbow, did he speak again. "By the way," he murmured huskily against the curve of her ear, "you are more beautiful tonight than ever before." She turned, surprised, to look at him and found his face very close, the gray eyes dark with a storm of desire. "Thank you," he whispered.

It would take very little, she realized, to destroy his control. A word, a touch, and he would let passion sweep them both away. It gave her a sense of power, to affect a man so strongly. But this particular man prided himself on his self-discipline. He needed his ability to plan and carry through, and he wanted tonight to be special.

Chloe lifted her chin, found a saucy grin somewhere within the swirl of her own yearning, and turned the situation around. "You mean, you like this better than the half-drowned urchin look? Don't they have a wet t-shirt contest at this dance?''

Peter gave a surprised shout of laughter. ''Maybe we can sponsor one,'' he suggested, opening the car door. ''Let's go and find out!''

SIX

They danced for hours. Before the champagne cock-
tail, after the crab-stuffed avocado, between the grilled
salmon and the raspberry tart, they danced—the waltz,
the samba, even, after darkness fell, the tango. Twice
when the music ended Peter and Chloe surfaced to find
themselves alone on the floor while the other couples
on the terrace applauded the performance they hadn't
realized they'd provided. Like the veteran she was,
Chloe gave her best curtsey and Peter managed a
smooth, if slightly embarrassed, bow. But when the
orchestra resumed, their audience might as well have
disappeared.

Nothing, in fact, seemed to penetrate the enchantment surrounding them. Lost in the ecstasy of romance,
Chloe could scarcely hear the music when his arm
caught her against him; she found herself relying on the
sensuous rhythm of Peter's body and the direction of
his hands for the beat of the dance. The freedom to
touch intoxicated them both. Her legs brushed against
his, his hands caressed her through the fabric on her
back and waist, and the slide of her palms across his
shoulders set them both to breathing faster.

They could give a seminar, Peter thought to himself

with a smile. "How to make love in public without getting arrested." But how long? he wondered. How long could he keep this up before the need became uncontrollable?

Often, in the closest steps, he placed his lips against her ear and gave her, in a soft, breathless voice, the words of the song. Funny, Chloe thought, the best songs to dance to are love songs. How would it feel if he meant it? Did he? Could they already be that close? Drawing back to look at Peter, she caught her breath at the depth of tenderness in his face, the glow in his eyes. Love? Surely not. Swept around in a turn, she melted against him and pushed the questions away, unwilling to accept more than the pleasure this moment offered and the promise of the night.

The candle on their table had burned down to a puddle of light when they paused for one last sip of champagne. Reluctant to do something so mundane as sit down, Chloe took up her glass and moved to stand at the marble wall of the terrace, looking down on the shimmer of the Potomac River and the lights of Virginia on the other bank. To her right stood the curving towers of the Watergate Hotel. And just behind her stood the man whose nearness set her heart racing, whose fingers on the slope of her shoulder kindled the most intimate longings of her body. With a sigh she leaned back against him.

His fingers tightened and his breath blew softly over her temple. "Last dance, Cinderella. Then the witching hour." Peter took the glass from her unresisting hand and put it on the table. She followed him silently out to the center of the terrace and moved without reservation into his arms, put her head to rest lightly on his shoulder, leaving the nape of her neck exposed enticingly to his mouth. His lips were so warm.

The evening concerts and plays at the Kennedy Center had ended more than an hour before. Tall, glistening windows were now no more than black mirrors reflecting the dancers outside and the lights beyond. Shadows crept out from the walls, the music slowed and softened, and the few remaining couples swayed to the sinuous, seductive sound. Chloe closed her eyes, giving herself up to the feel of Peter surrounding her, his left hand just barely avoiding a seductive intimacy as it pressed, caressed, really, far below the small of her back.

And then a deeper darkness flowed over her lids. Startled, she opened her eyes and realized that Peter had danced her around the corner and into the shadows, away from the terrace, the orchestra, and the crowd. The marble of the building warmed her shoulders as he pressed her against it; his mouth moved compellingly, hypnotically across her cheek, blocking thought. The fury of his kisses left her gasping for air, desperate for more, yet even as she turned her head to capture his lips, they travelled somewhere else, striking like lightning across her face and throat. She brought up her hands to hold him still, and he caught her wrists to drag them away, unwilling to be stopped.

"Peter . . ." she gasped, against the storm. "Peter, there are other people . . . oh, God," she moaned as his tongue blazed a path down the sensitive cord of her neck.

"I know," he whispered, even as his hands stroked firmly across her ribs to cover her breasts, which were already aching and swollen. "I don't care." Through the soft fabric he rolled the sensitive peaks gently between his fingers and Chloe whimpered at the pleasure-pain of his touch. "Do you?"

"I—"

His mouth prevented her answer, slanting over hers with an undeniable force. Tongues met and mingled in a wetly erotic duel, hands caught, gripped, and held fast as the tension coiling between them reached its peak. Time and place slipped away; in all the world there were only Peter, Chloe, and the ceaseless, driving need which consumed them.

What might have happened, there on the wall of the Kennedy Center with thirty people just around the corner, Peter never knew. A siren shrieked and he felt Chloe stiffen in his arms. In another instant their embrace was shattered. They broke apart, eyes wild, hearts pounding, as the painful wail split the night and the flash of red and blue lights stained their startled faces. For one horrible moment Peter expected to face the police. Dragging in a deep breath, he turned slowly around, trying to dredge up some remnant of sanity from his brain to make a rational explanation.

But the ambulance sped past on its way toward the hospital nearby and in only seconds, though it seemed much longer, the darkness closed around them again. Peter dropped his head back, staring up at the hazy indigo sky with a wordless prayer of thanks. Finally, with a deep breath, he turned to face his temptress, his siren, his own personal witch.

To find her laughing. Mopping tears from her eyes with the backs of her hands, still giggling. "Can you imagine," she gasped, breathless, "another five minutes, if they'd come down this way? What in the world would we have said? 'Don't mind us, boys. We're doing research for a book on the best spots in D.C. for getting it on. Your presence definitely knocks the rating down a point or two.' " Filling her lungs with air, she looked at him ruefully and sighed. "Oh, Peter, what fools we are."

He had to smile, and to agree. "More myself, than you, I suspect," he said, running a finger down her cheek. "I started it, as I recall."

Chloe moved away from the wall and caught his hand as it fell. "But you met no resistance from me. I'd say we both bear the responsibility for that close call."

Peter raised her knuckles to his mouth and brushed his open lips against her skin. "At least it brought me to my senses. It's time to get you home," he said. The expression in his eyes assured her that sleep was not part of the agenda.

Finding the parking garage locked tight with the BMW still inside was not part of the agenda, either. "I don't believe it!" Peter exclaimed, running his hand through his hair. "It can't be that late!" The streets around them were quiet and empty of traffic and people alike.

Chloe had to laugh. "You said it was the witching hour," she reminded him. "Strange things happen at midnight. Disappearances, apparitions, cosmic disturbances . . ." she catalogued in an eerie whisper.

Peter turned a skeptical eye on her and opened his mouth to inject some rationality into the situation. But before he could get out a single word, a cab arrived magically at the curb; almost, it seemed, appearing out of thin air. "You folks need a ride?" the driver asked through the window.

"Where did you come from?" Peter asked. The driver flashed him a smile, but didn't answer. And anyway, did it matter? With a fatalistic shrug he opened the door for Chloe and slid onto the seat beside her, gave the driver her address, and then took full advantage of the situation.

The cab got them back to Chloe's house in a very short time. More important, letting someone else do the driving allowed them to sit close, hands tightly joined, to kiss carefully and murmur softly. To behave, in fact, exactly like two people in love.

Which, of course, we aren't, Chloe told herself. While Peter called home to check on Eric, she had slipped into the bathroom to take appropriate precautions for the lovemaking she knew would come. Now, standing in the kitchen, filling a pitcher with water and ice, placing glasses on a tray, she tried to remember that what she had with Peter was not a relationship. It was just physical, she tried to convince herself. Just a reaction to the way he looked and moved and smelled. It had nothing to do with emotions, feelings, or love. They'd get it out of their systems and say good-bye. The end.

She had a little trouble with that concept, though, on her way back to the living room with the drinks. The thought of saying good-bye—forever—to Eric and his cocky grin brought an ache to her chest. And one look at Peter, slouched against the back of her couch, his jacket off and his tie loose, was enough to melt the strongest resolve. Without a doubt, the end was going to be hard to take.

Setting the tray down on the coffee table, she handed him a glass. "How is Eric?"

"Fine." He sat up to take a long drink, set his glass back on the tray and dropped back again. "He had another bath about 8:30 and fell asleep right afterward. Snoring ever since." His eyes caressed her face as she sat on the table across from him. "Tomorrow he'll be raring to go. Don't worry."

The polished look she'd left the house with six hours ago had suffered, Peter noticed. He'd wiped every trace of lipstick off her mouth; the memory of how it was done pierced him with pleasure. Gone were the dangling silver earrings, the black hose, and the "obsidian" slippers. The nails on her bare toes were painted a pale pink. In the lamplight she looked young, vulnerable, and very, very sexy. It was not a combination he could resist.

"Chloe?" She looked up, he leaned forward. "Do you want that?" he asked, with a nod at her drink. Holding his eyes, she shook her head.

He placed the glass on the tray beside his own, then reached to take her hand. Her fingers were wet from the condensation. Raising her hand to his mouth, Peter licked the water from her skin, rasping his tongue lightly across her palm to the music of her harshly drawn breath. He looked up into violet eyes gone sud-

denly black, lifted his head and ran his hands up her
arms. "I want you so much," he whispered.

Chloe nodded. It was all there in his face. He hadn't
needed words. "Please?" she said softly.

This time as he fell back against the couch he kept
hold of her arms and drew her with him. But when
Chloe would have come to sit beside him he shook his
head and, pulling more on one arm than the other,
brought her onto his lap, her knees nestled on either
side of his hips. He stared up at her as she knelt over
him, drinking in the softness of her skin and hair with
his eyes, almost afraid to make the move that would
wrench the world from its orbit.

And so it was Chloe who brought their mouths together, who sought out the first, irrevocable kiss. She
bent to him, seeking the firm, chiseled lips she'd
dreamed about. His mouth opened, their tongues tangled, but Peter allowed her to control the contact, to
tease and to demand, to plunder and withdraw. Chloe
let her mouth wander over his jaw, across his ears, and
down his throat, let her fingers explore the strong col-
umn of his neck. And all the time she rocked slowly,
sensuously against him, her womanly softness mas-
saged his increasing strength, setting them both on fire
with the promise of things to come.

Peter added his own fuel to the flames. His hands
drifted adventurously over her calves as they rested
along his thighs, and then across her knees to the soft
skin under the hem of her skirt. When she lifted to
move against him, he slipped higher, under her buttocks, encountering a drift of silk that barred his way
and yet urged him on.

"Your belt," he breathed. "Take it off."

Pulling away, Chloe fumbled for an instant and then
the barrier was gone. For good measure, she reached
to the back of her neck and released the pearl buttons
on the collar. Peter watched, debating whether to leave
the dress for a while or . . . no. Before his mind could

decide, his hands had performed, and the black chiffon lay like a deflated thundercloud on the floor.

"Beautiful!" he exclaimed softly. And she was. Small, firm breasts taunted him, daring him to conquer their rosy tips. Delicately arching ribs intrigued him with their texture, narrowing to her slender waist just below his palms. The silk he had encountered proved to be black, of course: a pair of tap pants wide in the leg and generous through the hips, practically inviting intimate exploration.

But first, he had a question to ask. "Why," he said unsteadily, "do you always wear black or white?"

Chloe heard the question with a smile. It did not stop her, concentrating as she was on releasing the studs that closed his dress shirt. "Magic. Mystery. Memory," she replied seriously. Then she lightened up with a laugh. "And easier. Fewer things to worry about."

Her hands on his bare skin had robbed him of breath, but he nodded. "Fair enough," he managed. She smoothed his shirt away with fingers that trembled, then smoothed again and again over his chest, smiling slightly at the pounding of his heart and his ragged breathing. Peter barely held on to his sanity as she explored the curve of his collarbone, lost ground at the pressure of her thumbs against the hollow of his throat, slid further down the slope as her palms covered his nipples and twisted, gently. His body tightened, but he mastered the instinct to thrust. Not now. Not yet. Seeking a focus outside the exquisite sensation she provoked, Peter raised his eyes to Chloe's face.

The pleasure in her eyes as she touched him shook to the core. Had a woman ever enjoyed him that way? He didn't think so. And it drove him wild. His palms against her back pressed her close, closer still, until he could taste her scent in the delicious valley between her breasts, could sample their silken slopes and the taut rosettes at their peaks. He closed his teeth gently on one nipple and tugged. Slender fingers writhed in his hair and her voice broke over his name.

"Peter, please—you're making me crazy—I can't take much more—"

He raised his head to look at her. In the soft glow from the lamp they stared at each other for a long moment, postponing—anticipating—the final step. Then something shifted in the depths of his stormy eyes. Chloe eased herself away and, with Peter's help, stood up. Keeping his hands in hers, she drew him off the couch, then turned to lead him down the hallway to her room.

As she crossed the threshold, Peter slipped his hand away and pulled her back against him. His tongue tasted again the satin of her shoulder while the smoothness of his palms took the place of the silk on her hips and thighs. The tap pants whispered into a puddle at her feet. He cupped her breasts, lightly squeezing her nipples, until she arched back against him, moaning softly. And then one hand skimmed over the flatness of her belly to find the tangle of curls at the juncture of her legs, damp with the need he had roused. Moaning softly, Chloe shifted to allow him entrance. With gentleness he found the very center of her desire and stroked her there, slowly at first, until the violence of her response demanded more. As she shuddered helplessly against him, he brought her to the pinnacle of excitement, then held her tightly as she went over the edge.

Chloe had never known such intensity of feeling. And she had never realized that she could feel so deeply and not be satisfied. Even as her body still throbbed with the pleasure he had created, she turned in Peter's arms, desperate to touch him. His shirt fell to the floor as her hands learned the planes of his back and her mouth explored the elegant strength of his shoulders and chest. The light feathering of hair on his chest teased the tips of her breasts as she moved deliberately, delightfully against him; his voice, telling her how she pleased him, drove her on.

It wasn't enough, for either of them. Capturing her hands, Peter brought them to the waist of his slacks, then he captured her mouth while she removed the last barrier between them. Chloe wanted to slow down, wanted to admire his slim hips and long legs, to explore the wonderful contours of his buttocks and thighs. But as he held her against him the silken heat of his manhood seemed to ignite a new, aching emptiness that must be filled. Her palms cupped his cheeks, drawing his eyes to hers, stilling his wandering hands.

"I want you inside of me," she said softly.

Peter nodded slightly, then rested his lips against her forehead. "Birth control?" he asked quietly.

"Done."

"Oh yes," he sighed.

At last they lay down together on her bed. Arms and legs tangled in a graceful moonlit dance as old as time, yet entirely new. Chloe wished the avalanche of sensation could go on forever, that she could spend eternity with the brush of Peter's skin against hers. But there were limits to his endurance. He knelt over her and she opened to him, ready to be swept away by the force of his need. The pressure of him against her drew a hoarse cry of pleasure from her throat.

And then, in the midst of passion, surrounded by the whirlwind of desire, they passed suddenly from the fury of the storm into its stillest center. She opened her eyes as he entered her, and the intensity of her stare drew his attention. Lost each in the other's gaze, they lay joined and quiet, motionless, absorbing the impact of completion. Her hand left his ribs to brush the hair from his eyes, and then stayed to trace the slight smile that shaped his mouth.

"I love you," Peter whispered against her fingers.

Chloe's eyes widened impossibly, until they seemed

to fill her whole face. Her head moved from side to side in denial.

"Yes," he insisted. "That's what this is all about."

To prove what he said, he took them back into the storm. His thrusts were the pounding of the wind-whipped rain, and the sounds they made together were the keening of the wind. They were drowning in the tempest, caught up in a flood of sensation and emotion too strong for the narrow channel of their bodies. But at the last second, when it seemed they must simply perish, release came with a flash of brilliant light and a powerful, thunderous roar. The wind subsided, the water calmed, and the glow of the moon shone once again.

Chloe found that she could, in fact, breathe. For awhile she thought she had stopped. And she found she needed to open her eyes again. When, she wondered, had they closed? She lifted her lids, to find Peter's smile waiting for her.

"Welcome back," he said softly, brushing her hair back from her face.

She tried a smile of her own. It must have worked, because his widened. Next she tried her voice. "Thanks," she whispered, still a little shaky.

His eyes told her everything she needed to know; he simply nodded in reply. Then he moved away. Chloe leaned up on an elbow to watch as he bent to recover the pillows they had scattered on the floor and the blanket which was somehow wedged at the end of the mattress. When her bed was once more as it should be, he drew her back against him, pillowing her head on his shoulder and twining her legs with his. "Rest," he instructed her gently.

The last thing Chloe saw before she fell asleep was the bedside clock, reminding her that her two weeks had expired yesterday. Did I win? she wondered. Or did I lose? There was no way to be sure.

* * *

Three hours of sleep: not her usual quota. Why then, Chloe wondered as she stood under the steaming spray of the shower, do I feel so refreshed? Rested, relaxed, and renewed? Could it have anything to do with Peter? Could it be the fact that he made her feel so incredibly alive, so marvelously, completely human? It had been so long since she felt so good. . . .

Lifting her face to the water, she corrected herself. It hadn't been *so long*—it had been *never*. Robert never made her feel like the center of the universe, even before they were married. And afterward everything went downhill fast. She had not known she could feel so much. It was the greatest magic on earth: a man and a woman, touching and joining.

And Peter had proved himself quite a magician. Not just in his lovemaking, although as she stroked the towel over her wet skin Chloe could all too easily recall the enchantment of his hands and his mouth. But he had achieved a far more impressive feat: he had gained her confidence. Even when she woke up alone in the dark, surely the single most dreaded outcome of a first encounter, she had known he wouldn't walk out on her.

In fact, she had found him in the dark kitchen, staring out into her backyard through the window over the sink. Beside him on the counter steeped two cups of tea.

"Do you always get up at 5:00 AM?" she had asked from the doorway.

He turned quickly at the sound of her voice. As she crossed the room he opened his arms, then folded them tightly around her as she nestled against him. Chloe felt him shake his head against her hair. "Not usually. I tend to stay up late writing instead."

She nodded against his shoulder. "Good. I'm a night owl, too."

The silence between them lengthened, but for once without tension. A sense of rightness, of completeness, had overwhelmed her. Words like trust, home, and forever drifted through her mind, words she'd sworn never to use again. And the scary part was how strongly Peter could make her believe in those concepts. With his arms around her, she could believe almost anything.

Now that she was alone in the house once again, the whole idea of a relationship seemed alien. Chloe had given up the prospect of permanence long ago. And yet, settling once again into the bed they had shared, she couldn't help wishing for the impossible.

"I love you," he had said. The sheer potential of those words was breathtaking. Being Chloe, she had tried to convince herself that Peter spoke out of desire, or out of need, or, perhaps, out of politeness. Men tended to say things like that, not meaning it, in the heat of the moment.

Being Peter, however, he had refused to allow her even that evasion. Hoping to be home before Eric woke up, he had left the house about six. They had been waiting by the front door for his cab when, without warning, he caught her chin with his thumb and finger, keeping her gaze on his.

"I meant what I said, you know." His voice was light, but serious. "I love you." As if for emphasis, the taxi announced its arrival with a toot of the horn.

Chloe had tried to protest. "I don't want you to love me, Peter. I don't want to love you. I don't want a relationship—not that kind. Please, let's just—"

He should have been hurt. Angry. Something besides slightly amused and, maybe, a little sad. "Well, whatever you want or don't want, my dear, facts are facts." The worried look on her face drew his sympathy. Stepping closer, he had placed a brief kiss on her forehead. "Don't let it worry you, Chloe. I'm not asking for anything. Relax." With the cab door open, he turned to give her a smile. "Go back to bed. I'll call you this afternoon."

So, after a shower, she was following orders. Except, Chloe thought savagely as she punched her pillow, following orders was something else she swore she'd never do. She was independent and she liked it that way. Commitment was a trap guaranteed to destroy everything she'd done.

She wasn't going to get so involved that she lost herself, she swore, blowing her bangs out of her eyes. The time with Peter would be a wonderful treat, something she'd look back on when she was too old and tired to do anything else. She'd just have to end it carefully, not let it tear her apart. Or Peter. Or Eric. Somehow she'd have to find a way to protect them all.

But it's not going to change my life. I can't let it.

Her resolve strengthened later that morning when she woke to Kirsten literally dragging her out of bed. Not only had Peter managed to undermine her hard-won detachment, but spending time with him was wrecking her professional life as well: she had slept right through the time she had set up for a rehearsal at the club. She had slept on as Kirsten hammered on the front door and rang the bell. Finally, her valuable and concerned assistant had used the key Chloe had provided for emergencies and had let herself into the house.

"Do you feel okay?" Kirsten asked as Chloe attempted to pull herself together after such a rude awakening. "Are you sick?"

Chloe peered groggily up at the blonde, sent a weary stare at the clock—which now said noon—and dropped her head into her hands. "No, I'm not sick," she mumbled. "Bewitched, maybe."

Kirsten nodded. "You went out with the professor last night," she said, stating the obvious. "It must have been quite an evening. But you scheduled a rehearsal for ten."

Running her fingers through her hair, Chloe struggled to get her eyes all the way open. "I know. I'm sorry. Go make yourself some coffee and I'll get dressed— quickly."

True to her word, in ten minutes she joined Kirsten

in the kitchen and found the other woman making sand-wiches. "You shouldn't have done this," Chloe protested. "I wanted to take you out to lunch as an apology for missing rehearsal!"

Kirsten smiled and placed two full plates on the counter. "It was no trouble. The tuna was here with bread and potato chips. Eat."

Chloe took a bite, and then another, appeasing an appetite she hadn't known she'd had. After demolishing half a sandwich, she stretched out her hand to touch Kirsten lightly on the arm. "You make great tuna salad," she said with a shy smile. "And you take great care of me. Thanks."

"Somebody needs to," was the enigmatic reply.

"I beg your pardon?"

Kirsten's blue eyes were friendly, but insistent. "You are not taking proper care of yourself. You sleep too little, and you eat almost nothing. You work too hard; you worry too much. And on top of it you want to push this man away, who would be so good for you. I am afraid something inside you is going to break."

Amazed, Chloe let her lunch lie ignored as she stared across the counter. "How did you—how do you know so much?"

"I watch," Kirsten said with a shrug. "I see your eyes when you think about him. I know how you feel about your work. But there is more to life than work."

With a sigh, Chloe shook her head. "Not for me. I tried to have a different life once, and I couldn't do it. But magic—that is something I *can* do. And as long as it's all I do, everything will be just fine."

It was Kirsten's turn to shake her head. "You are a woman and a human being. You need more than this fleshless sorcery. You will realize it one day." Without another word she began to gather up the dishes and put them away.

"But . . ." Chloe's protest died away as Kirsten turned a kindly inquiring look on her, but she pushed herself to continue. "You surely can't believe that a man like Peter—a college professor, no less!—could commit himself to more than a casual liaison with someone like me."

"Why not?"

"You know why not!" Chloe exploded. "My unorthodox profession. My questionable background. My inability to—"

Calmly, Kirsten interrupted. "The only real obstacle *I* see to a very satisfactory relationship is your inability to open up to him. You haven't explained anything about yourself, have you?"

Chloe let silence answer for her.

"Well, then, until you allow him the opportunity to know you, I suppose a casual 'liaison,' as you put it, is all there will be." With the dishcloth neatly folded and the kitchen cleaner than it had been in weeks, Kirsten walked toward the door. "Now, are we going to rehearse today? My babysitter must leave by four o'clock."

"I'm know I'm right," Chloe muttered to herself as she followed Kirsten out of the house. And to prove it, she ignored the telephone when it began to ring just as she shut the door. Of course, she was human enough to keep it open a crack, and so caught the beginning of the message Peter was forced to leave on the answering machine. *He needs to know*, she told herself righteously on the way to the club, *that I'm not sitting around waiting for him. I have my own life and I live it my own way!*

"Chloe is unavailable at the moment. Please leave a message at the tone."

Peter stared in disbelief at the phone, then pushed it back to his ear as he heard the beep. "Hi, it's Peter. Sorry you're not there. I hoped I could see you tonight after dinner. Call when you get in."

That sounds pretty awkward, he thought, for a poet.

But then, answering machines hardly fit in the same category with moonlight and roses. Would Chloe even like roses? He didn't know.

There was a great deal, he realized, that he didn't know—and probably should. Leaning back in the chair at his desk, he tapped his pencil against the wood and thought over some of it. Most of Chloe's life, he realized, was an absolute blank. The explanations she *had* made seemed a little threadbare, like the ones for why she didn't drive and why she hadn't read his book. And that boy in the picture looked enough like her to be her twin. Or her son. Her past was her own, Peter admitted, and she owed him nothing, not even, he supposed, the truth. But surely, if she cared about him, she would . . .

He flipped the pencil onto the desk and with restless energy went to stand at the window overlooking the campus fountain. The grassy square was deserted in the afternoon heat. That's the hitch, he told himself. Does she care? Last night's passion said yes. This morning's conversation discouraged him: "I don't want to love you," Chloe had said. If she was strong enough to stand by those words, life was going to get very difficult, very soon.

Because he'd spoken the absolute truth. He had fallen in love with the magician. The words had only come last night, but from the very beginning he'd been drawn to this elusive, compelling woman. He should have known that nothing else could make him quite as miserable as he'd been that last month without her. Nothing else could explain the incredible joy of being with Chloe and the intense need to see her again as soon as possible.

Which didn't mean, of course, that she returned his feelings. As far as Peter could tell, the slightest push from him would drive her completely away. It was one of the hardest things he'd ever done, to walk lightly, to be careful about making demands, when his blood surged in his veins and he wanted to shout his feelings to the world. But if he knew anything at all about this witch he loved, she would take off at the first whisper, let alone shout.

And yet she'd been so giving, so loving. Her enjoyment of him and the pleasure they made together was like nothing he'd ever experienced with anyone else. On a deep breath Peter turned from the window, glanced at his watch, and retraced his steps to the desk. His seminar should start in five minutes. Gathering his papers together, he tried to step back from the situation and gain a reasonable perspective. This, he told himself, is the twentieth century. It is possible to enjoy sex without benefit of clergy, or even love. Maybe she just likes your technique—you should be flattered. You're not getting older; as they say, you're getting better.

He paused at the door to flip off the light and then stood leaning against the door frame, staring into the darkened room. He'd take the risk, he decided and stay involved. Maybe he would solve the mystery of Chloe and come out with a woman and a relationship worth any sacrifice. And maybe, Peter acknowledged with a shrug, he'd come out with nothing but a sweet memory and a heart full of might-have-beens.

Footsteps in the hall cut short his introspection. Peter straightened up, shifted his books against his hip, and headed toward his class. Anyway, he reminded himself as he followed his students into the room, he'd always have Eric to fall back on!

But Eric, it seemed, had his own plans regarding his dad's new romance. Over dinner that evening he revealed just how far his ten-year-old sophistication extended. "So, Dad," he asked casually while carefully picking the green peppers out of Maia's excellent chicken and vegetable stir-fry, "did you and Chloe have a good time last night?"

Peter's fork stopped halfway between his plate and his lips. "Yes, very. Why?"

A nonchalant shrug. "I just wondered. She's a really neat person. I like her a lot." A fork filled with chicken disappeared into his mouth.

Scenting a trap, Peter studied his son carefully. "Yes, she is. I like her, too." When Eric continued to munch silently, Peter relaxed his suspicions and lifted his fork.

"Did you spend the night with her?"

Peter's answer was delayed several minutes. When he had stopped choking and could speak again, he used every ounce of parental patience he could muster to take a sip of water and calm down before he spoke. Even then, his voice shook. "Why—how—what makes you ask that?"

Eric flashed an impatient look at the ceiling. "Come on, Dad! This is nineties—and I'm not a baby. It makes sense."

"But, son," Peter began, then stopped. Should he deal with the substance or the form of the issue first? He tried again. "First of all, that's not a question you should ask. It's not polite and the answer isn't any of your business. Got that?"

The boy's eyes were round and innocent. "You're my dad. Of course it's my business. You'd be bugging me if you thought I was doing something like that."

"You're damned right I would, at ten years old. But not at twenty, or thirty. I hope I would give you the respect and privacy I want you to give me."

"Aw, Dad . . ."

Placing his elbows on the table, Peter rubbed his clasped knuckles against his lower lip while he directed a serious gaze at his son, then lifted his chin and rested it on his hands as he went on in an equally serious voice. "Secondly, Eric, what Chloe and I do together as adults is no one's concern but our own. Certainly not yours. Can you understand that?"

"But—"

"There are no buts here, son. I try to live my life

in a way that will make you proud of me, but I don't have to tell you about every aspect of it."

"I know, but—"

"If Chloe and I have a relationship, we will try to conduct ourselves appropriately so that nothing we do is an embarrassment to you—"

"Dad! Stop!" Eric screamed in his loudest, ten-year-old, outdoor voice.

Peter stopped. "Why are you yelling in the house?"

"Because," Eric complained in the same tone, "you aren't listening to me."

Looking at the flushed face and the hurt eyes, Peter could see that he believed it. "Okay, I'll shut up. What do you want to say?"

All at once, Eric was shy. But, shy or not, he was determined. "All I meant, was, well, that I think it's neat that you two are going out. I think you get along really great. And I like it when we do things together, but I wanted to tell you that you don't have to worry about me. I mean, well, I can find other stuff to do if you want to be alone with Chloe."

Suddenly, Peter had the whole picture. Eric was worried about being left out. Time to backtrack and mend fences. It would require tact, so he took it slowly. He sat back in his chair and pushed his hands into his pockets.

"Thanks, son, for your concern. I'm glad that you don't mind if I spend some time with Chloe without you. A lot of kids would be jealous.

"But I don't think of my life as just me, you know. I haven't for about ten years now. When a woman is interested in me, well, I expect her to be interested in you, too. We're sort of a package, you and I. So either we all do things together, or I suggest she might be happier with someone else."

Eric made a skeptical frown, and Peter nodded, with one eyebrow raised for emphasis. "Oh yes, my boy, it's happened more than once. And it wasn't a problem—for me, anyway.

"Chloe likes you, Eric. She was worried about you last night, almost to the point of canceling our date so I could come home and sit while you snored. I think she genuinely enjoys being with both of us. And so, whatever happens, we'll all be in this together."

As Eric nodded, pleased, Peter recognized the potential for disaster in this situation. "There is one other possibility, you know." He stood up and walked over to Eric's chair, placing a hand on the sturdy shoulder. "I don't have any promises to make about what happens between Chloe and me, Eric. It's complicated and it may not work out. She might not be with us for a long time."

Ten-year-olds can be quite stoical. Eric absorbed the warning with characteristic confidence. "I think it will work out just great, Dad," he said. "With your looks and my charm, how can we lose?"

SEVEN

Another frustrated groan from the direction of her living room brought Chloe out of the kitchen. "What's wrong, kid? Haven't got it yet?"

Eric sat on the floor in front of the mirror with a coin in his fingers. His mouth drooped and his eyes had lost their eager sparkle. "This is so hard!" he complained. "Are you sure I have to do this to be a magician?"

"Yep." Dropping her dishcloth on the couch, Chloe plopped down beside him. "A lot of the illusions you see are based on some kind of palming maneuver—you know, taking an object and moving it around your hand until it's hidden from the audience. And that requires a great deal of dexterity. Which requires practice." She took the quarter from him and demonstrated an intricate roll that involved all of the fingers on one hand and ended with the disappearance of the coin. "See?"

Eric grabbed her hand and examined it eagerly—without success. "Where'd it go?" he demanded in disbelief.

She smiled at him and tapped his foot. He lifted the sneaker off the floor and there sat the coin. "Unbelievable!'' he cried. ''I'm gonna learn to do that if I have to work all night!''

Neglecting her dinner preparations, Chloe watched him practice. She had wanted to maintain her independence from Peter, but she had forgotten to consider one factor: Eric. Her struggle against the affection he inspired was lost before it had truly begun. She loved his quick wit and his youthful eagerness, very different from Mikey's quieter approach, but it made her heart ache nonetheless. Their mutual interest in magic only strengthened the bond. He was a quick study and, despite his frustration, exceptionally dexterous for a boy so young; after only a few hours of work he had a repertoire of almost a dozen simple tricks that would amaze his friends.

''Is this a private party, or can anyone join in?''

''Hey, Dad! Look at this!''

Eric jumped to his feet and raced to the door where his father had entered so quietly that they hadn't noticed. Chloe got up more slowly, smiled in response to the wink Peter directed over his son's head, and then watched for a few moments as Eric demonstrated his developing skills.

Being with Eric meant being with Peter, of course, and it kept alive the emotions she so desperately wanted to die. Peter rarely touched her when they were with Eric—no hello kiss, no holding hands—yet one piercing glance from those gray eyes could weaken her knees and destroy her train of thought. Denying herself the pleasure and comfort of a relationship with Peter was not easy, but so far she'd managed to keep things under control. If he called to ask for a date, she often tried to manufacture an excuse. Of course, he called every day, and in the two weeks since their first night together, she'd weakened four times—not even counting the time they spent with Eric.

She had assumed the passion between them would peak, and then they would tire of each other. But as the days passed, she was beginning to wonder if that would ever happen. Chloe thought she might never forget the bars of late afternoon sunlight laid across Peter's body by the blinds in her bedroom, or the slide of his skin against hers in the shower. The demands of her job set an unusual schedule for their trysts. More than once she found herself wishing she could—just now and then!—spend a whole night with Peter. And the very existence of that whim scared her to death.

Shaking her head, she turned toward the kitchen and the dinner she had volunteered to prepare for the three of them. Coming back into the dining room with the salad, she found Peter had freed himself from his son and, with a familiarity that sent shivers up her back, had found the wine and was pouring them both a glass.

He handed her a goblet and lifted his in a toast. "To Monday nights with no performances."

She had to grin. And then topped his toast with one of her own. "And to six more weeks of steady paychecks!"

Peter lowered his glass. "Really? They renewed your contract? That's great! Definitely worth a toast!"

Muttering some excuse about checking the chicken, Chloe returned to the kitchen, unsettled by his whole-hearted approval. She'd known about the offer for days, had debated with herself about asking for his advice. Her first thought, when the manager offered the new contract, was how that would affect her time with Eric and whether Peter would mind. He'd already mentioned that the yearly trip to Greece had been postponed; Chloe had been ready to start an argument, fearing he'd changed their plans because of her, when he explained that Eric's mother had made plans to come to the States in October and would see her son then. *That* left her without a word to say on the subject.

Almost as an afterthought she consulted Kirsten, and then, remembering the security of a steady job and the worn tires on the van, she signed the papers. To hell with Peter Carroll, she'd thought defiantly. If he doesn't like it, he can lump it!

Except that what he seemed to feel was a pure pleasure in her success. "Did you get a raise with this new contract?" he inquired over dinner. "I know you must be bringing in business."

Did he think she was a moron? Of course she'd negotiated a raise. "I asked for a fifteen percent increase, based on receipts. He gave me ten." So there.

Peter nodded. "I'm impressed. You have him right in the palm of your hand. I'm sure he knows he's lucky to have you."

She stared at him, her fork dangling into her plate. He looked back at her across the table. The gray eyes laughed, but there was a message there, too, and as clearly as if he'd spoken aloud she knew what he was thinking: Don't pick a fight with me, magician. I'm on your side.

Eric forestalled the hostilities with a pertinent interruption. "When," he demanded imperiously, "do I get to see the show?"

After consulting Chloe, Peter brought Eric and his friend Andrew to the early show on the next Tuesday night. They sat at a front table, ordered Shirley Temples, and just barely restrained their excitement. The audience contained five or six other children and was unexpectedly large. Peter had no doubt that Chloe's reputation was pulling in more than the club's usual crowd. He noticed, thankfully, that the waitresses had on more clothes than he remembered from his earlier visit. This manager was no fool—he obviously gave the public whatever they wanted. What they wanted, in this case, was Chloe.

Promptly at eight-thirty, the lights dimmed and a man stepped to the microphone spotlighted in front of blue velvet curtains on the stage. Eric and Andrew gave one final wiggle a piece and then stopped dead as the announcer spoke. "Welcome, ladies and gentlemen, to the Street Scene. Allow me to present, for your pleasure, Chloe, Mistress of Magic!"

The curtains drew back toward the corners, forming an old-fashioned swag. A slender black figure stood on the darkened stage in complete silence for a long second. Just before the tension broke, the spotlight flashed with the crash of a cymbal and Chloe strode forward, smiling widely. As she reached the front of the stage she raised her hands and clapped them in front of her face. The cymbal crashed again and between her spreading hands was revealed a large, brilliant Chinese fan. As the audience gasped, and then applauded, she manipulated the large fan in a graceful dance, swooping and arching through the air to the lilt of a waltz melody. Suddenly, coming from nowhere, there was a smaller fan, then another, smaller yet, and the fans became juggling props, flying high in the air, open and closed, like obedient butterflies. When at last the fans fell with a snap into her palms, Chloe took her first bow to enthusiastic cheers.

"Thank you, thank you very much," she said, her voice amplified by a microphone Peter couldn't see. Her formal evening dress fit perfectly: Fred Astaire couldn't match her in white tie and tails. She looked crisp, cool, calm, and completely in control. And, Peter thought, irresistibly sexy.

"We're very happy to have you with us tonight," she went on over his lustful thoughts. "Let me introduce you to my assistant, Kirsten."

Kirsten glided smoothly on stage behind a velvet-covered table. Her regal looks were heightened by a dress of ice-blue sequins and her bow held the same assurance as Chloe's. She'd gained confidence, Peter recognized, in the weeks since he'd last seen the show. He spared a glance for the two boys at his table. They hadn't moved yet, had hardly breathed. A good sign.

"As you may know," Chloe continued, laying the

fans on the table, "the art of magic is an ancient one, recorded in the earliest histories of China and Egypt." The music, now more of an atmosphere than an actual presence, became, Peter noticed, faintly Oriental. From a stack of neatly folded cloths on the table, Chloe withdrew a red scarf. She flourished the silk in front of her as she talked. "There are many stories of sorcerers who could make an object appear and disappear at will. Something as simple as a coin," she said, as Kirsten handed her a silver dollar, "can vanish under a handkerchief, as you will see." Holding the coin in her outstretched hand, Chloe allowed the red cloth to float down over it. Just as the last flutter settled, she grasped a hanging corner and whipped the cloth away to reveal her empty fingers.

Against the sighs of disbelief from the audience, she protested. "What? You think my coin was tainted? You question my honesty?" Standing with hands on her hips, she stared sternly down at the crowd. "Very well. I will allow one of you to provide the coin. Does someone have a fifty-cent piece? Or a silver dollar?" No one seemed to have a large coin. "Well, then, a quarter. Can someone lend us a quarter?" A man in the back raised his hand. "Very good, sir. Could you bring it forward, please?"

As he stood at the foot of the stage, reaching up, she seemed to reconsider. "As a matter of fact, sir, I believe I will need your help with this undertaking. If you would come around to the steps on your left . . ."

Kirsten stepped to the side to show the man where to get on the stage. Chloe surveyed her audience. "Perhaps we need one or two others to verify our reliability. You, madam?" she asked, pointing to a young woman on the left, and "Would you help us, young man?" gesturing to Eric.

His son, Peter was amused to see, did not even look at him for permission. In a daze, he made his way to the stage. Once surrounded by her three "volunteers,"

Chloe explained the procedure. "First, sir, I ask you to label your coin with your name and the date. That way we'll be sure it is the correct coin." Kirsten provided a pen and the man wrote on the coin. "Now, I will hold your coin as I held the other, in my fingers, arm straight." Following her own directions, she stretched out her arm. "You, sir, are a fairly strong man, I think," she said to the man who provided the coin, "and I'm sure you don't want to lose your money. So," she twinkled, as the audience laughed, "why don't you grasp my wrist with your hand, just to be sure I can't move." The man took her wrist as directed and the audience laughed again at the grimace of pain Chloe produced. "Excuse me—I don't want to lose my hand, either. Loosen up just a bit. Good. Kirsten, the silk, please."

Once again, the cloth fluttered down. "Now I will ask each of you to check to be sure the coin is still present. Sir?" she said, indicating the man whose coin it was. He checked with his free hand and nodded. "Miss?" as the woman stepped forward. She nodded, too. "And now, young man, could you check, please?" Eric stepped forward and reached up under the scarf. Peter and those closest to the stage could see his small fingers tracing the edges of the coin under the cloth. He stepped back. "It's still there," he piped up in a loud voice.

"Very good." Chloe closed her eyes, the music got louder, and the audience stilled. Then she slowly counted, "One, two, three!" and pulled the handkerchief away with her other hand. . . .

The coin had disappeared.

Their surprise was tangible. The man on stage could have been knocked over with a feather; the woman laughed loudly. And Eric jumped up and down, swearing he had felt the coin. At last Chloe raised her hand for silence. "Where is the coin? Did it vanish into thin air? I think not." Turning to Eric, she instructed him to reach into the pocket of her trousers. "You will find a box. Pull it out."

Eric did as instructed, and produced a small, red lacquer box. He extended it to Chloe, but she shook her head. "Give it to the young lady, please. Let her open it."

The woman took the box and looked at it, puzzled. A ribbon had been tied around the box so that all four sides were secured by the bow on top. With a yank she released the bow so that the box could be opened. But when the top came off, she gasped. "Show the audience, please," Chloe commanded.

When the box was tipped, Peter could see another box nesting inside the first. When that top was removed, another one came into view, and so on, through five separate boxes. And then, the sixth box was opened, and with a loud ring and a bounce, a coin fell out, rolled across the stage and dropped onto the floor, where it continued to roll until it came to rest against the toe of Andrew's sneaker.

"Aha!" Chloe crossed her arms. The man on stage reached out as Andrew retrieved the coin and held it up. Shaking his head, he walked back to give it to Chloe. "No—I believe it is yours," she said, shaking her head.

His look expressed his doubt. But then he looked down at his hand. "Well, well,—I'll be damned!" he exclaimed in a loud Texas twang. "That's *my* quarter! It's got my name on it!"

"And you may take it home with you," Chloe said, smiling, as she shook his hand amidst wild applause. She thanked the woman and Eric, too, and sent them back to their seats. If Eric saw the lift of his dad's eyebrow as he wiggled back onto his chair, he was too consummate a performer to acknowledge it.

The show lasted well over an hour. All of the children in the audience had a chance to appear on the stage, as Chloe used their innocent delight as a foil for her talents. Andrew was given a closer look at the Chinese linking rings, only to come away shaking his head. Wands that produced scarves, ribbons that became candles, and another juggling sequence involving wine glasses and an open bottle of wine had the people in the audience on the edges of their seats with laughter and outright enjoyment.

Peter surveyed them all with relaxed indulgence, feeling somehow separate from the others in the room. He had watched one of Chloe's practice sessions and had developed an entirely new appreciation for the laborious effort that created such seamless illusions. At the end of three hours the magician had been sweatsoaked and exhausted, with her assistant nearly as drained. What looked so easy, he now knew, took a lot of work.

The finale stunned them all, even Peter, who had learned how it was done. Kirsten slipped offstage during the juggling, removing the velvet table, and returned carrying coils of thick, white rope. Taking the rope, Chloe retreated to the center of the stage, where the spotlight illuminated her white face and shirtfront against the black backdrop. The music modulated to a sinuous, intricate melody on an Indian sitar.

Chloe faced the crowd for the last time. "As a performer, I always find it difficult to leave a receptive audience. Thank you for your help and enthusiasm. You've been very kind."

With a wide swing of her arm, she threw the coil of rope into the air. One end fell back to the floor of the stage; the other could be seen suspended in midair, about ten feet high, with another ten feet or so of empty space above it. The sight of a free-standing rope was enough to bring a gasp from the onlookers.

Then Chloe began to climb. Hand over white hand, ankles clasped around the rope, graceful and at the same time incredibly strong, she pulled herself up on a rope standing by itself in space.

At the top, when the rope ended, she hung for a

moment, staring up into the empty air above her head. The music ended—all was silence. And then one white hand reached up. Firmly Chloe grasped the air above her head with her right hand, then her left. Her knees bent, her ankles pushed up, her arms pulled. Again. On the third effort the rope slipped from between her feet, but the magician kept going, pulling on thin air, another twenty feet, until, at last, she vanished from their sight. Her voice floated back over the room. "Good night!"

Deafening applause greeted her words. Cheers and cries of "Encore!" and "More!" went on for several minutes, to no avail. Chloe had gone. When the curtain closed, the calls began to die away, but the talk continued. Peter could hear comments all around him, ranging from "Incredible!" to "Miraculous!" to "I simply don't believe it!" Even Eric and Andrew took awhile to come back to life. They kept their eyes on the empty rope until the curtain hid it from view, and only then seemed able to breathe again. "Wow," they sighed, almost in unison.

Peter grinned at their satisfaction. "Quite a show, isn't it? What did you like best?"

That question released a torrent of words and a rehearsal of the entire performance that lasted through another round of drinks. When the room had emptied of most of the audience Peter stood up.

"Do you want to go talk to the magician, Andrew?" he asked. The two boys jumped immediately to their feet. Chloe had alerted the manager and staff, so they had no trouble getting backstage. Peter could read surprise and intense interest on Eric's face as he took in the dark, dusty, crowded nature of the world behind the lights. "Not quite so glamorous back here, is it?"

Eric shook his head, but if he was disappointed, Peter couldn't tell. They reached the door of the dressing room and knocked. "Chloe? It's Peter. I have Eric and Andrew with me."

The door opened right away. She stood framed by a gentle light, wearing a black robe and her stage makeup. "Eric! Hi! And Andrew—I'm glad to see you again. Come in!" She ushered the boys in and turned to Peter. He saw with pleasure that her eyes softened for him. "Hello, Peter. I saw you out there looking superior. Have you told them all my secrets?"

"Would I do that?" he responded lightly. "And it looks to me as if you've been doing the telling. That coin trick . . ."

She turned her smile on Eric, who beamed back and then turned to his father. "Wasn't it neat, Dad? Chloe and I worked on that one last week while you were at work, and she said that when I came to the show she would let me help. Could you tell what I did, huh? Did you see it?"

Peter shook his head. "It looked like magic to me."

Andrew broke in. "You mean *you* did the trick, Eric? You didn't tell me that! What did you do?" They wrangled back and forth, with Eric refusing to give up his secret. Chloe found a chair for Peter by throwing an armful of clothes onto a pile of boxes. She noticed his judgmental look.

"Yes, it's not much of a palace," she criticized, before he could. "But I think I'd rather have them give the money to me rather than some interior decorator."

He looked at her, both brows raised. "Don't jump on me—I didn't say anything. And I agree with you. I just think you'd be more comfortable with less junk." *Maybe a couch, or a bed*, he was thinking, *so I could come back sometime without the boys and take advantage of that silky robe that wants to slide off your shoulder and fall apart over your legs.*

She knew him well enough now to read even the subtlest signs. "Yes, well," she said dryly, "there's not much chance of that." Turning to the younger and more manageable guests, she asked, "What did you think of the show, guys? Did you have a good time?"

Kirsten came in while the boys were still raving and received her share of congratulations. And then Peter made a move to go, much to the disgust of his charges. "There's another show in just a few minutes, Eric," he stated firmly, with enough warning in his voice to quell the protests. "Chloe and Kirsten need a little peace before then. Say thank you and let's be gone."

Taking pity on *all* the males in the party, Kirsten volunteered to take the younger ones off to look at Chloe's trunks of equipment. Peter left the door as it was, slightly ajar, but came close to Chloe and took her hands. Raising them to his lips, he kissed her fingers. "You give a remarkable performance," he murmured against them. "I was awestruck at that last trick."

She clasped his hands and replied seriously, "You had me on my mettle. I haven't been that tense in years. I would have hated to blow it in front of Eric. Or you."

"It didn't show." He freed one hand to run his finger just inside the collar of her robe, sampling silky cloth against silken skin. "I'm supposed to take the boys back to Andrew's house to sleep. Yes," he said with a grin as she opened her mouth to ask, "I arranged it that way. Can I come back for the late show? Take you home? Spend the night?"

Staring into those wicked gray eyes, Chloe remembered the age-old caution: Be careful what you wish for; you might get it. And then, fatalistically, she gave herself over to the fulfillment of her desires.

"Of course," she agreed. "I'll see you then." His mouth on hers was the briefest of kisses, but even so he walked away with her lipstick. She called him back for a tissue, said another good-bye, then collapsed in her chair, her nerves tingling with anticipation. But at the same time she felt wary, even fearful.

How much longer could this go on before she couldn't give them up? When would it ever end?

The evening ended about 4:00 AM as they drifted into sleep together without even bothering, this time, to straighten the tousled sheets. Savoring the weight of Peter's arm across her body and the solidness of him in bed behind her, Chloe slept deeply and woke completely at her usual time, to the feeling of contentment she'd come to recognize as part of Peter's hold over her. She lay for a time indulging herself in an unusual game of fantasy, imagining how it would be to end every day with the comfort of Peter's arms around her and the exhausting passion of his lovemaking to welcome sleep.

And how would it be to start every morning with the sound of his slow, even breathing over her ear and the warmth of his skin holding off the morning chill? And then, as now, to feel the soft slide of his lips across her skin and the resilient stirring of his body as he woke up, wanting her again?

"Magic," she murmured, turning in his hold.

His heavy lids lifted a little and his mouth curved in a smile. "I think so, too." His hands drifted over her breasts and belly as he asked, in a still-sleepy voice, "So why do you avoid me? It could be like this," as she shuddered with pleasure, "much more often."

"Because," she whispered. And then forgot, as his mouth closed over hers, what she had meant to say.

A long time later, when they had recovered their breath—if not their strength—he returned to the conversation. He used the leverage of his fingers twined in her hair to bring her eyes to meet his. "Because . . . ?"

Gray eyes met violet; his were unyielding, hers resigned. She sat up away from him. "*Because*, Peter, every time like this strengthens the chain, makes it harder to break. Did you know," she asked in a softer voice, clasping her arms around her knees, "that there was a medieval torture in which the victim was tied up, arms stretched out, and had heavy chains hung around his neck until he either confessed or collapsed?"

Leaning on his elbow, running his hand over the interesting contours of her back, Peter had the nerve to laugh. "Is that how you see our relationship? Medieval torture?"

Chloe dropped back on the pillow and faced him. "No—or, at least, it's not painful. And anyway, this isn't a relationship. But—" She hesitated.

"Go on," he encouraged. "Say it all."

With a deep breath she continued. "If we don't stop soon, I won't be able to."

"Is that so bad?"

Again she caught the surprising current of amusement in his voice. How could he be this calm? Where was the hurt, the anxiety he should feel at what amounted to rejection? "Doesn't this bother you, Peter? Or am I worrying for nothing, because it doesn't matter?"

Now he rolled back onto the pillow, shading his eyes with the back of his hand as a bright shaft of sunlight struck him in the face. His answer came after a long silence. "It matters, Chloe," he affirmed in a low voice. "It matters enough that I don't want to push you away with emotions you can't—or won't—accept. Butterflies, as they say, are free. If you love something, you must let it go. That's rotten poetry, but reasonably sound advice.

"I can't hold you," Peter said, turning suddenly and pulling her into his arms, "if you don't want to be held. And since I want you as seriously as I've ever wanted anyone, it only makes sense to help you be comfortable with what is between us."

"But—"

"And so," he murmured into her hair, "I don't let myself be hurt by your doubts and your denials. I think you'll get here, where I am, in the end. And if you don't, well, there will be plenty of time for hurting then."

What could she say to that? His strength and his confidence in her defeated every argument; Chloe had

never been one to pursue a lost cause, so she fell silent
and savored his arms around her, even fell back asleep
for an hour or so. Hunger woke her the second time.
Peter got the bathroom first, and then left her with a
promise to make tea while she took her turn.

Looking forward to a shower, she was surprised to
find that no water appeared when she turned the handles. Shrugging on a short version of the black robe
that had so appealed to Peter the night before she
strolled into her kitchen, stopped dead in her tracks,
and screamed.

"My God! What happened?"

The kitchen floor lay under an inch of water, water
which sprayed like a fountain from the faucet in her
kitchen sink. It poured out the back door, which was
open, and was rapidly turning the carpet at the doorway
into a sponge. At first she couldn't even locate Peter
in the downpour, until she caught a misty glimpse of
him on his knees under the sink.

"Peter," she cried, sloshing over to him. "What's
wrong? Are you okay?"

He pulled his head back as she put her hand on his
shoulder and got a face full of spray. Spluttering, he
shuffled to the side on his knees. "I'm looking for the
water cutoff. There should be one under here, but I
can't find it," he shouted over the waterfall. "Got any
ideas?"

Chloe shook her head. "But what happened?" she
yelled. "What's broken?"

Grabbing the counter for support, he stood up, and
slid across the slippery floor. On the other side of the
spray, he picked something up from the counter. "I
went to fill the kettle," he explained, "and the faucet
broke off in my hand. The water is coming from there.
I opened the door so it would go outside," he pointed
out, with a look of apology, "and if I could just shut
it off, things would look better." He directed a look of

reproach mixed with laughter at her. "Don't you have *any* knowledge about your plumbing?"

"No!" she flashed back at him. "And I wouldn't expect a college professor to know much about it either!"

"Ah, but this professor helped his dad renovate the kitchen about twenty years ago, and learned all about pipes and traps and other nasty stuff. Well," Peter said, still at the top of his voice, "if we don't get this stopped soon, your water bill will equal the national debt. Give me a rag."

She found him a dishcloth, which he tried to stuff into the faucet pipe to slow down the gusher. The maneuver could not be termed a success. "I'll go look down there again. Meanwhile, you call a plumber."

Chloe threw up her hands. "I don't know a plumber. I've never used one before."

Already on his knees, Peter didn't glance back. "Well, then, look one up in the phone book. Anybody could do this kind of job. Just get one who can come right away." His head disappeared into the cabinet, leaving her with a really fascinating view of slim hips in soaking wet khaki slacks.

Several minutes later, he startled her with a shriek. "Eureka! I found it!" The water miraculously slowed until it only flowed into the sink. Peter backed out again and stood up with a groan. "I'm too old for this physical labor," he complained. He saw her waiting with a towel and slithered over to the dining room door. "Well, that's an improvement, at least. But your shut-off valve is leaking, too, and—obviously—" he nodded at the sink, "won't shut off all the way. How long until the plumber gets here?"

Chloe avoided his eyes. "I—I didn't call one."

"What?"

Sliding into the kitchen in her turn, she took the broom and started sweeping extra water out the back door. "Well, you know how plumbers in D.C. are, anyway. It takes forever to get one and then they always have to come back. I'll just get this cleaned up and—"

"Chloe!" he roared at her, exasperated. "That's insane! You need a plumber right this second. Water is pouring down your drain at the rate of a dollar a minute. Can you afford that?"

She kept sweeping. "I'll take care of it later, Peter. Why don't you take your pants off and I'll—"

Her kitchen was not very large, and she had pushed most of the water out the door so he could stride back across the room without fear of falling. The broom clattered against the counter, and then to the floor, as he took hold of her shoulders and gave her a slight shake. "This makes no sense, woman! You need to get this faucet fixed. So you go to the phone book, look up a plumber who has emergency service, dial the number written in the book . . ."

The real anger in his eyes frightened her. When he shook her again, she lost her head. "I can't!" Chloe blurted out.

"If the charge is the problem, don't worry. I can lend—"

"No, it isn't the money."

The despairing tone of her voice caught his attention. His eyes focused narrowly on her face. "Well, what is it then?"

"I can't look up a plumber in the phone book."

"Why, in heaven's name, not?"

"Because I can't read."

EIGHT

"You—" he started, and then stopped.

Chloe wrenched herself out of his grip and stepped back, drawing on her humiliation for a sort of anger that would get her through. "That's right, professor," she confirmed, with a biting emphasis on his title. "It's going to take me the better part of an hour to puzzle out the word 'plumber' in a phone book the size of the one in this town, and finding a company that has emergency service could take even longer. So, if you don't mind, I'll try to get the water out of the house, and *then* spend the rest of the day reading."

She started down the hallway to her bedroom, but stopped halfway down. "The dryer is behind the folding doors in the kitchen," she said without turning around, "if you would like to dry your slacks." Her door shut with a very firm thud.

They confronted each other an hour later in the dining room. Chloe, dressed in a white linen top and black linen walking shorts, looked cool and competent. Peter had asked for, and received, the rest of his clothes through the uncompromising wood of the bedroom door, and was unhappily aware of his still-damp slacks and wrinkled madras shirt. But as he watched her drop towels over the carpet and stand on them until the water puddled up between her toes, he knew that of the two of them, he felt more in control.

He broke the silence with a practical question. "Are there hardwood floors underneath?"

Her hair, shiny as always, bounced with her nod. She didn't look at him.

"I hate to say it, but I think you have to take up the carpet, or else the floor will be ruined. Do you have insurance?" She nodded again, still avoiding his eyes. "Good—they'll probably pay for it." They both stared at the drenched towels in silence for several seconds. "I've got one of those heavy-duty vacuums at home that will pick up water," he told her finally. "I'll bring it out later. The plumber will be here about three."

That news brought her eyes to his face. Peter stepped forward and caught her hand. "I called him. And now you and I need to talk."

He could feel her resistance as he pulled her into the living room, but she allowed him to settle her on one side of the couch. Taking the other end, trying to be close without threatening, he turned to rest one arm along the back and began. "You say you can't read. What, exactly, does that mean?"

With her eyes on his, she cautioned, "It's a long, long story."

"I've got time."

A sigh lifted her shoulders. She began in a soft, sad voice. "In the second grade, when I still couldn't recognize the alphabet, I was diagnosed as dyslexic." She flinched at the word as she said it, but went on. "My mother spent more money than she could afford taking me to Richmond, to a specialist, to get that information. I had a problem, he said, organizing visual signals."

Peter interrupted. "I've read about some therapies—"

She stopped him with an ironic glance. "Yes, there are some ways to help. But my school was out in the country, in a rural district that didn't have enough money for books, let alone special education teachers, as they were called. Mother tried to follow a program the specialist gave her, but she had three other children and a job. My father," she said with piercing bitterness, "left home when I was six."

The silence stretched between them. After a minute Chloe continued. "First grade. There is often, I understand, an emotional component to dyslexia."

"So, anyway, now you have a child who can't keep up with the class, whose father is not there for discipline or love or money, and who is angry about all of it. The anger caused trouble, with kids and with teachers. How many times can you flunk third grade? They passed me through just to get rid of me. I sat in the back of the room and drew pictures, or threw spitballs, as the mood struck.

"By seventh grade, with adolescence on the threshold, no one could manage me. More often than not I skipped school altogether, spent my time stealing cigarettes from the grocery store, slipping into the movie theater. I don't know why I didn't get involved with drugs, they were definitely available. And I didn't get involved with sex, either, but that's easier to explain. I was too skinny, with stringy hair, bad skin, and an overbite. None of the punks I knew was interested."

"You're too hard on yourself."

Chloe shook her head. "No. That's how it was." Taking a deep breath, she looked up at him for the first time in a while. "Aren't you sorry you asked?"

His gaze held steady. "No. Go on."

"The climax was funny, really. No one was in danger. They just used it as an excuse to get rid of me. I went to school, for once, and was smoking in the bathroom. The assistant principal started in the door. To keep from getting caught, I threw the cigarette in the trash where, of course, it set fire to all the paper towels.

The kids thought it was great—half a day off from school. I was a hero.

"The adult reaction was typical. And the principal, who had been doing research on the subject, suggested to my mother that a short visit to a 'therapeutic correctional facility' might do wonders. My poor, overworked mother agreed."

Peter held up a hand. "Do you mean—that sounds like another name for juvenile prison!"

Drawing up her knees, she inclined her head. "Not officially linked with the court system, if that's what you mean. Just a place to send your kid when you can't handle him. Or, in this case, her. It was sort of a cross between a hospital and boot camp. Very spartan."

"Where did your mother get the money?"

For the first time a flash of humor lit her eyes. It died quickly. "You know," she said frankly, "I have no idea. My brothers had left school by then, and were working, but I doubt that helped. Maybe some upstanding citizen in town did them all a civic favor by donating the money to get rid of me. I never asked. I just remember being driven, without warning, inside the chain link fence topped with barbed wire and left there. Screaming." With her face against her knees, she murmured, "I didn't want to leave home."

He gave her some time to recover, then asked, "How long did you stay?"

"Five years."

"What?"

The horror in his voice lifted her face. "You didn't believe the 'short visit' spiel, did you? They put me away in a place where they didn't need to see me or think about me again."

"But surely your mother came to visit?"

"Family visits were not encouraged."

Peter rubbed his hand over his eyes and tried again. "Chloe, this is the twentieth century we're talking about. People just don't incarcerate their children—"

Her look pitied him. "Of course they do. And any-way, Peter, it was the best thing that ever happened to me."

"Why?"

"Because of Chuck Dillon."

"Who?"

"A nurse and drill sergeant combined, the only one who took pity on the kid crying all night, every night, and sat with her, talking, until she fell asleep. Who tried to teach her to read and, when he couldn't, began reading *to* her, something no one had ever done before."

"Your mother never—"

"And whose hobby was magic."

Understanding dawned. "So he taught you—"

"Everything he knew. And when I knew it all, he brought books to read. We practiced at night, after lights out, until we'd memorized the local library books. Then he went to Richmond, once a month, got a card there, and brought more books back. Chuck taught me the history of magic, and biographies of all the great magicians, and he read the tricks to me, so I could do them. He made equipment, if I needed it. And when they couldn't keep me at the home anymore, when I turned eighteen, he took me to my first magic show to celebrate. It was David Copperfield. I'll never forget a single minute of that night." The enchantment of it still lighted up her face.

"He must be a very kind man. Do you still see him?"

"Oh, no," she sighed. "Chuck died four years ago. He smoked, and spent a long time fighting lung cancer. Which, I guess," she said ruefully, blinking back tears, "is something else he did for me. I haven't picked up a cigarette since he first got sick."

Chloe dropped her feet to the floor, stood up and reached for the ceiling in a long stretch. And then, spreading her arms wide, she gave him a direct look.

"So there you have it, Peter. You wanted to know about me, and now you do. Are you satisfied?" Surely, now that she had revealed so much of her past, he could let it alone.

To her relief, he could. Braced for the worst, she watched as he got smoothly off the sofa and walked to where she stood. His hands came up to rest lightly, warmly, over her shoulders. When her eyes met his, she found only tenderness and comfort in his gaze.

He saw her apprehension and greeted it with a slight shake of his head. "Guess what?" he said softly. Chloe tilted her head to the side in question. "I'm still here. You've revealed your weakness, and I'm not running away. And I'm not staying to take advantage of you, either. You can't read, but you're still yourself—and that's enough."

"Eric?"

Peter shrugged. "If it comes up, we'll explain. It's not something we need to rush out and tell him. When the time is right, we'll know." With a squeeze of his hands he stepped back and turned to look at the room. Hands in his pockets, he made his way to the desk and stood looking at her tape collection. "So, this is the way you compensate. I wondered," he told her, flashing a grin over his shoulder, "that day I called about Eric's birthday, when you kept repeating everything I said. You record all your appointments?"

Feeling exposed, she stayed where she was. "Yes."

"You must have a phenomenal memory, to keep everything straight." He moved to the case with her stereo components and tape collection. "And you have an incredible collection of literature—in audio format! Poetry, novels, biographies," he catalogued, scanning the titles. "Who makes your tapes?"

"Chuck made them for me at first. And then Dallas."

"Did they know each other? Were they friends?"

Her eyes widened with surprise at the hint of envy

in his voice. "Oh yes. Chuck had an affinity for lost causes. He picked Dallas up on the highway one afternoon and brought him home. We were the scandal of the county: two men and a young woman living in the same house, none of them related. It didn't matter— we *felt* like a family." She rubbed her wet eyes with her fingers. "Anyway, that was about a year before Chuck died. When I decided to try working here, Dallas insisted on coming with me. For protection, he said. I think Chuck made him promise to look out for me."

"Now he's gone, too."

Chloe managed a laugh. "I think he knew his replacement had arrived. I'm afraid he turned me over to you. As if," she said, almost under her breath, "I'm not capable of taking care of myself!" Peter's only response was an ironic look in the direction of the kitchen. She lifted her chin in defiance. "I would have gotten it taken care of, Peter! And without, I might add, quite so much embarrassment."

He took what she had come to call his professorial stance: arms crossed over his chest, hips braced against the edge of a desk, legs crossed lightly at the ankles. The light stubble over his jaw, the shaft of hair falling uncombed across his forehead, and the disaster of his clothes did nothing to diminish the authority of his attitude.

His words, when he spoke, were crisp. "I don't think you've put the correct interpretation on this situation, Chloe. You seem to classify us as overprotective males, standing in the way of your freedom." She flinched as he came so close to the truth. "But I see it differently. I think Chuck and Dallas recognized a valuable and beautiful human being, in danger of being destroyed, and took the necessary steps to rescue you. In the process, you discovered your wonderful gift for magic and, with their help, refined it."

Although he didn't move, the look in his eyes made her feel, suddenly, as if he'd stepped closer. "I'm not so altruistic. I want more than just your talent. But I'm not interested in *owning* you—I only want to share."

Shaken, Chloe turned away, only to find herself looking into the mirror and, through it, at Peter again. His name escaped her on a long sigh. And then, with a pitiful sniffle, she buried her face in her hands.

In an instant she felt him behind her, absorbing the sobs that shook her with his own body. He stood and held her, for a long time, while the tears dripped through her fingers. And he held her through the quiet, while she gathered the courage to lift her head and look at him again. His smile was waiting. "More water on the carpet," he complained in mock despair.

It got a laugh. A weak, but healing laugh. Dropping her head back against his shoulder, she covered his hands with her own. "When do you have to leave?"

"About thirty minutes ago."

She lifted her palm and peered down at his watch. "Your class starts in an hour."

"True."

"Too bad."

But when he had left, she felt relieved. Relieved, first, because at least she didn't have to pretend anymore, didn't have to hide her handicap from the man she cared about. But relieved, as well, because she needed to recover her equilibrium, an impossible task with Peter around. He filled the space, somehow, and brought the empty rooms of her house—and her heart!—to life. "I only want to share," he'd said. Could she believe him? Did she dare let herself accept the love he'd offered so . . . so selflessly. Would she be able to return it?

Wandering through the house, checking out the still-leaking faucet, the almost-dry kitchen, and still-sopping carpet, she pondered that question. Finally, she ended up in her bedroom, where the unmade bed scolded her into constructive activity. With the covers smooth, she sat down and bent over to open the nightstand drawer.

Mikey grinned up at her, and she brought the picture out.

Propping her back against the pillows, she rested the picture against her drawn-up legs and grinned back. Then she pulled the telephone over to rest beside her hip and picked up the receiver. In a few seconds, the ringing stopped.

"Hello, Trudy. It's Chloe. How are you? Is Mikey home? Could I—" She stared at the ceiling and bit her lip, waiting. He must have been outside, because it took a long time. And then, at last, he was on the line. "Hi there, big guy," she said roughly, then cleared her throat. "Haven't talked to you for awhile. How's it going?" She glanced at the clock. "I thought you might be home since you don't have school. What are you doing this summer? Baseball? Really, a home run? Hey, that's fantastic! Tell me all about it."

As a first in the history of Washington, D.C., plumbers, this one came early. Chloe heard the doorbell with an inward groan, covered the phone with her hand, and shouted "Just a minute!" toward the front of the house. She thought she heard a faint "Okay" and turned her attention back to the blow-by-blow account of Mikey's latest fishing expedition. "That sounds great, son. I'm so proud of you!" She listened to his questions and smiled. "As a matter of fact, I have a really good job right now, and I work five nights a week. No, I haven't had time to work on any new tricks for a couple of months. If you come across one when you're reading, let me know. I'd love your help."

The plumber was getting impatient. He knocked on the door again, "Listen, honey, hold on a second, okay? There's someone at the door." She slid off the bed, started to put the phone down on the pillow, then brought it back to her ear. "Mikey? Stay right there, okay? Don't hang up. I'll be right back."

With anxiety on one side and impatience on the other, the encounter at the front door was belligerent.

"What took you?" growled the plumber, pushing past her into the house.

"I was on the phone, long distance," snapped Chloe. "The kitchen is through there." She pointed, then headed back down the hallway to the bedroom. If a plumber couldn't find the kitchen by himself, she doubted he'd be able to fix the sink anyway.

"Mikey?" At the sound of his voice piping over the line she relaxed again. "Sorry, sweetie. So what else are you doing this summer?"

There was so much to say, so much to catch up on, Chloe couldn't believe it when she glanced at the clock and saw that they'd talked for almost an hour. A call every other week just wasn't enough; she wondered, as she listened to the latest best friend story, if Robert would let her call once a week. She'd get Kirsten to write a letter tomorrow.

Or Peter could do it, if she asked. Except that Peter didn't know the truth. And how she would tell him, she couldn't begin to think.

Mikey had wound down—she could tell he was ready to get back outside. "I'm glad you're having such a great summer, son. I'll try to call next week. Oh, okay, if you won't be there I won't call. Where are you going? Disney World? Wow."

She listened to more vacation details and wiped tears off her cheeks. "What a great trip, Mikey. Have a wonderful time. Send me a postcard. I'll call in a couple of weeks then, when you're home, and you can tell me all about it. Tell Aunt Trudy thanks for me. I love you, Mikey."

Chloe replaced the phone gently and pressed the heels of her hands into her eyes. What she wanted to do was indulge in another crying jag, hold Mikey's picture against her and wail until she fell into forgetful sleep. But she hadn't heard anything that sounded like progress from the direction of her kitchen. She'd better go light a fire under that plumber or the faucet wouldn't

get fixed. Peter would come back at five with his vac-
uum and make pointed comments. And her eyes would
be puffy and red for the show tonight.

In the kitchen, the plumber was finishing up a meat-
ball sub. "My last call ran over," he replied to her
gesture of protest. "Can't work on an empty stomach."
He hauled his significant bulk out of her kitchen chair,
crumpled up the greasy wrappings of his sandwich, and
only then seemed to really see the situation he had to
confront.

"Jeez, lady," he wheezed, "you got a real mess
here!"

A comment which, as far as Chloe was concerned,
just about summed *everything* up.

"Tent bag."

"Check."

"Sleeping bags."

"One, two, three. Check."

"Coolers."

"Big green one. Little red one. Check."

"First aid kit."

"Ch—oops!"

"Eric . . . !"

"I'll get it, Dad. Just a second."

Shaking his head with a rueful smile, Peter watched
his son scorch up the walk to the house and slam the
door open in his haste to get started on their trip. In
twenty seconds he was back, panting, with the kit.
Peter nodded and looked at his list again. "Okay. I see
the lanterns, the grate, and the toolbox. Did you remember to put in extra socks and an extra hat?" he
thought to ask, eyeing the turtle-green and neon orange
item on the boy's head with aversion.

"Yep. *And* my jacket *and* a sweatshirt *and* a rain
poncho."

"Good boy. Stow the kit while I lock the front door
and we'll head out." Once out on M Street, threading

their way through Friday morning rush hour, Peter gave in to his anxieties and brought up the subject one more time. "Are you sure," he said, with a glance at Eric, "that you don't mind having Chloe with us this time? We've always gone alone before but I don't want you to feel—"

"Dad, give me a break!" Bouncing his head against the back of the seat for emphasis, Eric made his point. "*I* was the one who invited her, remember? Chloe is a lot of fun and I think we'll have a good time *if* you stop bugging me about it!"

"Okay, okay," Peter conceded, laughing. "I quit. And I agree that we'll have a good time, as long as you don't do anything crazy."

"Right, Dad," came the irritated reply.

When they pulled up in front of Chloe's house, Eric barely waited for the car to stop before he had the door open and was sprinting across the yard, yelling at the top of his lungs. "Chloe! Chloe, we're here! Let's go!"

She opened the door, laughing. Peter watched her, leaning his arms on the roof of the car, as she dealt with Eric's boisterous hug, his imitation boxing punches, and his nonstop patter. The way she had changed, in the month since that crazy day of the flood, took his breath. From a shy, reserved caterpillar, she seemed to have transformed into a fluttering, open, graceful butterfly. Gone was the hesitation, the unwillingness to take part, to belong; they had all become an accepted part of each other's lives. Chloe and Eric had become the best of friends. Even Maia now accepted the magician with nearly the same degree of quiet affection extended to Peter himself.

Most important, the magician had accepted *him*. Oh, not in so many words. But there were no evasions now, no more rejections. What time she had free, she gave to him. Or to Eric, or to them both. *I think*, he told himself, *that in just a few weeks, I can ask her. She might say no, the first time. But eventually, maybe by*

Christmas, she'll say yes. We could honeymoon during spring break in March.

He interrupted his own daydream to call, "Hey, you two, are we going to camp in the backyard, or in the Blue Ridge Mountains? The day is marching on and we're standing still!"

Chloe lifted her face from Eric's with the glow in her eyes reserved for Peter alone. Then with her hands on her hips, she yelled back, "Well, if you want to get going, you'd better come get my luggage."

Taking his own quick strides up the walk, Peter claimed a brief kiss before asking, "Luggage? What luggage?"

"Only three suitcases," she threw back over her shoulder, leading them into the house.

"Three?"

"Chloe!" Eric protested. "You can't take suitcases on a camp-out! Why, you—" and stopped, with a look of reproach, when he saw the single duffle bag on the floor of the living room. "You were just kidding!"

"Of course. But I bet it's too heavy for you," she challenged.

"Oh, right," he scoffed. "I'll show you!" He grabbed the handles and tugged. If the bag was heavier than he'd hoped, he didn't say so but took it straight out the door to the car—only stopping two or three times on the way to "shift his grip."

Peter took advantage of the moment. The kiss ended long before he was ready. "Mmm, that was nice." His head lowered to repeat the experience, and then he pulled back. "We're sleeping in the tent with Eric. Much more of this will have me dragging you into the underbrush and scandalizing the squirrels." He looked at her laughing eyes and groaned, "Why can't I get enough of you?"

"Someday," she promised. Peter lifted a skeptical eyebrow at the comment, but let it pass.

As they headed out to the car, Chloe admitted to

herself that it seemed unlikely she could ever have enough of this man, or have enough time to spend with him and his son. Quite a pair they made bent over the map on the front of the car: Eric in his fatigue pants and t-shirt, an absurdly colored cap crowning unruly blond curls, and his meticulous father, controlled and pulled together, as always, even in worn jeans and a blue cotton work shirt that was softened and faded by use. Well, maybe not always in control, she thought with a smile. She had found several ways this summer to drive him crazy and shatter that cool, rational facade.

Those memories struck sparks in her eyes as she joined them. "Where's your bullwhip, Indiana?" she teased, referring to the soft fedora hat Peter wore pushed back on his head.

He grinned and nodded toward the back of the Jeep. "In the back. Just for emergencies."

She looked into the back window at the equipment he'd brought. "Are we coming back?" she inquired. "There's enough gear here for a permanent relocation! And where did you get this car?"

The route settled, Eric hopped into the back seat while Peter walked around to the driver's side, folding the map into its original conformation. "Parking in Georgetown being what it is, I keep it at my parents' house," he explained, referring to the rural Virginia estate he had taken her to several weeks ago.

Chloe didn't know what he had told his family about her, but the visit had been more comfortable than she had ever expected. Peter's father, a retired lawyer, had been gracious and kind in the same composed manner that characterized his son. His mother, a small, merry woman with her grandson's brown eyes, had embraced everyone when they arrived and immediately drew Chloe and Eric off on a tour of the barns to see her prize-winning pigs. Chloe had never known pigs could have so much, well, personality. Or that parents could be so easy to know.

"We drove out yesterday and left the BMW there," Peter was saying. "My mother sends her love."

She finished buckling her seatbelt and looked at him, feeling the warmth of a flush stain her cheeks. "You're making that up," she accused. "Just to be polite."

His eyes on the traffic, Peter shook his head. "No, I'm not. Eric can confirm. That's what she said."

Chloe was not going to get into a childish argument involving something so silly. What did it matter, anyway. As they pulled onto the Beltway, a ten-lane ring of Interstate 95 that circled the city, she changed the subject. "How long will it take us to get to the mountains?"

In two hours they had reached the foothills. Within three, the mountains hung in front of them, just barely visible in the late August haze. But as they began to climb, the heat diminished, the greens became more vibrant. Blue and purple slopes shimmered above their heads. In spite of the sheer drop-offs, which left her breathless, Chloe was enchanted.

"It's so beautiful, so—so majestic!" she exclaimed at one particularly mesmerizing vista. "I never knew!"

They had turned off the air conditioner in favor of mountain breezes. Eric, busy testing the rushing wind with his fingers out the window, turned at that to ask, incredulously, "Haven't you ever seen the mountains before, Chloe?" She looked back at him and shook her head. "Never? Not in your whole life? Really?"

"That's enough, Eric," Peter warned, casting her a brief glance in apology for his son's lack of empathy. "It *is* fantastic," he agreed. "My favorite time is autumn, when the colors are at their peak. The sleeping is a little colder, but during the day you're walking around in a jewel box."

He shifted gears to start up a very steep incline. There was not, Chloe noticed, much in the way of a shoulder between the road and a slide down five hundred feet or so to the bottom of the hill. With a deep breath, she turned back to look at Peter's face.

"Eric and I usually come back in early November. Maybe," he suggested, then hesitated. "Maybe you could come with us this year."

For a second they both seemed to be holding their breaths. And then Chloe said, softly, "I would like that."

Peter nodded, once. He didn't speak again for a long time, But, seeing the curve of his mouth and the glint in this eyes, Chloe knew without a doubt that she'd made him very happy.

They arrived at their campsite around six o'clock, just as Peter had planned. Chloe laughed when she realized that their equipment had been loaded in the order it would be needed, and then had to admit that the system worked beautifully. Within an hour their tent stood taut and ready, sited with a view of the valley just beyond their hill, and a roaring fire warmed the slight chill of the mountain dusk. At the folding camp table Eric had buttered bread and wrapped it in foil to be baked on the coals, while Peter put together something he called "hunter's stew": separate servings of hamburger, potatoes and vegetables also wrapped together in foil and cooked over the fire. In a very few minutes the crisp, clean scent of pine was joined by the more satisfying aroma of dinner on its way.

As the least experienced member of the crew, Chloe had been assigned water duty. "This," she told them, on her third trip with a full bucket, "is humiliating. I feel like a serf."

Eric grinned at her, and Peter nodded. "That's about it," he agreed. At her cry of protest, he relented. "Now, now, don't get depressed. Tomorrow I'll let you cook. Look at tonight as a, well, a vacation."

Eyeing the grooves on her palms made by the handle of the bucket, Chloe cast him a dirty glance. "Vacation? Right!"

After dinner, though, with the dishes washed, the food stowed back in the Jeep, and a warm cup of coffee between her hands, she changed her mind. What could be more relaxing indeed, than to lean back against a log in front of the fire, with Peter on one side of her and Eric on the other, listening to the alien, but somehow not frightening, sounds of a mountain night? Eric's tales of past camping mishaps, including the first time Peter had pitched a tent only to have it come down on top of them in the middle of the night, kept them all laughing.

And when the little boy, who had bounded from his bed at 5:00 AM, at last gave in to the yawns that overtook him, Chloe found a special kind of magic in the smoldering embers, with Peter's arm firm around her shoulders, his warm breath stirring her hair. They sat for a long, long time, saying very little, until the fire fell apart into glowing embers. Peter let her go, finally, when the coals no longer kept the cold away, banked the fire for safety, then turned and extended a hand to help her up. His strong pull drew Chloe back into his arms for a sweet, stirring kiss.

"I'm so glad you came," he whispered.

"Me, too," she murmured against his cheek. They blended together again, a single black silhouette against the blacker darkness and then moved apart, breathing fast. Chloe stepped into the tent first and sat down on her sleeping bag to take off her boots. After entertaining her with several gruesome stories of unwary campers who had put on their shoes only to find them inhabited by irate reptiles, Eric had suggested that she seal her boots in a plastic bag. She was following his advice when Peter made his way inside.

He chuckled as his flashlight caught her out. "I'm going to zip the screen on the tent. You don't really need to worry about snakes."

Her eyes smiled back at him, but her mouth was firm. "You don't want to know how I react to snakes," she warned him. "Let's be cautious—I don't want to spend the rest of the trip hanging from a tree limb."

With a low laugh, he sat down on the other side of his son and unlaced his own boots. "Do you want to wrap mine up, too?"

One slender white hand reached out, wordlessly answering his question. Finally all the footwear had been protected, the flashlight switched off, and they lay in the deepest night Chloe had ever known. Eric still snored softly between them.

"Peter?" she said softly.

The poet didn't answer; he had fallen immediately asleep. Chloe smiled to herself and burrowed a little deeper into the sleeping bag. *It can wait*, she thought. *I'll find a chance to tell him tomorrow*.

Dawn arrived, it seemed to Chloe, unreasonably early. Almost before she had fallen asleep, the tent was filled with light and the smell of coffee drifted through the screen. Groaning, she covered her head and tried to recapture her dream. But when the aroma of bacon sizzling reached her, she gave up and reached for her boots.

Outside, a glorious morning awaited her. Their campsite was still shaded by tall trees, but the mountainside across the valley shone brilliant gold in the first light of day. Even more wonderful, she found, was the cocky grin Eric flashed her way in greeting, and the gentler, deeper smile of his dad, who gave her a cup of coffee and a lingering kiss. "Hello there, slug-a-bed."

Chloe lifted her chin with dignity. "Some of us have been working five nights a week until 3:00 AM for the last two months. Resetting a biological rhythm is not, I would have you know, accomplished in an afternoon!"

"Yes, ma'am!" Peter said with a snappy salute. "How about some breakfast?" Drawing her to the fire circle with an arm around her waist, he offered her a choice seat on the log and filled her plate with the biggest breakfast she'd ever seen.

"Peter—stop, for goodness sake! I can't possibly eat all of that. Eggs, four strips of bacon . . . I thought you don't eat bacon?"

"Ah, but you do. So we brought some along. Eric and I are having kippers."

Her mouth dropped. "Fish? For breakfast?"

Eric came to take his plate. "It's good, Chloe. You should try some!"

Casting her eyes skyward, she shook her head. "No thanks. I wouldn't want to deprive you and your dad. Who, by the way," she added, with a grin at Peter, "has managed to cook my eggs completely. Thanks!"

"Anything," Peter replied, half-laughing, but half-serious, "the lady wants."

The big breakfast stood them all in good stead. Peter supervised a meticulous site cleanup, and then they scrambled into the Jeep for a corkscrew ride down a narrow road to the river bank. There Chloe's eyes widened as she saw the incredibly small rubber raft in which Peter proposed they travel down a waterway composed, as far as she could tell, mostly of large boulders and frothing foam.

"You—you're not serious?"

It seemed he was. Three hours later they stepped out of the sturdy vessel, drenched to the skin and laughing.

"What did you think of your first white-water trip?" their guide asked her.

"Wonderful!" she had to admit and saw Peter smile. "I loved it!"

Their clothes dried on the four-mile hike back to the Jeep. They stopped for lunch on the shady top of a gigantic rounded rock they found along the trail. Peter took off his knapsack and produced cheese and bread and apples, all in waterproof wrapping, and an insulated jug of sweet, cool tea.

Chloe stared at him in amazement. "Were you a

Boy Scout?" she asked with wonder. "Are you *always* prepared?"

"Yes," he said in answer to the first question and, "I try to be," to the second. "Being prepared is the best way to avoid problems. But then, you know that. Isn't that how you work your magic?"

Her mouth full of cheese, Chloe just nodded. It was Eric who said, "We don't usually eat this good, though. Mostly we have cereal for breakfast and hot dogs on sticks."

Chloe exploded with laughter at this innocent exposure of the special treatment she was getting; for only the second time since she'd known him, Peter flushed red with embarrassment. His head buried in his arms, he said, only, "Well, Eric."

"Well, what?"

A fresh fit of giggling caught Chloe. "We don't usually eat this *well*," corrected the much-tried father.

"Oh, yeah. I'm finished, Dad. Can I look around?"

Lifting his face, Peter nodded. "Stay where I can see you."

As Eric slipped down the side of their boulder, Chloe folded up the last of the wrappings. Peter pushed the leftovers back into the knapsack, zipped it up, and then stretched out on his side with the bag as a pillow.

"Come here and make me feel better," he requested, pulling her back against the curve of his body. "There's nothing like having a ten-year-old to prick your vanity."

Turning sideways, she leaned lightly on his hipbone and laid her arm along his side. With the other hand she flicked his chin. "It's good for you. You tend to be arrogant."

He closed his eyes. "I know. You and Eric must have a conspiracy to knock it out of me."

"Me?" she protested, looking around to be sure Eric's orange and green cap could be seen. He was closer than she'd expected, examining a fallen, rotten tree.

"Mmmhmm."

With a relaxed sigh, Chloe pulled off her wide-brimmed Australian stockman's hat and tossed it to land gently on top of the already discarded fedora. A gentle breeze lifted her bangs. Following an impulse, she ran her fingers through the light, glinting hair falling over Peter's forehead and found out that he hadn't, as it appeared, fallen asleep. At her touch he smiled, but didn't open his eyes. "Having a good time?"

She sighed with pleasure. "Oh yes."

In fact, Chloe was afraid she might burst with the joy she was holding inside. To be safe, she decided to share some of it. She leaned close and placed a kiss on his cheekbone. Her voice was soft and low as she said, gently, "I love you, Peter."

NINE

His lids lifted, revealing a clear, shining, gray gaze. For a long time there was just the two of them, lost in each other's eyes, celebrating the moment without a word. They sat on the top of the world and they were in love. Lifting his hand, Peter touched her full, trembling lips with his fingertips, then exerted a gentle pressure against her cheek to draw her face down to his. She came easily, willingly. . . .

"Dad! Chloe! Look at this!" Eric came scrambling up the trail and stood at the bottom of the boulder. "An arrowhead! I found an arrowhead! Is it old, Dad? Come down and look at it!"

"Just a minute, son." Peter sat up and, regardless of their audience, pulled Chloe tight against him. "One kiss," he murmured over her protest. "One kiss to make it true."

On the ground, Eric looked up, did a double-take, and then grinned widely. With unusual tact he turned his back to the rock and fiddled with the arrowhead. "Way to go, Dad!" he cheered under his breath.

They spent the afternoon playing in the stream near their campsite, where they met another family staying close by: a Virginia couple and their two young daughters. Eric was good with the little girls, helping them splash in the icy water and look for special stones in the shallows. After a dinner of hotdogs and chips, over which Peter took an excessive amount of teasing, they made a visit to their new acquaintances, for fire-cooked popcorn and cool watermelon.

And then they came back to their own hearth for another peaceful evening. Chloe contributed stories of mysticism and magic to the entertainment, and Peter recited several of the more haunting poems in his memory. When Eric stumbled sleepily to the tent, Chloe again sought the haven of Peter's arms, where everything was the same, and yet, after today, wonderfully, breathlessly new. The beat of his heart under her ear was nearly as familiar to her now as her own—and more important. *It's time*, she thought. *Do it now*.

"Peter," she said quietly, without moving, "I have one more thing to tell you."

"Mmm?"

"You were right."

"I usually am," he pointed out, tightening his arm. "About what, in particular?"

"Mikey."

She felt his attention sharpen. "Your nephew?"

"My son."

Still he didn't move. But she felt his breathing stop and then start again. "Go on."

Chloe studied the toes of his hiking boots and, beyond them, the dying fire. "I was twenty, living with Chuck, polishing up my act, with plans to move to Richmond and start work as a magician. I had even done a few birthday parties around town. One of them happened to be for Trudy Morrison's little girl, Amy. Amy's uncle Robert came to the party. He asked me out.

"I went. Chuck had played Pygmalion with me, you know: took a dirty, ugly, awkward little girl and over the years gave her the confidence and help she needed to be a real person. But I had never dated *anyone*. Robert was—is, I suppose—very persuasive. He's a banker, the only son of a banker, well-respected, well-liked, and quite an important man in that little town. I guess I felt flattered, even honored, by his attention. And he took me to the houses that I had only seen from the outside, so that suddenly I was part of the country club set. Maybe it doesn't seem like much," she added, suddenly realizing how that could describe *Peter's* lifestyle, "but at the time, I was overwhelmed.

"Six months after our first date, we were married. Three months later, I was pregnant and Robert still didn't know I couldn't read. He found out when he brought home a book on pregnancy and childbirth and discovered he would have to read it to me. He tried to be nice about it, but of course everything started to change. Important bankers do not have illiterate wives. Nor, as a matter of fact, do they have wives who work as magicians. Even before Mikey was born, I knew we had made a mistake.

"But Mikey was so sweet, such a dear baby, that for a while we managed pretty well. I was a reasonably competent mother, and Trudy had turned out to be a good friend, someone I could call on for help. Mikey turned one, and I had started to hope we would make it after all."

The memory of her son on his first birthday kept her silent for several moments. Peter hadn't stirred. Afraid to look at him, she took a deep breath and went on. "Robert's mother had never been quite happy about me. She didn't like the idea that I had been living with Chuck. And she hired a private investigator to dig up everything: my 'troubled youth,' my juvenile record, my incarceration. She kept quiet, to do her justice, until Robert let her know we were unhappy. Then she laid the whole story out in front of him." This time it was Peter who took a deep breath. He blew it out very slowly.

Now came the hard part. Suddenly tense, Chloe sat up and hugged her knees, keeping her eyes on the fire. "I was at fault. I know that. I—I always tried to take a tape recorder with me, so that when people gave me instructions I could replay them later. But . . ." She had to stop again, and take a deep breath. "Mikey got sick. I could tell he had a high fever. As luck would have it, the doctor had his office in a house just across the street, and I hurried right over. But because Mikey was screaming and I was panicked, I forgot the recorder.

"He had an ear infection. No big deal. Antibiotics and a medicine for the fever. I listened to the doctor's directions, I really did, but the baby was still screaming and wiggling and I just couldn't concentrate. And, of course, I couldn't read the labels on the bottles. Trudy was out of town. Robert was in a meeting at the bank, not to be disturbed. The doctor's office closed. And Mikey was still crying. I had given him one dose of pain reliever—thank God, I at least understood what one dose should be. He was still hot two hours later. I thought and thought, and finally, gave him another. And, an hour later, another."

She felt Peter sit up behind her and turned her head to look at him. His face, in the firelight, was horrified. She gave him a nod. "You, competent single parent that you are, realize that it was too much. So did Robert, when he finally got home. We spent the night in the hospital, making sure that it hadn't been a toxic dose and that Mikey would be okay. When they drew his blood, he screamed. Over and over, he screamed."

Sometimes, in her nightmares, she could still hear Mikey's screams.

"And that was that. Robert filed for divorce and sued for custody, claiming I was unfit. With my background and my handicap, and with the added evidence of my mistake, the judge was more than happy to agree. I got visitation rights—three times a year, for a week. Until he was five, Trudy had to be with us. Now, that he's older, we go off by ourselves. We talk on the phone. Until now it's been every other week, but I've asked Robert to let me call more often. I think he will. And Mikey writes me. I'm sure Robert reads the letters, though, so I don't know if they really say what he thinks. He's a great little boy. Like Eric, but a little quieter. And although he thinks my magic is fun, he doesn't have Eric's passionate interest. I . . .'' What else was there, really, to say?

After a long silence, Peter got stiffly to his feet. Walking over to the other side of the fire, he took up a heavy stick and leaned over to stir the glowing coals, pushing them apart to let the heat die down. In the darkness the crickets sounded louder, and the rustle of the wind in the trees seemed more alive. Chloe couldn't read his face, and so she looked beyond him to where the blackness of the mountains blended into the blackness of the sky. Only the stars, impossibly bright, distinguished heaven from earth.

His voice came quietly across the clearing. ''I'm glad you told me. You've answered the last of my questions.'' Her eyes, now accustomed to the dark, found him standing with his back to her, hands in his pockets, staring at the same view. ''I hope you know how many people who can read make the same mistake you did. I gave Eric too many antibiotics once,'' he reminisced. ''I thought the diarrhea would never end!''

He turned so suddenly that she didn't even see him move until he stood over her and, reaching down, pulled her to her feet. Even face to face, the darkness hid his expression. ''Are you still in love with him?'' he asked, with a tense grip on her fingers.

''Who?'' she asked, genuinely bewildered.

''Robert Morrison. Is he the reason you never got involved?''

Chloe managed a laugh. ''No! Not because I still loved him. I did try to contest the custody arrangement.

Having your every sin dragged out for public digestion by the man you lived with kills love. No, I don't care about anybody but Mikey."

"And Eric," he reminded her gently.

She agreed, with a deep sigh. "And Eric."

"And me," Peter ventured.

"Yes." But her tone was hesitant.

Don't push, he told himself. "Are you ready for bed?" he asked.

Her violet eyes flashed up to his face. "That's it? That's all you have to say?"

He shrugged. "What do you want? My assurance that I don't blame you? I don't—everybody makes mistakes. My regret that you don't see your son every day? I do regret it, but I don't think it's your fault. My promise that it doesn't make a difference in how I feel? I haven't had any choice about loving you from the first time I saw you. If you don't understand that by now, saying it doesn't matter."

Relief, shame, anger all boiled up inside of her and ignited her temper. Chloe jerked her hands away, put them on her hips. "Such logic, such eloquence! You drive me crazy, do you know that? I tell you the worst about myself and you sound like you're lecturing a class on what kind of paper Shakespeare wrote sonnets on! Doesn't *anything* ever get to you?"

"Damn you!" Peter growled. His hands bit into her shoulders, his kiss demonstrated just how crazy she made him. So much for control, for understanding, for concern: the force of his need took them to the edge of passion and then flung them into space, without a rope or a net. Ruthlessly, he crushed her lips against his, until the violence caught in Chloe as well.

Then her trembling hands sought his skin, jerking his shirt out of his belt and smoothing roughly over his ribs. The stroke of his tongue against hers weakened her knees, but Peter brought her with him as he knelt on the ground. She arched against him, feeling in the tautness of his body the strength of their hunger. He ran his hands firmly, even harshly, over her back and hips and bottom, and then, boldly, his hand slipped between their hips, resting hotly at the very center of her desire. The whisper of his fingers against the denim of her jeans was not enough. "Peter, oh, please. . . ."

Cold night air caressed her bare hips and belly, until his hands warmed her. The black mountain night filled with streaks of light and color, as Peter's hands and his mouth burned like wildfire across her skin. At last she could wait no longer. Her clumsy fingers found his belt, then his zipper, and she released the power of his manhood. With a groan he managed to fall softly to his side, then pulled her down onto his body, so that she could lift herself over him and make them one. From the dust of the fire circle they soared into the limitless blackness of the sky. Seeking, and, at last, finding . . . love and the peace of starlight.

Eric's eyes popped open at dawn. He sat up, completely awake, ready to go. Only two obstacles kept him down. One: his dad didn't like for him to go outside unless an adult was awake. Two: beyond the screen, the morning was shrouded by a thick blanket of white. The heavy mist that made the mountains a dangerous place to be had come back. On his hands and knees peering through the zipper, he couldn't see the table or the fire ring. If he stuck his hand out, which he did right away, it disappeared about twelve inches in front of his face.

So he sat back on his heels, pulled the zipper down, and fell backwards onto his pillow. *You'd have to be crazy*, he told himself, *to wander around in that! The next thing you knew, you'd be sliding down the mountain! Of course, that might be fun, kind of like a giant sliding board. . . .*

In the dimness of the tent he could see his dad next to the wall, sleeping peacefully on his back with his hands folded on top of his sleeping bag. On the other side cuddled Chloe, not much more than a big ball under the heavy covers, with only the shining top of her head exposed. Maybe they'll get married, he thought as he reached under his pillow to pull out his arrowhead. That would be excellent: a magician for a mom! And she was a neat person, too—always ready to play or talk. Those stories she had told the night before were really scary. It would be cool, Eric decided, to have Chloe for a parent. And after that scene on the rock yesterday, it just had to happen. Why would anybody kiss a girl if they didn't want to marry her?

As if disturbed by the thought, Peter opened his eyes. The heavy silence outside, where there should have been bird song, warned him about the weather. And a movement he caught out of the corner of his eye told him that his son, the earliest of all birds, was already awake. He shifted over to his side with a yawn. "G'morning, Eric."

Bright brown eyes snapped his way. "Hi, Dad!" he said, too loudly, then ducked his head when his father shushed him. "Sorry!" he managed in a stage whisper. "The mist is back."

Peter nodded. "It will probably burn off when the sun gets up. We're not so high that it should hang around all day." He peered at his watch. "Only six o'clock? It could take a while." His eyelids drifted back down in gratitude. With everything that had happened last night, he hadn't fallen asleep until well after 1:00 AM.

"Dad?"

Even through the whisper, Peter could hear an unusual note in the boy's voice. He looked over.

Stretched out on his stomach, Eric kept his eyes fixed on the arrowhead revolving between his fingers. His legs, bent at the knee, swung casually down, bounced off the ground, then back up again. The bomb dropped. "Are you going to marry Chloe?"

On the other side of the tent, the woman in question had not stirred. Was she awake? He didn't know. Did it matter? "I would like to," Peter confessed to his son. "What do you think?"

"Have you asked her?"

An open line of communication between parent and child could be, in Peter's opinion, a dangerous thing. But it was too late to change now. "Not yet. It can take a long time for two people to be sure they care enough about each other to get married. That's not something you do without thinking long and hard."

"Do you think she'll say yes?"

Good question. He rolled onto his back, put his hands behind his head. "I hope so, Eric. But I can't promise anything. Would you like it if she did?"

"Sure," the boy said, but a question clearly remained.

"But . . ." Peter prompted.

"Would you . . . would you. . . ." He seemed to be having trouble with this one. Peter didn't know how to help him, and it took several minutes of silence for Eric to work it out. At last he rushed into speech. "Would you have other kids?"

Another good question. He liked the idea, right away. Creating a child with Chloe would be miraculous. Elaine had denied him any part of her pregnancy with Eric; he'd give a lot to share that experience with Chloe. Before he could follow the fantasy too far, however, he remembered the other kid already in the picture.

Eric was waiting for an answer. Peter sat up and rubbed his hands over his head while he thought over his answer. When he had raked his hair smooth again, he rested his elbows on his knees and began. "You're asking me a question I can't answer, son. Chloe has a career, you know, and babies take a lot of time. You should be sure, though," he assured his son, with a firm squeeze on a sturdy shoulder, "that having a dozen other children wouldn't change the way I—the way *we*—feel about you.

"And, Eric," he continued, as something in his voice brought the boy's face around to his, "you ought to know that Chloe has a son of her own." Brown eyes grew round. "She was married a long time ago, just as I was, and got divorced. Her son, Mikey, lives with his dad in Virginia. He's just about your age." There, it was done.

"Cool!" came the unexpected response. "Can I meet him?"

Between relief and surprise, Peter had to laugh. "Do you want to?"

"Oh, yeah!" Eric bounced into a sitting position. "I bet he's fun. Does he do magic?"

"Keep your voice down," warned his father. "I don't know. No, wait, Chloe said he's not as wild about it as you are." A glance out the door took in the thinning fog. "Let's get dressed and go outside so we don't wake her up. We'll talk more later."

Chloe, however, was wide awake and had been for almost the entire conversation. Her ears had signalled the word "marry" and sleep had rushed away. Now, with the tent to herself, she could stretch the tension out of her muscles, cramped with lying unnaturally still, and sort out her reactions.

Marry Peter. Live with him and Eric for the rest of their lives as a family. She hadn't had a real family, ever. Mikey could visit, and the four of them would be a family. Or, the five of them, with a baby. A thrill shook her, thinking about carrying Peter's child. Without realizing what she did, her hands came to rest lightly, protectively, over her stomach. There could be, she thought suddenly, a baby already! Not expecting a chance to be alone, neither she nor Peter had brought birth control. But last night . . . Then she stopped and did some quick thinking. No, the dates weren't very promising for a baby. Oh, well.

Hearing the clink and clank of dishes, she pulled herself up and out of the sleeping bag. The clothes she'd worn yesterday had gathered too much dirt last night to be worn again. She folded them to be put away, noticing that Peter had torn one of the buttons off of her shirt.

He had made love to her after hearing about her deception. He stood by her every step of the way, seemed to want to make her happy without changing anything, asked only that he be allowed to share her life. She could almost believe in happily ever after with a man like that. Meeting his welcoming smile as she stepped out of the tent, Chloe was more than ready to believe.

Three people puttered around the campsite that morning, all thinking about the same thing and, as a result, not saying much to each other. Peter conjured up another gigantic breakfast, with pancakes and sausage, which fortunately took a lot of time to clean up. Then Eric set himself to finding just the right stick to fit his arrowhead, while the adults lingered silently with coffee and the clearing view.

About noon, Peter suggested fishing. Chloe hesitated, not being fond of worms, but Eric greeted the idea with enthusiasm. They took their tackle to the same stream they'd visited the day before, but this time they walked farther down, where the water deepened and silver streaks could be seen flashing among the rocks. Under the shade of a magnificent oak tree Peter helped her bait her hook and cast it into the water. Eric insisted on taking care of himself, and only pricked his finger twice before getting the worm down to the fish. And then they sat.

After fifteen minutes, Chloe understood why she didn't like to fish—and it had nothing to do with the worm and the hook. The heart of the problem, although she didn't mention this to Peter, was that fishing bored her to death. There was nothing to do! No talking, no activity; if they were going to be this still, she thought, they might at least be asleep! *That* would accomplish something! Instead they sat, quiet and motionless, in the hot afternoon haze, staring intently at an almost invisible thread disappearing into the foaming stream. She tried thinking about magic effects and found herself jerking out of an uneasy nap. The third time it happened, she'd had enough.

At least she tried to be polite about it. Laying her pole down on the ground, she stretched and stood up, planning an excuse that would leave Peter's masculine pride intact. Eric, a little farther down the bank, looked over and waved.

But Peter, leaning back against the trunk of the tree with his hat pulled down over his face, didn't move— and then she knew the truth. With a grin, she walked over and nudged him with her foot.

"Okay, Peter!" she said loudly as he started up out of a sound sleep. "This might be your idea of the perfect way to take a nap, but I disagree! *I'm* going for a walk!"

He looked as sheepish as anyone would who'd been caught snoozing, but he recovered quickly. "Some people," he pointed out in his most arrogant college professor voice, "do not appreciate the more sophisticated pleasures of life."

"Fishing?"

The eyebrows went up. "Of course! Communion with nature, a peaceful contemplation of wildlife and the natural environment, fellowship with the planet, the ancient battle for life. . . ."

With a snort she turned on her heel and walked down toward Eric. "I'll be back in about an hour," she called over her shoulder. Peter's lofty monologue rolled after her and she could have sworn she heard, somewhere in the middle, a comment about cold beer. Men! she thought to herself.

As she expected, Eric, found sitting still as painful

as she did. He jumped at her suggestion of a hike and would have rushed eagerly away except that she insisted he go back and check with his father first. Peter listened to his son and then looked over at Chloe. Across a hundred yards of stream bank, she couldn't read his face, but she saw him nod and give Eric a gentle cuff on the shoulder to send him back. And she heard his voice, carrying even across the water noise.

"I trust you," he said, and her heart turned over.

The area boasted a fine series of hiking trails, ranging from easy strolls to rigorous climbs. Chloe had been relieved to discover that the paths were marked, not with words she would have to read, but with colored circles painted on rustic wooden markers that blended easily into the woodland. At some points, carved wooden maps had been posted to guide the way. Some of the signposts, especially at the scenic overlooks, held explanations or identifications, but those she could ignore.

She and Eric started out enthusiastically on one of the easier trails, which led them past the waterfall and over a short rope bridge crossing the rock pool at its base. Eric raced to the middle of the span, planted one foot on each edge of the plank, and started to rock.

Chloe had gotten about a fourth of the way across. As the bridge began to swing she caught at the rope rails and sent the little devil a laughing look. "Are you trying to drown me?" she shouted. "Cut it out, Eric!"

His answer was a wide grin and a bigger swing. "Please, you little monster!" Chloe begged, barely keeping her footing as the bridge moved in a slippery arc. "I'll turn you into a toad," she threatened, still laughing. "Let me off this bridge or you'll spend your life in the mud!"

Eric had no interest in being a toad and more than a little faith in Chloe's magical talents. He whirled and raced away, leaving Chloe to make her way across the bridge which still rocked beneath her feet. Before she could reach the other side, Eric disappeared from view under the leaves of the trees. She chased him, still smiling, and found him at the top of a steep hill, surveying a fork in the path and the map above it. "Our trail goes that way," he pointed to the yellow circle they'd been following, "but this blue one heads back to our tent."

Chloe glanced at her watch. "We've been gone about half an hour. We'd better start back."

The blue trails were the most difficult. This one led on up the slope, at an angle that had to bring them at some point to the top of the mountain. Even Eric's normal chatter came less often as they used their hands as well as their feet to get them up. Thank heavens, she thought panting, for all that rope climbing!

Just when she was beginning to wonder if the trail ever ended, Eric gave a shout and disappeared into a cluster of trees. Then she heard him whistle. "Wow!"

She came out of the trees behind him and gasped. They *had* reached the top. The tip of the mountain was a small, clear table of grass, sloping steeply away on all sides into the forest. Standing there in the sunshine, speechless, they saw on every side the rolling, climbing green of the country's oldest peaks, roofed by the wispy blue and white of the summer sky. The only sound—the song of a bird—sounded as clear as a tiny bell in the thin air. "Awesome!" pronounced Eric.

"You're so right," Chloe told him. Awe was precisely the word for what she felt. The ancient enchantment of the mountains took her, for a moment, out of herself. The spirit of the hills touched her soul, demanded worship. Never had she experienced such infinite quiet, such perfect peace.

Except, she realized, with Peter. This was the feeling he brought her in those moments after loving, when, their bodies still joined, he held her against him and gave her this same precious contentment. *And it can be like that forever*, she thought with anticipation. *I can feel this way every day for the rest of my life!*

Suddenly needing to be with Peter, she turned from the view to locate one tempestuous little boy. "Eric!" she called. "Your dad will start to worry if we don't get back. Let's go down." With minimal protest he came to her side and together they located the trail sign on the other side of the mountain.

Their path picked up with an angle as sharp as the way they'd come. For a long time they had to back down, just to keep from falling. And when the trail did level off, they found the way blocked by fallen trees and rocks. "There must have been a storm," Chloe panted as they climbed over their fourth, and largest, tree trunk.

"Or an avalanche," Eric offered with relish. His attitude remained chipper, but she noticed with concern that he seemed tired.

"How much longer do you think we have?" she asked as they crossed a flat stretch.

He shrugged. "I don't think Dad and I ever saw this trail before. I'm not sure where we are."

Great! Chloe thought to herself. *All I need to do is get lost with Eric in the Blue Ridge. That will just about . . .*

Her dialogue of worry died as they came around a hairpin curve in the trail. At their feet stretched a wide, open valley, filled with light. Four feet from the edge of the path the ground dropped straight down to the river sparkling several hundred feet below. At the point of the turn, directly in front of the drop-off, stood one of the wooden sign posts. Eric leaned over it, looking down.

Chloe quickly admired the view, but didn't want to linger. "Come on, Eric. We need to move." She turned to continue, but he called her back.

"Wait a minute, Chloe! There's a watch here. Somebody might want it."

With impatience, she swung around. "Eric, it's been here for years. Just leave it."

"No it hasn't. It's still ticking. Just let me . . ." He ducked down underneath the marker and crawled over to the watch, which lay just at the edge of the cliff. His fingers snatched it up.

"Eric—"

With his energy renewed by his find, the boy jumped to his feet. Lithe, athletic, conditioned, his balance was perfect. But the old mountain, injured by torrential spring rains and weakened by a long, hot summer, was not so resilient. With a groan and a shudder, the ancient earth surrendered to time. Before Eric could take a step, while Chloe's voice still hung in the air, the cliff edge collapsed into the valley, taking Eric with it.

TEN

It was funny, Peter reflected, but fishing had lost its appeal. After only half an hour of majestic—and lonely—communion with nature, he left the stream, took the fishing poles back to camp and started on the hike from the other end, hoping he would meet Chloe and Eric coming down. He even stopped to fill the jug and pack some fruit and crackers into the knapsack, thinking they could have a snack on the way back. There was, he remembered, a remarkable view of the valley not too far away. It would be a great place to relax.

Despite Chloe's inexperience, he hadn't worried about sending them off together; he and Eric had hiked the blue trail last year with no problem at all. But seeing how the terrain had changed as he started up that afternoon, Peter began to regret his carelessness. If he had known, he thought as he climbed around a boulder, he would have told them to stick to the yellow trail and come back later. He should have checked this out first. Chloe would look for the quickest way down. He hoped they were taking it slowly.

He was only a hundred yards or so on the way when

the quiet mountain air fractured across a shriek of sheer horror.

The second scream confirmed what he thought he'd heard: Chloe's desperate, shredded voice, crying "Eric! Eric, can you hear me? Eric, please . . . please answer me!"

And then the sound of something—someone?—crashing along the trail. He picked up his pace, heard the sobs, and started running.

Chloe fell into his arms. Peter tried to soothe her, to make her sit down and relax, but her hysteria gave her irresistible strength. Before he could make out any of the words in her panting, crying panic, she was pulling him back up the trail.

And then, at last, he understood. "Eric fell? Where? Is he hurt?" He stopped dead in the path. "How far? You called him—did he answer?" When she shook her head, he closed his eyes.

After a long second, they opened again on her face, tear-streaked, scratched and bruised. His voice sounded quite calm. "I'm going for a rope. Go back up there, try to talk to him. Call him, see if he'll answer. I know the place, I'll be there in a few minutes." Without waiting to see if she understood, he turned back down the trail, moving at a fast jog.

But she had heard what he said. She tried to run up the trail, but the effort took more breath than she could find. After what seemed like hours of walking she came back to that horrible place. The cliff now ended at the marker, as if its wooden posts held back the rest of the mountain. But, because of the missing ground, she had been able to see that Eric had not fallen all the way down. He lay on his back about twenty-five feet below the trail, on a narrow ledge of rock. Afraid to trust all of her weight to the cliff, Chloe lay down across the trail, put her chin near the edge, and tried to wake the boy up.

"Eric!" she shouted, as loud as her sore throat would

allow. "Wake up, Eric! Are you there?" He didn't move. She inched forward, trying to sense if the earth beneath her had shifted. "Come on, Eric, wake up! I need to talk to you!"

In the silence, she could hear her echo: "you . . . you . . . you . . . you." But still no sign from the boy. Useless tears filled her eyes and threatened to destroy what little control she had left. Resting her forehead against her arm she tried to clear her mind and steady her breathing. Then she started calling again.

Before she could have believed possible, she heard Peter coming up the path. She inched back across the trail and stood up as he cleared the trees. Over his arm he carried a big coil of heavy rope. The first aid kit dangled from the other hand. His face was a mask of pain, with no color left in it.

"Where is he?" he demanded in a jagged voice.

She looked toward the cliff. Peter followed her eyes, and then his gaze snapped back to her face. "Didn't you . . ." he started and then stopped.

Chloe answered what she thought was his question. "I've tried calling him. He doesn't answer."

Peter dropped the rope and the first aid box, then slipped the knapsack off his back. He stretched himself out at Chloe had done and looked over the edge.

"Eric," he called in his turn. "Hey, son, come on. Eric!"

They waited in an agony of silence. And then, above the rustle of leaves, they heard it. "Dad?"

Peter's head jerked up. "Eric? Can you hear me?"

"Dad—where—I don't—" The faraway voice sounded very weak. Chloe bit down hard on her knuckle waiting for more.

Peter inched a little farther out on the edge. "It's okay, son," he called hoarsely. "We're coming to get you. Don't move, okay? Stay absolutely still."

No answer. She saw him drop his head against the

ground for a moment, until the quavery words floated up to them. "Okay, Dad. I hear you."

"Good boy!" Peter whispered, then crawled back and sat up on his knees, reaching for the rope.

He began talking and tying at the same time. "I found Jim Holt, the man from Virginia, at his camp. He's driving down to the ranger's office to get some help. It will be at least an hour. I'm going down to Eric."

"My God, Peter, how?"

He checked his knot, then lifted his gaze to the trees around them. "I'll tie the rope to a tree, then around my waist and lower myself down there. Simple."

She didn't stop to think. Her hand on his arm slowed his movements. "Let me do it, Peter."

His gaze flickered over her face and beyond, assessing the tree trunks. "No. You couldn't."

Gripping tighter, she brought his eyes back. "You're forgetting. I've been climbing ropes five nights a week for the last two months. I'm used to it and I'm good at it. I'm lighter than you are, but not as strong. I don't know if I could help you if you leave me up here, but you could probably help me. Let me go."

His stony eyes stayed on her face, but his gaze looked through her as he thought it out. It took a long time until, finally, he decided. "Okay. I'll winch the rope around this tree," he told her, walking over to the biggest trunk available. "Tie a bowline around your waist and I'll lower you down."

She followed his instructions, grateful for her magic-oriented practice with knots. But something bothered her, and she finally spoke up. "Peter, I—" she started. He didn't look at her, but continued splicing a rope to tie the first aid kit to her waist. "Peter!"

"What?"

"That tree is the wrong place."

He looked up at that. "What do you mean?"

She pointed to the cliff. "If I go straight down over

the ledge, I might bring some of the cliff with me to fall on Eric. Let me go over here," she said, walking slightly down from the point, "so that the dirt will fall away. I can swing over when I get down there. The tree isn't as big, but it's sturdy enough."

Still without emotion, he studied her suggestion. "Fine," he replied with a blink.

Chloe waited quietly by the tree while Peter wrapped the rope twice around the trunk. He dropped the rest of the coil on the ground at his feet, wove the line near the trunk through his hands and over his arm, and then looked across to her.

She expected at most a curt nod. But for just a second his gaze softened and she saw tenderness in his eyes. "Good luck, magician," he murmured. And then he gave her a thumbs-up sign.

Testing the feel of his weight on the other end of the rope, Chloe backed slowly across to the edge of the cliff. When she saw the emptiness behind her heels she stopped and glanced up at the tree. Peter, his arms corded with tension, forehead beaded with sweat, managed a grimace that passed for a smile.

Blanking out her mind, Chloe took a deep breath and let herself fall back into space. It felt like she had dropped off the edge of the world. Feet against the mountain, she slid several feet, then dug in her heels and stopped. Her breath seemed caught down in her stomach; she took a second to let it out and then draw it in again.

"Okay?" she heard Peter growl.

"Sure," she yelled back. The cliff face in front of her was almost vertical. With a push against it, she hopped out, away, and then back, crashing into the rock with her knees. She cried out, and Peter called, "Chloe?"

"I'm okay," she shouted hoarsely. *No time to think about pain. Forget the burning of the rope.* Push again, hop, crash—her side, this time, as the rope twisted. *If*

Peter's strength gave out . . . don't think about it. Don't look down, either. You only have to go twenty feet or so. That's all. It's Eric, remember. Push, hop, crash. *That was a good one, glad I have my boots on.* A quick glance down between her knees inspired panic. *God, I'll never make it.*

When, after a few more crashes, the ledge appeared beside her, she was startled. And scared. How would she get there? She had told Peter she could swing over—quite a swing, now that she looked at it, about ten feet —but there was nothing to catch onto when she did. Eric had fallen onto a smooth, flat shelf of rock, with no handy trees or rocks to hold. What would keep her from swinging back?

At least the ledge looked better than it had from above; it extended into the cliff as a shallow cave, which would give her some room once she arrived. *If* she arrived. She hung there above the valley, thinking. It was so long that Peter called down again. But at least by then she had a plan.

"I'm here," she panted. "Hold steady." Just below her knees ran a lovely horizontal crack in the rock, a little pathway that could deposit her nicely onto Eric's ledge. All she had to do was move lower to reach it, work herself across with her fingers, and then pull back up to the ledge. Simple.

"I need three more feet," she called. When she tugged, it came, and she walked herself down to the crevice. But then she spent precious time trying to find the nerve to let go of the rope.

"I can't do it," she admitted out loud. "I can't let go of the rope."

"Sure you can," she told herself. "You're solid, you've got a rope around your waist. Just let go."

"No way."

"How about just one hand?" she bargained with herself. "Then you'll still be holding on."

Her more cowardly half seemed to find that idea acceptable. Slowly, painfully, she loosened her right hand, ignored its trembling as she slipped her fingers into the mountain. So far, so good. Next step, move to the side. Stretching out her arm, she pulled herself to the side, using the toes of her boots for traction. Carefully, breathlessly, she began to inch herself toward the ledge.

The rope caught, jerked her backwards. Her fingers scrabbled across the rocks, dragged free of the crevice, and grabbed for the rope. "Peter!" Chloe shrieked, swinging free, scared to death.

Scariest of all, when she calmed down enough to lift her eyes, was Peter looking down at her over the cliff. She hung there for a second, feeling her heart pound against her breast, trying to believe she wasn't about to fall.

"What—who?" she stuttered, not daring to look up again.

Peter understood. "You're secure up here. Holt is on the other end of the rope. What can we do?"

There was no strength left to talk. She shook her head, moved sideways again, carefully regaining the ground she had lost, then making more progress until at last the ledge hung just above her head. Now the simple part. She drew her fingers out of the crack, and put her hand on the sharp rim of rock. Tested. It seemed sturdy. Using her feet, the rope, and what little support the ledge provided, she pulled up. Miraculously, nothing slipped. Her elbow, then her shoulder, then her side rested on the warm, dusty rock. With a final scrabble of her feet, Chloe pushed herself over and let the ledge take her weight, praying it would hold them both. She must have lain there for a long time, just breathing.

Eric. With that thought she moved, rolled to her hands and knees, started crawling across the ledge. She passed his feet, his dusty, denim-covered legs. The arm closest to her was obviously broken; the bones in his lower arm bent in a sickening zigzag. She reached his shoulder and stopped, put a gentle hand on his cheek.

"Eric?" she whispered. "It's Chloe. Can you hear me? Can you see me?"

His eyes opened. Their usual brown was turned a fathomless black by widely dilated pupils. A cut over his eye still seeped blood into the blond curls, and the rock under his head was red and wet. He stared at her a long time.

Then he blinked. And grinned—a little less confidently than usual. "Of course I can see you!" Eric said in a weak, thready voice. "But what's a nice person like you doing in a place like this?"

"Thank God for summer."

The words penetrated slowly, but after a few seconds Peter heard them. He dragged his eyes away from the activity on that hellish ledge to look at the ranger. "I'm sorry—what do you mean?" Surely the man was not making small talk. Not now.

The tall man nodded toward the light-filled valley. "Any other season of the year, we'd be fighting darkness. As it is, we'll get this taken care of before the sun sets. Makes it easier," he commented in experienced understatement.

Peter could only nod, while his eyes returned to the ledge. If *this* was easier . . . God!

One of the men from the rescue squad had reached Eric. Equipped with rock-climbing gear, his trip had been easier and taken far less time than Chloe's, even though he'd gone down the same way. He stood on the ledge, looking up.

"What is he doing?" Peter demanded, trying to keep his anxiety under control.

"They're sending down a spine board," the ranger explained. "He'll strap the boy to it, immobilize his head, to keep him from moving until the doctor can check him out."

Peter nodded again. There could be injuries to Eric's neck or back. Only when he reached the hospital would they know. Chloe had said, during her first few minutes on the ledge, that he could wiggle his toes and the fingers on the arm that wasn't broken. Still . . .

Shifting his feet, he changed his grip on the tree trunk, keeping his eyes on Eric. He had discovered his observation post a few minutes after the rescue squad arrived, when they made it very clear that he was nothing but in the way. This bluff sloped, rather than dropped, away from the trail at a right angle to the side of the cliff, about thirty feet away from the ledge. It was stabilized by a thick covering of mature trees, making it a safe vantage point, as long as he held on to a tree. The ranger had joined him, he had to think, as a gesture of comfort.

"See, it's coming down." And indeed, a pitifully small yellow plank was floating down the cliff. The climber grabbed it and pulled it to him, quickly detaching the ropes. Then he placed the board next to Eric on the shelf. "They'll need to stabilize his neck," the ranger pointed out. "Can that woman follow directions?"

"She'll do it." Peter could not afford to think about Chloe, beyond an intense gratitude for her courage. He blocked everything else out of his mind.

"I can't believe she got over there, with just a rope. Is she a climber?"

"A magician." *Someday, I'll call this man up, thank him for everything, and really talk to him*, Peter told himself. *I can't manage it now.*

The rescue worker knelt at Eric's feet and blocked their view. When he stood up and moved, they could see the boy lying on the board, with Chloe still kneeling by his head. "They put sandbags on either side of his neck," explained the ranger. "And tape his head down. Then—" he started and stopped, as a beating sound filled the valley.

A helicopter. The rescue squad had insisted, over parental panic, that the safest and fastest way to get Eric down was a helicopter. *This is a nightmare*, Peter assured himself. *I watched one too many episodes of MASH and I'm dreaming.* He opened his eyes, and was forced to acknowledge reality. The chopper hovered over them, stirring the leaves and the bushes on the mountain with its wind. He looked up and jumped. "What the hell—?"

The ranger glanced at him. He thought the rescue squad had explained. "They're lowering the litter."

Peter stared at him, shaken. "You mean . . ." He hadn't understood this part of it.

The ranger kept his gaze on the dark object descending from the belly of the helicopter on a swinging cable. "A Stokes litter. A heavy metal cage, really. They'll tie the boy into it and pull him up into the chopper. Only takes a few minutes."

He was right. With appalling precision the helicopter adjusted its height until the litter swung gently into the hands of the rescue worker on the ledge. With Chloe's help he pulled it down on the shelf. Thank God, Peter thought, they have enough room to work. In another minute Eric had been wrapped in a blanket and fastened inside the cage.

They could see Chloe kneeling again, saying something to Eric. She looked up at the rescue worker and nodded, then scooted back to the wall of the cliff. The loose line of the cable tightened. The litter lifted off of the ledge, guided by the man still standing. Slowly, it went beyond his reach, and he dropped his hands to his hips, still watching. Swinging gently, Eric's cage floated out over the valley below and, gradually, was drawn upward to the helicopter itself. At last, it disappeared inside. The doors closed. Sweeping the sky with a graceful arc, the helicopter turned for home and disappeared.

"Now let's get you down there, too," the ranger

said, turning to his companion. Peter was not there. He had taken several steps back up the hill to the trail and then stopped to lean against a tree as a cold shiver overtook him. The whole world seemed to be spinning inside his head, and he thought he might be sick.

After a few seconds the whirling stopped. The ranger stepped up beside him and offered his handkerchief. Peter wiped the sweat off of his face with a word of thanks.

"No problem. If it were my boy, I'd feel the same way."

At the top of the trail, the rescue squad was making preparations to get Chloe and the climber off the ledge. The team chief came over to Peter, nodded in greeting to the ranger, and reported. "That went very well. Billy—the man who went down—says it looks to him like the little boy will do fine. His vital signs are stable, and he's alert and oriented. Feisty as hell, is the way Billy put it." He looked over at his crew and acknowledged a wave. "Two of my men are ready to go down and can give you a ride to the hospital."

Peter's face had regained a little of its color. He shook his head. "I need to be sure Chloe is safe. I can't leave until she's off—"

"Hey, Tom!" The shout came from the edge of the cliff.

The team leader went over, followed by Peter and the ranger. "Something wrong, Al?"

Al, a big, heavily muscled man, lying prone on the ground with his chin on the edge, shook his head. "The lady wants to talk to the dad. Is he still here?"

Peter crawled over and stretched out. "That's me." He inched himself up to look down at the ledge. "Chloe! Are you okay?"

She sat with her back against the wall, as far away from the edge as she could get. Her face lifted at his voice. "Peter, I—" He couldn't see her expression, but he heard the break in her voice.

He tried to reassure her. "I'm here, Chloe. I'll wait for you right here."

"No!" Her shout drew the eyes of the men behind him on the trail. "I don't want you to wait. This will take too long. You need to go to Eric. He's okay, Peter, he was making jokes the whole time. But he'll be scared without anyone there. Please go right now!"

Backing away from the edge, Peter found himself, for the first time he could remember, unable to think. His son needed him. Of course. But how could he just drive away and leave the woman he loved in such danger? He stood up and rubbed his eyes, trying to make a decision.

A hand clasped his shoulder. He looked over into the face of Jim Holt. "You go down to the hospital," the Virginian said. "I'll stay right here and make sure she gets back up. These guys don't look too worried. Everything will be fine. Then I'll help her pack up your gear and she can meet you there."

Relief drowned his mind. Peter knew there was a problem with this plan, but at the moment he couldn't think what it was. He shook his head to clear it. Chloe would work it out. She could handle it. Gripping the other man's hand, he said only, "Give her my love," before making his way down the mountain.

Solid ground. Somebody tried to hold her up, as they led her away from the cliff, but she slipped through their arms to rest on solid ground. They let her stay where she was. A blanket like the one they'd sent down for Eric covered her shoulders and a cup of water was pressed into her hands. Chloe tried to hold it, but by then she had started shaking. With a gasp she dropped the cup and covered her face with her wet fingers. She sat perfectly still, except for the shakes.

The men milled around, finishing up their task, with frequent glances at the huddled figure on the trail. Billy, her rescuer, came over, at last, and hunched down by her side. "Chloe, we need to check *you* out. Can you look at me, honey?" He placed warm, gentle fingers on her wrist, taking her pulse and offering comfort.

She raised her head. The drowned purple of her eyes barely recognized him. He slipped the blood pressure cuff around her arm without meeting any resistance. "Peter?" she whispered.

Jim Holt sat down on her other side. "He went down to the hospital, Chloe," he reminded her gently. "He told me to give you his love."

With a deep sigh she accepted his words. Billy tilted her chin and flashed a light into her eyes, watching the reaction. "Okay, honey," he said softly, "I need to ask you some questions. What's your name?"

"Chloe Smith," she whispered.

"What year is it?" She answered without a pause, and went on to identify the month and day, the current U.S. president, and her home address. Satisfied, Billy stood up and spoke to Jim. "I think she's fine. A few scrapes, but nothing that soap and water won't take care of. What she needs most is rest." He put his hand on her head. "You did a good thing today, Chloe. That boy would have been a lot harder to handle without you there. Thanks for your help."

Staring straight ahead, Chloe barely heard his words. The rescue squad departed, unnoticed. Finally she sat alone in the woods with Jim Holt patiently waiting by her side. Dusk had crept into the valley in front of them. Under the trees, it was darker still. Jim put a hand on her arm. "Let's go down to camp," he suggested.

She shook her head and felt him start to protest. Placing her fingers over his, she spoke at last. "You go on, Jim."

"Like hell!"

"I'm fine." Her eyes, meeting his, did seem more confident. "You ought to see your wife, let her know everything is over. I need to be alone for a few minutes. I won't stay very long. Please?''

He left her there, finally, with the flashlight he always carried clipped to his belt. She heard his steps on the trail, and then the silence of the forest surrounded her. In a minute or two, she hoped, her legs would be strong enough to hold her up. She couldn't let him carry her down, so she'd just sit there and wait.

Night fell completely while she waited. She flipped on the flashlight and played it over the ground in front of her. The dry earth had not held the footprints of the men working there that afternoon. Nothing but the uprooted sign post testified to their close brush with tragedy. Chloe was sitting, as it turned out, right beside the sign. Her light flashed over the carved lettering and paused.

Her free hand reached out to touch the letters. She traced the first with her finger. Applying some concentration, because she didn't recognize it right away, she finally decided it might be a B. Or a D. The next one was easier: Chuck had told her a single tent would be an A. Another spiky one: W? M? N?

Six letters formed the first word. As she had warned Peter, so long ago, it took forever to figure it out. On her knees, though, tracing each groove and puzzling over the options, she read the sign. DANGER! CLIFF EDGE UNSTABLE! STAY AWAY!

Calm poured over her like an icy bucket of water. Her knees had stopped wobbling; she got to her feet. Looking down at the sign, folding the blanket over her arm, she had a sudden flashback of the look on Peter's face when he first saw the place where Eric fell. He'd looked over at the cliff edge, she remembered, and then back at her. "Didn't you . . ." he'd asked and she'd assumed he wanted to know if she'd tried to call Eric.

That wasn't his question, she now knew. What he'd started to ask, in that first minute of horror, was "Didn't you see the sign?"

Of course she had *seen* it. She just couldn't *read* it.

"Amazing," Chloe said out loud, "how life goes around in circles." She talked herself down the path in pitch black darkness, trying to avoid roots and rocks and snakes. "Every time I get involved, I endanger someone's life. It's getting more and more spectacular, too. First, a little overdose. This time, a fall off the mountain. Next time I'll probably blow up the White House. Or the World Trade Center. Something really big. Except," she swore softly, stepping over a log, "there will never, ever, be a next time."

The fork for Holt's camp came sooner than she expected. The trail, in fact, ran almost straight downhill from that last horrible turn. Chloe smiled grimly as she realized that she and Eric had been *this* close to home, to safety . . . to happiness. In the distance she could hear the children, could see a glimmer that might be a lantern. Or a fire. Their own site, only a few more yards down the hill, would be deserted. She wished she could go there. It would suit her to be so totally alone. But Jim would come searching in the dark, endangering yet another person. The least she could do would be to return his flashlight. Tomorrow, she thought, would be soon enough to be alone. Again. Forever.

Squaring her shoulders, she made her way down the path and into the welcoming light.

ELEVEN

"Mr. Carroll? Mr. Carroll, wake up."

Despite the gentleness of the hand on his shoulder, waking up felt like running head first into a brick wall. Peter opened his eyes, wondering if somewhere in this hospital he could get an aspirin for his headache. "I'm awake. Is Eric—"

The nurse smiled and stepped back. "Eric is fine. Still sleeping," she pointed out in a low voice. "But someone is at the ward desk asking for you. Turn left as you come out of the room." With professional concern, she moved over to the bed, checking the patient's pulse, the tuck of the bandage on his forehead, the coolness of his skin. When she had poured a fresh glass of water, in case he woke up thirsty, she left.

Peter pulled himself out of the reclining chair the hospital provided as a courtesy to the parents of pediatric patients. Still feeling foggy, he stood by the bed and checked everything over, much as the nurse had done. The new cast looked uncomfortable, with only the tips of the chubby little-boy fingers peeking out the end. Eric had been ecstatic, in a tired way, to find out he would have to learn to write with his left hand. The realization that most magic takes two hands dampened his spirits quite a bit. But even that obstacle could be overcome. "I bet Chloe can teach me some one-handed tricks, Dad! And I can get really good with my left hand, to make it even more amazing when I have two again. That will be cool!"

Chloe. That must be her, waiting out by the desk. A quick swipe at his face with some cold water from the bathroom did little to make him feel better, and he couldn't focus well enough to tell if it made him look more human. But she would understand, and she'd feel better when she heard the good news.

He stepped quietly out of the room, left the door open, and turned left as directed. The ward station was about halfway down the hall, across from the elevator he vaguely remembered using late last night, when Eric's tests were finally finished and his cast complete. The big clock on the wall above the desk said 10:00 AM, he noticed with surprise. He hadn't expected her until about noon. To get the camp packed up and make the ninety-minute drive to the hospital before ten must have taken a real effort. The nurse at the desk looked up as he stopped in front of her.

"Someone is looking for me—Eric Carroll's father?"

"Yes. In the waiting area," she said, indicating a room beside the elevator.

In two strides he was at the door. "Chloe? How are you—"

Jim Holt turned from the window. "Hi, Peter. How's the boy?"

Peter took the hand he extended, not even trying to hide his confusion. "Believe it or not, he's fine. But . . ."

The other man nodded. "Kids are like that, you know. They do something that you think will surely kill them, and come out of it smiling. Anything serious, besides the broken arm?"

A survey of the room had proved that no one else waited for him. With an effort Peter brought his attention back to the man who, after all, had made a difference between life and death. "Eric has always had amazing luck, thank goodness. He got a nasty gash on the back of his head, a concussion, and broke both bones in his lower arm. Otherwise, he's in excellent shape. We should be able to leave around noon. Jim," he said abruptly, "where is Chloe?"

Hands in his pockets, Holt shrugged, looking as bewildered as Peter felt. "I wish I could tell you."

"Didn't she come down with you?"

"Oh, yeah, sure. She spent the night in our camp." He saw Peter's sigh of relief and shook his head. "Not, as you might think, in the tent with us, although we had plenty of room. Two little girls don't take up much of a six-person tent. No, I left her last night sitting by the fire, and when I got up about five, she was still there. Still awake, still staring at the dead coals."

The picture he painted was chilling. "So . . ." Peter prompted.

"So we got both camps packed up by about eight. I didn't realize she couldn't drive, but—" he said, lifting his palm, as Peter took in a deep breath. *That* was the problem he'd tried to remember and couldn't. *Chloe didn't drive.* "It was okay. My wife drove our van and I drove your Jeep. We stopped for breakfast at a little place I know just outside the park. Good food. She— Chloe, I mean—didn't eat."

Peter walked over to the window. He could see the top of the building next door, with all its air-conditioning machinery going full blast. "You got here and . . ."

Holt's voice was puzzled. "She disappeared." Peter looked around. "We walked across the parking lot together. I tried to give her the keys to give to you, but she wanted me to keep them, said she knew I'd want to come up and see Eric. We got on the elevator together. The thing didn't stop at all until it got to this floor. We got off, I spoke to the nurse, turned around, and—poof!—she wasn't there." He was, Peter could see, genuinely distressed.

Walking back across the room, he clapped the other man on the back. "Don't worry about it, Jim," he said, with all the assurance he could muster. "She might have gone into the restroom. Or down to see Eric. You've done your part—more than I'll ever be able to thank you for. It's time to get back to your own life." With sincere expressions of gratitude, he walked Holt down to peek in on Eric, who slept on, and then to the elevator. "I'm sorry we ruined the end of your trip," he said as the door opened.

Holt stepped in and shook his head. "It happens. I'm just glad I could help. Take care," he managed, as the closing door separated them. Without the need to perform, the energy Peter had drawn on suddenly evaporated. He shuffled like an old man back to Eric's room and dropped into his chair.

He had been afraid of this. All night, in the back of his mind, he knew this would happen. She had taken the blame for Eric's accident onto her own shoulders. And, typically, she had disappeared out of their lives. Damn!

Eric woke up for lunch. By then, Peter had gotten his release papers signed and had made the first of many phone calls to an answering machine in Washington, D.C.

"Where's Chloe?" asked Eric, surveying with distrust the better-than-average hospital food on his lunch tray.

Peter had even less enthusiasm. He pushed his own meal away, untouched. "Um, I don't know."

"Well, she was here. Where'd she go?"

Of course. Peter looked over at his son. "What do you mean, she was here. At the hospital?"

Mouth full, Eric nodded. When he could talk, he said, "I woke up, sometime, and you were gone but Chloe was sitting right here," he said, trying to pat the right side of the bed with his arm in a cast. Frustrated, he reached over with his left hand to point. "Right here. I saw her."

"What did she say?"

Eric chewed and concentrated. "Not too much. She was messing with my hair, the way she likes to, you know, and when I opened my eyes, she stopped. Then she said something like, 'I love you' and—weird, Dad!—she called me Superboy. I guess after that I fell back asleep. So where'd she go?"

Honesty being the best policy, Peter took the bull by the horns. "This is complicated, son. I have a feeling that Chloe blames herself for your fall. She—"

"But that's crazy," protested Eric.

"I know. But—"

"It's not her fault I fell!"

"I'm sure you're right. But she didn't read the warning sign and—"

"Well, of course, she didn't. She can't read. But *I* did. And I climbed out there anyway. I'm the one who was stupid."

Peter stared at his son a long time. In clear, short sentences, he had dropped a bombshell. "You know that Chloe can't read?"

Giving up on rubber gelatin, Eric nodded. "She never looked at menus, when we went out. And she doesn't have any books at her house, even though you can tell she knows a lot. We talked about it one day."

So much for his own adult insight—he'd never guessed Chloe's secret; he'd needed to be told. "So you saw the warning on the cliff—and ignored it?"

Shamefaced, Eric nodded again. "I really am sorry, Dad. I'll be more careful. I promise," he said, trying to cross his heart with his bandaged hand.

Several versions of the standard "I-told-you-so, why-don't-you-listen-to-me?" lecture came to mind as Peter stood there by his son's bed. But the brown eyes staring back at him were, for once, completely serious. There was even, he thought, a slight tremble in the lower lip. Forgetting the lecture, Peter dropped onto the mattress and pulled Eric into his arms for a hug.

"It's okay, son," he murmured into the blond curls tickling his chin. "I'm just glad you made it."

"Me, too." And then, lifting his face from his dad's shoulder, Eric delivered his news. "That helicopter ride was really neat, you know? They gave me some earphones because the noise was so loud. Maybe I could be a pilot when I grow up, Dad, and do rescues like that one. It was wild, swinging around in the air in the litter. It's called a Stokes litter, they told me, and it comes from the military, where they have to do a lot of that kind of stuff. Maybe I should join the Air Force or the Navy, you know, so I could . . ."

It's worth it, Peter groaned to himself, *to have him alive!*

Chloe got home after a ten-hour bus trip and two cab rides that wiped out the last of the money she had with her. She hadn't eaten, but she had slept almost the whole way on the bus. The phone was ringing as she unlocked the door, but she let the machine get it. Kicking aside the mail that had fallen through the slot onto the floor, she dropped her duffle bag on top of it, and walked through her house. The hiking boots she still wore sounded loud against the bare floors. She started thinking about why the carpet had come up, then quickly blocked the memory. The past was just that.

Her refrigerator boasted a loaf of bread and a jar of jelly. The pantry did not offer peanut butter, so she made herself a jelly sandwich and walked back through the dining room to the answering machine. Nine messages in four days. She pressed the button and prowled around the room, listening.

The first five calls were job offers. Two birthday parties, two clubs, and a convention. Not bad. The sixth call was a hangup, as was the seventh. She'd almost relaxed by the eighth.

"Chloe, it's Peter. Eric is okay. If you get this before 2:00 PM call me at the hospital. If not, we'll be home about eight tonight."

Her stomach cramped. She threw the rest of the sandwich in the trash. Message nine came on. "Chloe, we're home. Eric is tucked into his bed, sound asleep. I need to talk to you. Please call." Standing in the center of the room, her head bowed, she heard the strain in his voice, the pleading behind his words. Tears gathered and fell.

Even as she stood there crying, the phone rang again. She could hear the announcement and the beep. Then Peter's voice. "Don't do this, Chloe. Don't run away. Give me a chance—" Abruptly, the line went dead.

She took a shower, tears blending with the water, then dressed in a white shirt and jeans. She could rent the house furnished until she found a new place, she decided, pulling empty boxes down from the attic. Then she could sell it. Kirsten's husband was in real estate. He could manage it for her.

Where to go? she asked herself, pulling out suitcases. Not New York. She'd never be able to see Mikey. St. Louis? New Orleans? Atlanta might be a good choice— lots of conventions, lots of people, not too far from Virginia. She'd call the shipping company in the morning, arrange to have her stuff stored until she found a place there. And she'd have to find somebody to drive the van down.

Even though she'd been expecting it, the knock on the door made her jump. And it wasn't a knock, anyway; it was an assault on the doorbell and a pounding that threatened to wake up the entire neighborhood. She ignored it for five whole minutes.

Then he started shouting through the door. "Come on, Chloe, I know you're there. I saw you through the window. I can keep this up and you can call the police.

Or you can let me in." The quality of the beating changed and somehow she knew he'd picked up that garden trowel she'd left on the step and was using it against the door. "Let me in, Chloe!"

He held his fist raised over his shoulder, ready to knock again, when she flung the door back. Quick reflexes kept him from smashing her face. Instead he tossed the trowel into the bushes and pushed past her without a word—or an invitation.

Chloe closed the door and turned to face him. "What do you want, Peter?"

In the light he looked as if the emotions of the last two days had torn his features apart and then put them back together differently. Nothing remained of the calm, sophisticated poet; the man facing her had come perilously close to losing everything he cared about all at once. It showed in the breakup of his face. "You," he said in an equally fractured voice.

Chloe lunged away from the door and grabbed a handful of tapes to drop in the box on the couch. "Well, you had me. And it was good, but now it's over. Time to move on."

His fingers around her arm were excruciating. "What the hell do you think you're doing?"

She stood still because he wouldn't let her move. But he couldn't make her look at him. "I am packing. Leaving. Now."

With a shake he pushed her away. "Another disappearing act? Why?"

"It's my specialty. Remember?"

Peter dropped down on the couch and rubbed his hand across his face. His eyes looking up at her were bloodshot and angry. "Yes, I remember. I also remember an afternoon in the mountains when you told me you loved me. It's a little difficult to reconcile that memory with what you're doing now."

She stood before him, hands on her narrow hips,

breathing fast and talking hard. "Look, Peter, I told you after we made—after the first time that I—"

"You might as well call it what it was, Chloe. Every time I've touched you, we've made love."

The black fringe of her hair swirled across her eyes as she shook her head. "I told you—I don't want to get caught here. I am not looking for relationships. We enjoyed each other. Let's leave it at that and let it go." She turned away, biting her lip to keep the tears back. How many more lies would it take to convince him?

His fingers bit into her shoulders and she gasped as he turned her around. A rigid hand pushed her chin up so he could see her eyes. "Is that the way you live your life, Chloe? A little fun here, a little sex there, and off you go? Give him what he wants so he'll, if you'll forgive the kinky pun, get off your back?"

Before she was even aware of it, her hand connected crisply with his cheek. "Don't you dare say that, you bastard! I'm not a whore!"

He hadn't even flinched. "Then why are you acting like one? Why do you want to make believe that what we have is nothing but games?" With his hands still clamped on her shoulders he forced her to walk backwards, guiding her around boxes and the coffee table until he could shove her down onto the couch. And when she would have bounced back up, he pushed again and followed her down to sit in front of her on the table, leaning forward, hands pressing her into the back of the sofa. She couldn't move if she wanted.

The red blaze of her hand marred his cheek. "Talk, Chloe," he ordered. "Tell the truth."

Eyes on the ceiling, Chloe gave up the battle with tears and let them slide. She licked her lips and tried to do what he wanted. "I—I can't."

Peter was not feeling generous. Or merciful. "Can't what? Talk? Or tell the truth?"

Her hands twisted in her lap. "I can't stay," she whispered. "It's too hard."

"What is too hard? Come on, Chloe, spell it out!"

Her gaze dropped from the ceiling to clash with his. "That's just it, damn it, I can't spell! I can't get close and I can't promise forever and I can't read! Why won't you leave me alone?"

Peter dropped his hands to his knees. His right eyebrow lifted as it always did when he found something unbelievable. "Explain what you think your dyslexia has to do with this."

Like a rag doll she lay limp against the cushions, no longer trying to get away. Her voice was a distant echo of her thoughts. "I lost one son because, when all is said and done, I can't read. And I made myself a promise that I would never hurt that much again. I never got close enough to anybody to worry about it, until you—and Eric. For awhile I thought it might work, that I could have the things I've starved for: love, a home, a child. But yesterday, on the mountain, I saw it all come apart again."

His voice finally gentled. "But not because of you, Chloe. You can't blame yourself!"

Her violet eyes widened. "Of course, because of me, Peter! You saw the sign—you started to ask me about it. Well, I was there a long time after you left and I finally took the time to work it all out. DANGER, it said, CLIFF EDGE UNSTABLE. STAY AWAY." Thin shoulders lifted in a huge sigh. "If I could read like normal people, I would have kept Eric away. He wouldn't have fallen. He wouldn't have needed rescuing."

Peter stared for a long minute at the downcast eyes and tense fingers twisting in her lap. Then he reached out to cover her hands with one of his own. "Chloe, Eric can read. He saw the sign, he told me, and decided to ignore it." He squeezed her fingers as her gaze came up to his. "I'm telling the truth. He's ten; he has to take the responsibility for his own actions sometime. Maybe last night he learned a lesson," said the father who had offered anything, in his frantic prayers, if his little boy would be okay. "You risked your own life for my son, Chloe. Your special talents made it possible for you to help him as no one else could. Don't you see that?"

Chloe shrugged. That was all well and good, but it didn't change much. "Thanks for making me feel better, Peter. But I've been alone too long. It makes you unfit for company, after awhile." She saw his skeptical look and pulled her hands away. She went on calmly. "I can't be what you need, Peter. I—I do crazy things, on top of being dyslexic. What would the faculty say if you married a magician? What would the college do if they found out about my juvenile record? About losing Mikey because I was deemed unfit? And I am, you know. Yesterday was just an example."

"That," said the poet, "is garbage." Without warning he moved over to sit beside her on the couch, overruled her protest and pulled her tight against him, with her back to his chest and his lips in the silk of her hair. "I don't give a damn about the faculty or the college. I don't believe you could have ever been less than loving and caring with your son, and I'd be glad to stand by you while you fought for him, if you wanted to."

Her fingers tried to find a hold on his wrists to pry his arms away, but the effort was futile; she gave up after a moment and simply held his hands.

Peter gentled his hold. His voice was purple velvet as he whispered against her ear. "What I need is a magician in my life. You have given me a glimpse of the sun. With you in my arms I have the mysteries of eternity at my bidding and I am the most powerful man on earth. How could I ask for more?"

Chloe let her head drop back onto his shoulder. Peter took advantage of the opportunity to taste the cord of her neck with his tongue. She shuddered against him. "You see what I mean?" he murmured. "There is no more magical force in all the universe than what we are, together."

Her breathless voice tried to argue. "It's just sex, Peter."

His eager hands had done their work and he shook his head against her bare shoulder. "No, Chloe, it's not *just* sex. It's love and passion and commitment. Yes," he said as she tried to deny him, "you were committed from that very first day, Chloe. Just as I was. Admit it."

She knew he was right, but for his sake she kept trying, struggling against the tide of desire he raised in her. "I can't read your books, Peter. I can't read stories to babies. I can't—"

With a smooth twist of his shoulders he shifted their bodies. Now she lay back on the sofa; he leaned over her, his hand roaming freely across the porcelain of her breasts, blazing a trail that his lips followed.

"Damn it, Chloe," he growled, "forget the books. I'll read them to you. And I'll read the stories. You," he whispered against the blue-veined silk of her skin, "can teach them magic. Games. Fun. Laughter. All the things you are. All the things you've taught me."

She reached to bring his head up to hers. With her fingertips she caressed the mark on his face. "I'm sorry, Peter." Soft pink lips drew away all the hurt. "And you're right. I love you, have always loved you, will always love you."

Peter lifted his head, drew back slightly to look into her eyes. What he saw there was more than he had dared hope for—the absolute commitment of love shone steady and true from the depths of her purple gaze. Reflecting the depths of her heart.

He took a deep, shaking breath. "Oh, Chloe. At last."

His mouth touched hers, once, gently, in welcome. Her lips parted under his; passion, wild and raging, surged anew, melding them together with a force infinitely more powerful than the most formidable magic. And leaving, in its wake, a union infinitely more sweet.

Much later, Peter found the strength for a light laugh. "And anyway," he murmured against the midnight tangle of her hair, "you have to lure Eric back to magic. His new career choice turns my hair white."

Chloe looked for evidence of this phenomenon, running her fingers through the insulted gold strands. "I think just being on the same planet with Eric could do that. But let me guess: helicopters."

Why should he be surprised? They were on the same wavelength. "Right."

She met his eyes, a teasing laughter in her own. "But, you know, there are some really remarkable illusions that can only be accomplished with helicopters. Why, I've seen . . ."

Peter closed her mouth. And though it was not done in the most efficient way possible, they both agreed it was by far the most satisfying.

EPILOGUE

The graduating class filled two rows of the auditorium. Friends and family overflowed the rest of the seats and stood along the walls. Each graduate received a cheering ovation with their diploma. They stood in their royal blue academic gowns to be pronounced "official graduates of Lincoln B. Johnson High School" and proudly moved their white tassels from the left side to the right of their flat-topped blue caps. Another cheer hit the ceiling. And then the audience, graduates and supporters, settled down into their seats—or onto the floor—for the valedictory address.

The head of their class stepped forward. She looked at them all in silence for a moment, and then focused on the two rows of her classmates. A smile broke over her face and, lifting the paper on which was written her speech, she spoke directly to them. "*I wrote* this!" she exclaimed.

With a cry, the blue gowns leaped to their feet. The celebration lasted several minutes as they gave rein to their joy, their sense of accomplishment, their pride in each other and themselves. And then the valedictorian, used to controlling a crowd, calmed them down with a single raised hand.

When all was quiet, she continued. "Graduates, Friends, and Teachers: We have every right to celebrate. Today we have completed a remarkable journey, a journey which has set us free. We began in the shadow of ignorance, our only guide a small hope that somehow we could break the chains of habit and fear and pride which tied us to the past, that we could realize the potential we saw in ourselves. The price of the struggle has been high. We have neglected our families, our homes, even our jobs to reach this point. Some of the friends who started with us did not make it this far. Perhaps they will finish later.

"But *we* have arrived. For the first time in our lives we can take our places in society as full, functioning adults. *We can read!* At last our opportunities are limited only by our dreams. Now we have the tools to accomplish any task, great or small. But, more important, we are supported by the knowledge of what we have already achieved. What could be beyond a person who has traveled, in a few years, from the black hole of illiteracy to this place? A person who could not read a menu, but can now read—or write—the great classics of literature? Whatever you choose for the rest of your life, the strength of your commitment and dedication will provide a solid foundation for every effort. God bless you all!"

They waited for her outside the auditorium, as arranged. Chloe rounded the corner of the building, laughing at the comments of a fellow graduate, and caught sight of her family. Peter, with baby Kate asleep on his shoulder. Eric, chasing after two-year-old Samantha, who had just learned to run and constantly chuckled with the joy of it. And Peter's parents, talking to a tall, black-haired young man in a blue sports jacket. "Michael!"

To hug him, she had to reach up. He topped her by two inches. "Hi, mom," he said in his new baritone voice. "I'm so proud of you!"

Drawing back, she looked him over. "I'm very proud, myself. When did you get here?"

"Peter picked me up at the airport about twenty minutes before the ceremony. We only got two speeding tickets on the way back."

Peter stepped up and transferred Kate to her mother with experienced ease. "Why," he asked conversationally, slipping an arm around his wife's waist, "does it take so long to get a baby ready to go anywhere? It seems like I'm always late, these days."

Eric, carrying Samantha, arrived in time to hear the question. "I don't think it's the baby, Dad. It's this little spitfire, who got two other dresses dirty before we could get out of the house. And who," he said with a wince, as chubby fingers tangled in his blond curls, "has this thing about pulling my hair. Ow!"

With more laughter they moved across to the parking lot. Buckling Kate into her car seat, while Peter did the same for Samantha, Chloe became aware of a friendly argument taking place outside. She straightened up and asked, "What's the problem, guys?"

"I want to drive home," Eric said.

"So do I," replied Michael, with a playful punch at the other's ribs.

Looking at her boys—two sixteen-year-olds determined to act ten years older—she couldn't repress a grin. They competed, it seemed, in everything. If Eric bragged about soccer, Michael made sure they heard all about his championship baseball team. His annual summer visits had always turned into contests of some sort: who could swim fastest, or climb highest—that was the reason, she remembered, that Eric broke his *other* arm! In the winter they went skiing, and in the fall Peter took them camping. And in every activity they challenged each other to excel.

Yet the rivalry concealed a real affection and respect that Chloe would never have expected. Michael admired and applauded Eric's ever-improving skill with magic, without seeming jealous of the closeness it inspired with his mother. And Eric freely approved Michael's undeniable talent with words, which Peter had discovered and eagerly fostered. As for the little girls, well, Chloe had only their brothers to thank if they were spoiled absolutely rotten!

Now both boys had taken a course in driver's education in school that spring. Each, evidently, had earned his learner's permit license.

"Well," she said logically, "why don't you drive the BMW with Peter, Eric, and Michael can drive the van with me."

"But I wanted to talk to you," Peter whispered plaintively in her ear as each of their sons took a set of keys and threw himself behind a steering wheel.

She turned to him, found the gray eyes smiling as usual. "We can talk at home," she promised him. "Kate woke up, fussing because she's hungry. I'll have to feed her as soon as I get home. Stay with me while I nurse her."

His hands on her shoulders, he drew her close. "Do you think she'll go back to sleep?"

Chloe shook her head, a regretful look on her face. "I doubt it. And I promised Sam I'd read her a story before dinner. Your parents . . . Michael . . ."

"I get the picture," Peter sighed. "They all want to celebrate with you. So," he told her, with a light kiss to seal the bargain, "I'll wait. But tonight . . ."

She drew him back for another, longer embrace. "Tonight, we'll have our own private celebration," she assured him. "With candles, music—"

"Come on, you two," Eric called, with a blast on the horn. "You can't do this in the parking lot. Let's get home!"

Resting his forehead against hers, Peter groaned. "This mob! Don't you have some magic that would make them disappear?" he suggested. "Just for an hour or so?"

Smiling, Chloe looked at her family, at the crying baby, at the two-year-old who'd been pacified with a lollipop and now had red candy all over her white dress, at the two youngsters who were almost men. Then she brought her gaze back to the man who had made possible everything she'd ever wanted out of life.

This, Chloe knew, was the magic. The love, the caring, the closeness. The beautiful messiness of it all. No illusion in the world was more exciting than her life with Peter.

"I'm afraid I'm not that good a magician," she told him, attempting a sigh of regret and failing completely. "But I promise to show you some of my levitation tricks later on. You wouldn't believe," Chloe said in a voice pitched for her husband's ears alone, "the objects I can make rise!"

Peter got the point, and the last word. "Oh, wouldn't I?"

SHARE THE FUN . . .
SHARE YOUR NEW-FOUND TREASURE!!

You don't want to let your new books out of your sight? That's okay. Your friends can get their own. Order below.

No. 17 OPENING ACT by Ann Patrick
Big city playwright meets small town sheriff and life heats up.

No. 18 RAINBOW WISHES by Jacqueline Case
Mason is looking for more from life. Evie may be his pot of gold!

No. 19 SUNDAY DRIVER by Valerie Kane
Carrie breaks through all Cam's defenses showing him how to love.

No. 20 CHEATED HEARTS by Karen Lawton Barrett
T.C. and Lucas find their way back into each other's hearts.

No. 21 THAT JAMES BOY by Lois Faye Dyer
Jesse believes in love at first sight. Will he convince Sarah?

No. 22 NEVER LET GO by Laura Phillips
Ryan has a big dilemma. Kelly is the answer to *all* his prayers.

No. 23 A PERFECT MATCH by Susan Combs
Ross can keep Emily safe but can he save himself from Emily?

No. 24 REMEMBER MY LOVE by Pamela Macaluso
Will Max ever remember the special love he and Deanna shared?

Meteor Publishing Corporation
Dept. 393, P. O. Box 41820, Philadelphia, PA 19101-9828

Please send the books I've indicated below. Check or money order (U.S. Dollars only)—no cash, stamps or C.O.D s (PA residents, add 6% sales tax). I am enclosing $2.95 plus 75¢ handling fee for *each* book ordered.

Total Amount Enclosed: $_____.

___ No. 138	___ No. 7	___ No. 13	___ No. 19
___ No. 2	___ No. 8	___ No. 14	___ No. 20
___ No. 3	___ No. 9	___ No. 15	___ No. 21
___ No. 4	___ No. 10	___ No. 16	___ No. 22
___ No. 5	___ No. 11	___ No. 17	___ No. 23
___ No. 6	___ No. 12	___ No. 18	___ No. 24

Please Print:

Name _____

Address _____ Apt. No. _____

City/State _____ Zip _____

Allow four to six weeks for delivery. Quantities limited.